Why was everything happening to her? First her husband dies, leaving her to support her children alone— and now this...

Annalee woke up suddenly. Surprised and alarmed, she smelled smoke! Then she became aware of crackling sounds coming from the kitchen. Awake now, she saw by the faint glow of early morning light outside her window, smoke came pouring through her open bedroom door. When she heard the roar and the crackling of a roaring bonfire right inside the house, she knew something wasn't right. What was burning? Her sleep-fogged mind sprang fully alert and she coughed from the choking smoke as it rushed through the hallway into her room.

With her eyes burning from smoke, she leaped out of bed, pulled on her robe, and ran out of her room. Then she saw her living room engulfed in flames. She gasped at seeing the blazing fire running up the walls and across the ceiling. The way to the door was already burning, the linoleum flaming up, leaping, crackling, and creating thick, black smoke!

"Oh my God in heaven—the kids!" She ran into their room. They lay asleep as the smoke grew thicker, choking her and making her eyes water. She slammed their door shut to keep out some of the smoke. Then she grabbed Bucky and pulled him up. "Wake up, Bucky! Get up, the house is on fire!"

She grabbed Sarah in her arms and, touching the door, felt the burning heat of it.

There was no way out through there. The kids' little bedroom had already filled with smoke. Flames crept under the door and licked upward.

She's left with nothing and has no means of survival...

In the Depression-plagued rural Wisconsin of 1932, Annalee Lines loses her husband to an accident and her home to a fire within a few short months of each other. The abusive husband she can do without, but with her home and possessions totally destroyed, Annalee and her two children are now destitute. She'd been supporting her family by caring for the daughter of a widowed engineer, but with no home of her own, she can't even do that. With memories of her brutal marriage fresh in her mind, Annalee vows never to tie herself to another man—but unless she wants to live with her sour-faced and forbidding parents, she may have no choice.

He offers everything...but at what cost?

Widowed engineer Jack Harrison mourns the loss of his beloved wife. Left with a small daughter, Sissy, Jack turns to Annalee for daycare while he works. Since he's not interested in remarrying, the arrangement is perfect—until Annalee's house burns down and she's left with no option but to move in with her parents. If she does that, she'll no longer be around. He's unwilling to leave Sissy with anyone else but Annalee won't risk her reputation by being a live-in babysitter, so Jack comes up with a plan: they'll get married, Annalee and her children will move into Jack's house, Annalee will take care of Sissy, and Jack will provide everything she and her children need. Annalee reluctantly agrees, after extracting a promise from Jack that this will be strictly a business arrangement, with no intimacy required or expected. Everything goes according to plan—until Jack kisses her at the altar. Now Jack no longer wants to keep his promise and Annalee is terrified. Her first husband was cruel, and Annalee doesn't care for intimacy...but how long can she keep her new husband at arm's length?

would not ask her to have sex with him. Reassured (silly girl), Annalee marries him and moves into his home. It doesn't take long for Jake to decide their agreement isn't working and he wants more. Now she has a new dilemma—how to keep her hunk of a new husband at arm's length. Forrest is one of my favorite authors, due to the fact that her characters are so appealing and easy to emphasize with and her settings are so authentic. A Marriage of Convenience is equally well thought out. I found the book to be a thoroughly entertaining read. ~ *Regan Murphy, Reviewer*

A

Marriage of

Convenience

Ramona Forrest

A Black Opal Books Publication

GENRE: HISTORICAL ROMANCE/WOMEN'S FICTION

This is a work of fiction. Names, places, characters and incidents are either the product of the author's imagination or are used fictitiously, and any resemblance to any actual persons, living or dead, businesses, organizations, events or locales is entirely coincidental. All trademarks, service marks, registered trademarks, and registered service marks are the property of their respective owners and are used herein for identification purposes only. The publisher does not have any control over or assume any responsibility for author or third-party websites or their contents.

DEDICATION

I dedicate this book to each and every unwitting soul who married the one they loved so dearly, trusting to be loved, cherished, and cared for by a loving spouse, only to find their dreams of happiness shattered at the hands of an uncaring, battering soul who never had the ability to understand the bliss and rewards of a fine, loving, relationship.

Chapter 1

Annalee Lines sat in the front row of the faded, whitewashed Baptist Church. That area, by custom and long use, had always been the designated area for close family mourners. She let her tears flow—they were a cleansing thing for the heart, as well as the soul. As she wept, she comforted her four-year-old son, Buckley, and held her two-year-old daughter, Sarah, on her lap. Sitting close beside them were her two closest friends, Amy Lassen and Carol Woods. They sat there to hold and support her in her loss.

Before her a modest casket lay positioned at the front of the church. Dressed in the only suit he'd owned, lay her husband of five years, Gerald Lines. He'd met his death in an accident while working for the WPA. The foreman, his weathered face a mask of regret, had explained to her how he'd slipped in the mud as his horse pulled a loaded scoop down an embankment. Somehow, the scoop, heavily loaded with wet sand, had overturned.

The man said that the metal rim of the scoop had caught Gerald under the chin, dealing him a fatal blow. It had happened in an instant, he'd said.

Annalee wore long sleeves today, though it was a gently warm, early spring day in this small town of Delano, Wisconsin, in the year 1932. She carefully touched her upper arms, feeling the tender and painful bruises left there only three days ago by that still form laid out before her.

Her son Buckley tugged at her arm and murmured, "Momma, is Daddy asleep?"

She put her finger to her lips to caution silence as she shook her head. She'd tried her best to explain the concept of death to him, but wondered how much he understood. The boy shed no tears today. His little face was pale and still. Sarah lay quietly in her lap. She had only shuddered and turned away when she looked upon her pale, dead father. Annalee well understood the child's fear, even of a dead man. How well she knew about that.

Going back over her life with Gerald Lines, she had few good memories. Those were of the first few months she'd known him. She thought back to the way he had been, a tall, very handsome, dark-headed man with deep black eyes. He'd had a seemingly pleasant manner and a charming smile. She had fallen hard, quickly, and deeply in love with him. Oh how exciting it had all been—back then.

He'd appeared from somewhere else—another state, Illinois, he'd said. Strangely, he'd never mentioned his family, other than the fact that he'd had a brother. She'd had no address to inform any other family member of his loss, having never met mother, father, sister, or brother, or any other of his people. After a short courtship, they had married. Annalee remembered how happy she'd been that day, marrying this handsome, church-going man. Several of her friends had looked fondly on him, too, but he had chosen her. She'd felt like a queen on her wedding day.

Annalee felt a frown cross her face as she remembered how quickly things had changed. Living day-to-day with him, she'd never thought of him as a lazy man, just one who never found the right job to suit him. Along with a very meager living, she'd quickly discovered that Gerald Lines was a hard man to live with. It had begun with a very brutal wedding night. She'd been unable to forget the way he'd forcefully attacked and painfully initiated her into the life of a married woman without any thought or consideration of her untried, virginal state.

Other than the nightly pain of the marital bed, he'd been pleasant enough, and they'd had fun together at times, too. But after living a few happy months with him, something happened—a small incident really—to change even that. In an anger-filled instant, he'd changed toward her.

A few months into the marriage—after Gerald had gone from job to job, never able to keep one for more than a paycheck or two—Annalee had dropped an egg on the floor. It had seemed a small thing to her, a simple little accident. But Gerald had suddenly changed, becoming enraged with her. In surprise, she'd watched his handsome face turn red with fury. And on that day, she'd felt the back of his hand for the first time.

The stinging pain of it had sent a soul-shattering shock through her. The memory of that first incident had become permanently burned into her memory. From that day on, an icy coldness had crept into her heart and never left.

Her father had never treated her like that, and certainly not her mother. But in a rage devoid of thought or reason, her husband had struck her as if she had done something evil. But dropping one small egg on the floor? Maybe she had been to blame for that little mistake, but she had never imagined a man would hit a woman so cruelly over something as minor as that, or for any reason, come to think of it.

Annalee knew it wasn't right for a man to brutally strike a woman, especially not a woman he'd promised to love and cherish. She'd stood her ground asking him, "Why worry about one egg, when you can't keep a job for more than a month or two?" She was in the family way by then, and they had a coming child to worry about.

In shock, she'd seen his eyes narrow at what she'd said. His clenched fist had wavered in her face as he'd grabbed her shoulder in anger. He threatened her and shook her cruelly. And after that day, he seemed almost eager to take out his rage on her. She had only to look at her battered body in her mirror to be reminded of it. She continually wore bruises of many colors, both healing and fresh. After that incident, getting the back of his hand had become a regular event until his punishment had advanced into utter brutality. From then on, when she looked at him, she no longer saw a handsome face. And she felt nothing but fear and revulsion.

Annalee had always been careful to hide the shame of her bruises. She made sure she wore long sleeves and longer skirts to hide the marks on her legs, and used powder on her face if she had a disfiguring bruise to hide.

After the abuse began, Annalee, upset and fearful—in pain and shock—had gone to her parents. At that time, they still lived in her small town of Delano. In tears, she'd related to them the details of Gerald's brutality.

But she'd found no comfort there and came away deeply disappointed in her parents. They offered her no support.

Her mother had only said, "I'm very sorry to hear about that, but you've made your bed, my daughter, and now you must lie in it. You must be careful how you do things, and do try to make him happier. Then Gerald won't feel the need to strike you like that." Her mother had turned her back on Annalee. "We cannot interfere in your marriage, nor can we help you."

Her father had reddened in the face and clenched his fists, but he'd never uttered a word or made a move on her behalf against her husband.

Her mother, a good, church-going woman, believed that the man was the head of the home. When you married, you lived with your husband and did as he wished. "God will guide you, my girl, just keep praying and he will change, you'll see."

Her words had finally come true, but if it had come about through fervent prayer, it was certainly not in the way her mother had expected. Instead, God had stepped in. Annalee felt a sense of gratitude to Him for the release she felt this day. Maybe God had no hand in his death, she didn't know, and she had no idea of what the future held for a widow with small children. But she was free of her husband's hateful vengeance and, deep inside herself, she was glad he was gone.

In her heart, Annalee felt no guilt that she secretly rejoiced at seeing her husband laying in that box, cold and stiff. How many times, with her jaw clamped tight, had she thought, *God forgive me, but if he would die—I would be free of his ugly, staring looks and his nasty, evil temper.*

Annalee frequently looked at that casket sitting up in front of the church on two sawhorses that had been covered with a deep-red velvet throw. With her teeth tightly clenched, she silently swore to herself, *If I die for it, no man will ever touch me in that ugly way again—Gerald's way. If I die of starvation, I will never allow it to happen to me again—never! And if any man ever touches one of my babies—God help him!*

Annalee felt herself getting heated and angry over a problem she no longer had. She quickly got hold of herself and quelled her wayward thoughts. She raised her eyes and then bent down to kiss the top of her daughter's head, carefully directing her attention to Pastor Benson as he intoned the traditional words to send her husband on his way to heaven—or that other place—and to lay him in the ground.

Her reddened eyes had dried. If she had wept at all this day, it was from a deep sense of relief. Or maybe a beginning stab of fear about how she could care for her babies. If those attending the services thought she was a heartbroken, grieving woman, she was glad for her reddened eyes. It helped create the picture of the bereft widow, and she was satisfied if they thought that.

Annalee truly believed she'd been a failure as a wife and as a woman. She had no doubt about those things. But she was a good mother to her babies and had pride in that to cling to. Otherwise, her sense of trust, self-worth, and her confidence as a woman had been shattered by that cold man lying in the box at the front of this simple little church.

The feeling that she should never have had to endure such treatment from any man was always with her, and that alone brought frequent tears to her eyes. She never could understand why her husband had been so cruel. That question had never been answered. Maybe it had something to do with his family. She didn't know, but she strongly suspected harsh treatment somewhere in his younger years. What else would cause such anger and fury? Maybe that was the way he'd been treated and the reason he no longer cared to acknowledge any one of his relatives.

Yes, she had cried today, mostly from fear and uncertainty of the future, but not for her own sorrow or losses. Annalee had done a lot of thinking over these things. Positive that those frequent incidences had seldom been her fault, her head rose a bit higher. Life alone wouldn't be easy. She already knew that. She faced living on her own with two babies to bring up. But, in spite of what lay before her, she believed she could find a way to feed them and care for them without the dark, threatening shadow of an angry man hovering over her, a man ever anxious to hurt and brutalize her, and seemingly without thought or reason.

Their rented home might be small, and had often seemed crowded, but she'd kept it clean, and things were always done up. Worries nagged at her mind about her children, Buckley and baby Sarah.

Her husband had barely made enough to keep them

in food, kerosene for the stove and lanterns, and coal and firewood for the big, cast-iron cook stove they used during the winter months. Annalee had learned to get by with as little as possible, but with the children, there were things she had to have. There were a few jobs out there for men to work at—but a woman with babies, as far as she knew, had little chance of earning her way.

In these lean Depression years, working for the WPA, the federally sponsored Works Progress Administration had been the only work her husband could find. It was a government created public works project to keep some of the people busy and put a bit of money into circulation. Many folks snickered behind their hands, referring to that group of workers as "We Poke Along," but for a woman, there wasn't even a public works job like that available.

She'd never told her pastor about the abuse, in spite of the fact that she and her husband were regular church goers. She felt if her parents offered her no help, her pastor no doubt held the same beliefs about marriage as her parents, and she couldn't bear to hear that business again about the man being the boss. Having decided that, Annalee believed she had nowhere to turn.

Her thinking of the past was interrupted by her close friend, Amy Lassen, who nudged her and whispered, "What's going on with you? Are you all right?" She looked at Annalee. "You had such a far away, an almost lost look on your face."

"Just thinking of things in the past, that's all," Annalee whispered back.

She'd never told her best friend about the abuse she'd suffered, either, and that had kept her even more isolated. But she'd been unable to face the shame of Gerald's abuse and tried her best to keep things looking normal.

Returning to the present, she hugged her son and daughter close and directed her attention on the choir as they began to sing one of her husband's favorite hymns, *The Old Rugged Cross*.

Another nearby friend, Carol Woods, had been very quiet. Yet, Annalee had seen so many tears streaming down her friend's face she'd began to wonder about it. Who did Carol cry for—surely not Gerald? Annalee wondered what could possibly occasion that much sorrow for a man who wasn't hers. Of course, her friend was being supportive—a good friend, offering sympathy.

Her parents sat in the row behind. They had driven in from Arnott to be here for the services. They had relocated three years ago, and the drive took them nearly an hour. She believed their old Model T was barely running by the way it shook and rattled as it moved along the graveled roads. It looked so rickety, she wondered what would happen if they hit a rock.

Her husband had owned a Model A Ford Coupe, which was fairly new. She hadn't driven it much, as Gerald usually had it at his job if he had one. Gas was up to ten cents per gallon these days and too much for her to pay with her husband's inadequate wages. She'd found she'd rather walk for her needs. Their small village of Delano, Wisconsin, was small enough that nothing was very far. She used the kids' little red wagon for hauling them and the few groceries she could afford. Of course, they enjoyed the outing as well.

She'd been glad to see her parents but no longer

looked to them as a source of help. They barely kept their own heads above water. Sadly, she'd noticed this time that her father had suddenly appeared to have grown older. He seemed even more bent over from his job at the Arnott Creamery where the local farmers brought their milk to be processed. Her mother's hair had turned totally gray by now, too. Annalee wondered how much longer she would have them and felt a few more tears flow.

The service had ended in a prolonged prayer and almost before she realized it, her friends were escorting her out to the waiting cars. Her parents came along behind. Her mother had given her a quick hug, and it had felt strange, like some distant relative or someone she barely knew. Touching had never been their way, never having been demonstrative or affectionate. Her mother did manage to offer in a weak voice, "Annalee, if you can't feed your babies, you are welcome to come home to live with us. We'll manage to take care of you somehow."

Her mother's hopeless tone did nothing to encourage Annalee to give that offer a lot of thought. If she stayed with her parents, she would have to suffer all over again her mother's continual negative comments and ways. Annalee had been away from home too long, and her own housekeeper, to want to return to that.

"Thanks, Mom. We'll be all right." Annalee did her best to sound hopeful, and hoped she had.

She wondered if her husband had an insurance policy. She'd heard of people having a thing like that and hoped it might be true. She decided to look into his belongings when she got home, to see if a policy might exist. If so, it would be a great deal of help to her now.

The casket was carried out by six men chosen from

Gerald's work crew and loaded into the faded, old hearse for the trip to the local cemetery. What flowers there were had been loaded in with the casket. She and the two children were taken in her parent's old car for that last ride. During the drive, her father asked, "Any idea how you'll get on now with Gerald gone, Annalee?"

"We'll be all right, Dad." She wasn't sure of that at all, but she didn't plan to burden her aging parents. She'd find a way. Others had, and she knew she would—somehow.

As they drove into the cemetery, the narrow graveled drive took them past monuments dedicated to many others, and of many generations. There was a large WW monument in the center of it, dedicated to soldiers lost in the Great War, as it was called. She realized she wasn't the only one to suffer a loss. And after driving through the rows of grave markers, it came home to Annalee that death comes calling to everyone at one time or another.

When the car lurched to a halt, Annalee saw a mound of dirt piled high beside a deep hole in the ground. Seeing it, a shock ran through her as she imagined lying in an airtight box, all those terrible feet below the surface. Her throat tightened at the thought of the blackness and suffocating closeness. Even Gerald, for all his cruelty, didn't deserve a thing like that. She hugged her children close and shook her head to rid herself of those upsetting thoughts, as she and her children took their seats before the open grave site.

Annalee told herself that the man who dwelt in that body was gone. He was no longer even a part of that body. All that was physically left of Gerald Lines would eventually become dust as Pastor Benson had just said.

Over the years, she'd visited the cemetery with her parents to place flowers on a long-dead relative's grave. She'd known that feeling then, and felt it. That person they'd come to visit was no longer there—merely a name of someone lost. But now, she understood far more deeply that change and the way it affected a family and those left behind

She settled back to listen to the pastor's final words, and noticed her stomach felt empty. *I should be feeling guilty for thinking of the food we'll have after this burial service, but I don't. And I don't feel guilty for being glad Gerald is gone from my life.*

The table at her small home was groaning from the many dishes her neighbors had brought to her. It was their usual way of offering what comfort they could at this sad time. It was customary—everyone did it, including Annalee.

Mary Jensen, her close neighbor, often watched her children when Annalee did her shopping alone. Mary had asked to take the children to her home after the services were over, and Annalee planned to take advantage of her offer. They needed to be away from this depressing event.

She turned her attention to the pastor again to hear, "…ashes to ashes, dust to dust," as he tossed a handful of earth down onto the casket.

When had they lowered it? She hadn't really noticed, being lost in thought the way she'd been.

But she'd paid attention when Bucky had grabbed her arm and cried, "Momma, where are they putting my daddy?"

She did her best to explain as much as possible, in

hushed tones, that his daddy was no longer in that body until the pastor motioned for her to toss a handful of dirt down onto Gerald's casket.

Annalee didn't mind doing that. It was a final gesture and one she found easy enough to do. She dropped the handful of earth and brushed her hands together, as though washing her hands of an unhappy period in her life. After the final intonation, she took her children by the hand and slowly walked away.

She felt a hand on her elbow. "This way, Annalee. You're wandering." It was Amy who guided her along toward their car. "Are you all right, An? Losing a husband and father has to be about the hardest thing for a family to endure."

"Yes, I just forgot where we were going. I didn't notice where your car was for a moment." Annalee uttered a slight, embarrassed groan. "Thanks, Amy, you're a good friend." She looked around. "What happened to Carol?"

"I don't know," Amy replied. "She seemed awfully shook up for some reason. Wonder what's the matter with her today." Amy lowered her voice. "Did you see the way she was carrying on? It was like she'd lost a husband, instead of you."

Annalee thought Carol was pretty hard to figure out at times. "I don't know, Amy. Maybe it brings back some bad memories or something."

"Or something," Amy said, a distant tone in her voice. "Sometimes I wonder about her. She's married, but she doesn't seem that happy. They haven't had any kids yet, either. Did you ever hear why that is?"

"Never heard, but I can't worry about her life right now. I've plenty of my own problems to face, Amy, and I confess I'm worried that I can't handle things alone."

They reached the row of parked cars.

"Why not ride with me and Derrick? "Amy said. "We're your friends, An, and will do whatever we can to help, you know that. And don't you be so stiff-necked about asking, now, will you?"

"Thanks, Amy." Annalee hadn't even noticed Amy's husband, Derrick, in the crowd. "We'd love to ride with you both. I'll just signal my folks."

After she waved to her parents, she herded her little ones and herself into Amy and Derrick's fairly new Buick. The soft, cushiony seats were covered with heavy maroon velvet, and she sank happily into them.

The car smelled like 'new car' to Annalee and, as Derrick drove, it seemed to glide along like they were on a slick tarred road.

"This is a nice car, Amy." Annalee felt herself melting into the luxury and softness, and quietly wondered if any time in her life she would own a car like this. She uttered a soft sigh.

Amy turned and looked back over the front seat. "Annalee, I will help you in any way I can, you know that." Her expression was serious, but her eyes held a sparkle of excitement. "Maybe you could take care of kids. Why not? You're good at it and wouldn't have to leave your house. You could take in some money that way, you know, to help out."

"That's a good idea, Amy. If you hear of anyone needing that kind of help, please put in a good word for me." Annalee felt a touch of excitement and a renewed sense of courage. She would be good at that kind of work. She certainly knew that job. Her house was small, but she could manage. After all, kids were small, too.

They reached her modest home and had gotten out to enter, when her parents came up. Her mother huffed, "We were all set to give you a ride, Annalee." She seemed a little put out judging by the sour expression on her face.

"Well, Mom, Amy was right there. We've been good friends for quite a while now." She introduced Amy and Derrick to her parents, and they walked into her home together. They were met with a houseful of well-wishers and mourners. Several ladies from the church had begun serving food.

Annalee let Mary Jensen take her children to her home across the street. She felt herself taken about, meeting the people who had come on this sad occasion. Many hands offered comfort, pity, and enough suggestions to set her mind in a whirl.

She gratefully and thankfully waited for them to finish eating and slowly depart. She craved time alone after the services and people crowding around.

The business of burying her husband had made her feel frustrated and tired. She appreciated everything, shed many tears, but her body was stiff with fatigue.

Later on, Mary Jensen brought her children back home, and they wandered about, lost in the confusion. Her mother had tried to hold them and talk to them, but they didn't know her well enough and shied away. Little Sarah cried and reached out to Annalee.

She apologized to her parents, seeing they were hurt by the children's rejection. "Don't be upset with them, Mom and Dad. They don't see you enough to know you very well."

But they were upset as they took their leave, and Annalee waved them off with a sigh. Being left alone with her children to begin life anew as a young widow was all Annalee wanted right now. As the last person departed, she slowly shut the door and heaved another sigh.

She took baby Sarah on her knee and held Buckley close against her body. "My darling babies, I will do my best for you. We can do this together." She repeated her thoughts aloud, "I can do this. I know I can."

Chapter 2

Annalee put out a small sign at a local grocery store, Bartig's, to see if she might attract some babysitting. A few days later, hearing a knock on her door, she opened it to see a nicely dressed young woman.

She wore a fox fur piece around her neck, and her other garments were of equal quality. Hoping this might be someone in need of child care, Annalee opened the door wider and bid her come in.

The woman looked about and Annalee could almost see her nose curl upward as she sniffed. "Oh my, you certainly have a small, little place here. Where do your children play? I don't see any sort of garden area for them to get outside for fresh air." At that moment, little Buckley ran in from outside with muddied hands and, reaching up with tears in his eyes, he grabbed his mother's dress, smearing it heavily with mud.

"Momma, I faw down," he cried. Big tears rolled

down his chubby little cheeks, and Annalee knelt down to wipe them away.

The woman with the fancy fur piece carefully placed about her slender neck was forgotten for the moment.

Annalee looked up from her crying son to see an expression of revulsion cross the woman's face. She knew instantly she would never take care of a child belonging to this snooty woman with her nose held so high in the air. Annalee decided that the woman was lucky it wasn't raining today.

The woman sniffed. "Well, I see you are very busy, Mrs. Lines. I am sorry to have bothered you."

With that she turned and walked through the front door and down the crumbling sidewalk that had led to the street where the woman had parked her gleaming new Chrysler sedan. Annalee watched her go, speechless at the woman's uncaring attitude for those she obviously considered beneath her notice.

"Well, maybe it's for the best. I would never be able to please that woman, no matter what I did."

Annalee did wonder who the woman was, and if she had come to her home because of the little ad she had placed in Bartig's. It was the closest store, and the one Annalee frequented the most. There were other stores where she might place her hand-lettered card as well. Thinking of the woman who'd come to her door, she wondered. *Does a fancy woman like that even shop for groceries?*

After she had settled her son from his fall and cleaned his muddied hands, she sat him at the table and ladled him a bowl of soup. Then she went to get her little girl up from her nap. Her crying as she'd come awake had set Annalee to worrying. *Am I doing all right? Can I feed my children? What will I do if they get sick?"*

As time wore on after her husband's death, she'd begun to worry. She had almost used up what money she had found in Gerald's pockets and all the gifts from the funeral letters.

She'd been happily surprised by the amount in Gerald's pockets. He'd had over $200.00 dollars there. But why he had that money secreted away from his wife, she couldn't imagine. Had he kept this money back for some special reason of his own? Eyebrows furrowed, she wondered about that, realizing there were many things about Gerald she had not understood. Where had he gone at certain times, why, and what had he been doing?

She fed her little daughter some of the thin soup she had simmering on her kerosene stove. At the same time, she wondered what they would eat for dinner. She'd always kept back a large bag of cornmeal, a food she kept for those times when she had nothing else. It made a tasty meal, especially with the syrup she made from sugar and Mapelene flavoring. Her mother had used that plenty of times when food got scarce in the house. She could also mold it in a pan, slice it, and fry it, as well as serve it as mush.

❧❧❧

Derrick Lassen sat in his office chair, tilted back, wondering about Annalee Lines. His wife Amy had done a lot of fretting about her friend, and it bothered him, too. He believed there ought to be some kind of government support for people like Mrs. Lines—a widow with two little ones to rear and little means of making any sort of a living for herself.

For himself, he felt very lucky to hold a job with the local power company. He was an engineer and worked for a utility company, Wisconsin Light and Power. They provided electricity throughout the small town. Electricity was fairly new, but it had quickly become a necessity that everyone had to have in these modern times. His position afforded him a good living when so many were out of work and standing in food lines all about the country. The poverty and lack of jobs all over America in 1932 was called The Great Depression by some. He believed it was certainly that, all right.

One of his co-workers walked by and stopped for a chat. "Say, Derrick, how're things with you?" He leaned against his cubicle wall, and Derrick saw how it gave a little—Jack was a good sized man.

"Going along all right," Derrick said. "Damned glad to have this job, I'll have to say that." How about you, Jack, things all right with you?"

Derrick and Jack Harrison had been friends for a long time, worked together, and socialized in off hours. Their wives had been good friends as well.

Jack had lost his young wife, Amelia, several months ago to a severe bout of pneumonia. Derrick also knew they'd been a happy couple and very much in love. He guessed that closeness with his young wife had made Jack's loss that much greater. And Derrick had often seen that lost look on the man's face when he thought no one was watching.

"All right for me, I guess, but I'm worried about my little girl. Cecelia's only three. She misses her mother so much, Derrick. I hear her crying at night all too often." He had a frustrated look on his face. "It tears my heart out, the way she also cries every time I take her to that woman who watches her while I work. She is so unhappy there it makes me wonder what goes on during the day." Jack frowned. "Is she good to my little girl? I can't help but wonder about that when Sissy cries every time I take her there." He shrugged and heaved a sigh. "The woman tells me she pretends to have a belly ache at times, too. She says it's because Sissy doesn't want to eat or do what the woman asks her to do. She claims Sissy is just making up an excuse. I don't know where to turn with this, but I need to find someone else."

"Are you sure Sissy's all right? Maybe she isn't making it up. I know how kids are. I have a couple of them at home myself, but…" Derrick wondered if Jack might want to leave his daughter with Annalee Lines. He knew she was having a tough time financially. "I know of someone," he offered. "She's a family friend. She just lost her husband a few months ago, and I'm sure he didn't leave her enough to get by on. She's very proud and won't admit it, but that's what my wife and I believe. I'm sure she could use the money. In fact, I know she could." Seeing the look of interest on Jack's face, he added, "She has two little ones of her own and it might give your daughter someone to play with."

"Well—" Jack hesitated. "Tell me where she lives and I'll go check it out. I've got to find a better place for my Sissy." He straightened up, ready to walk away. "When I go see the woman, I'll take my daughter along and keep an eye out—see what happens. Might be a good idea. Thanks, Derrick."

Derrick, as an engineer himself, thought a lot of Jack as a co-worker. He was the engineer in charge of running the power crews—the men who built the lines to install new electric connections to homes within cities, smaller towns, and villages. The REA planned on electrification of farm homes in the near future, and he and Jack were excited to have a part in that new enterprise as well. In fact they had recently been offered a part in the planning.

The men under Jack Harrison kept the lines up and running. Derrick had heard they called themselves high-wood walkers. He guessed it might be because they climbed those high poles with spikes fastened to their legs. Standing on those spikes, the men did their work about sixty feet in the air, usually with dangerous hot wires buzzing right beside their heads. One false move and another man could easily be lost on those jobs. He applauded their bravado, respected their ability, and was glad he sat at a desk.

ℰↄℰↄ

It was coming dark when Annalee heard a knock on her door. She opened it to see a tall man wearing a nicely cut business suit. He held a tiny girl, with thick blonde curls, in his arms.

Surprised, she asked, "Yes, may I help you?"

"Mrs. Lines," the man said. "I came to see if you might consider minding my daughter during the days I work, usually Monday through Fridays, but often on a Saturday as well." He waited to see if she would allow him to enter her home.

Surprised that the man knew her name, she asked,

"How did you know I did child care? Did you see my advertisement in the grocery store?"

He smiled down at this young woman, who seemed a bit nervous. "You were recommended by a good friend of yours, one of my co-workers at the light company, Derrick Lassen."

He looked her over as she stood before him, and Annalee understood it. She would have done the same if she were in his situation. "I need to find a new place for my daughter while I'm at work," he continued.

"Please come in then, won't you?" She opened the door wide and waved the father to a chair in the shabby little sitting room. Then Annalee knelt down to meet the tiny girl. "And what is your name, little one?"

"I'n Thithy," she lisped, as she clung to her father's leg.

"My daughter's name is Cecelia," her father explained. "But we call her Sissy."

"We?" Annalee asked, wondering why he needed child care.

"I'm sorry, my wife passed away about six months ago. I'm afraid I haven't gotten out of the habit of saying 'we.'"

He had a deep look of sorrow about him, almost one of hopelessness. Annalee's heart went out to him and his daughter as well.

"I see," she said. Annalee knew a lot about learning to live without your marital partner and the support he could bring into the home. However, she didn't know the loss of a beloved marital partner, only the loss of a nasty, hot tempered brute. "I am sorry for your loss, sir," Annalee replied.

In her case, the loss of a spouse had been a great relief, but she'd always kept that fact carefully hidden.

"My name is Jack Harrison. I'm a co-worker of Derrick Lassen's, the one who recommended you."

He managed a smile and she saw that his face had a
gentle look to it—no harsh lines that could so easily
change into anger and cruelty if he was displeased. Annalee saw nothing to set her heart racing in fear. She also
noticed his teeth were white and even, and that he was a
very tall man, yet trim. His darkly streaked blond hair and
deep gray eyes only added to his overall good looks. His
daughter was blonde, too.

But it was his caring attitude with his child that ap-
pealed to her more than any other consideration. He
seemed a good sort and she understood his loss. Her heart
went out to the motherless child, knowing how terribly
she must miss the softness of her mother's touch and the
gentle, loving tones of her voice.

Her own two had come into the room. They stood
quietly watching the man and his daughter, their eyes big
as saucers. But it wasn't long before Buckley came forward to stand in front of Cecelia and stare at her. Annalee
was proud of her son. He had the dark hair and dark, almost black, eyes of his father. Yet, he was a gentle child
and tried to be helpful when he could. He had cried for
his father, but not for long.

"These are my children," Annalee said. "Buckley
aged four and my daughter, Sarah. She's two."

She indicated a small dark-haired child with deep
dark eyes as well. Buckley stood before Cecelia, his
hands on his hips, looked her in the eye, and asked,
"Wanna see my blocks?"

Cecelia, instantly mesmerized by Buckley, nodded her blonde curls. Jack soon watched his little girl being led away to another room. Little Sarah toddled after them, jabbering away. "She seems to like your boy," he said. "I don't think the other place had any other kids—never saw any." He hesitated. "Would you consider taking my child during the day? I work during the week, off most week-ends. But with the new lines going in, looks like I'll be working some week-ends for a while."

Annalee felt this child was an answer to a prayer. "Why yes," she replied. "I'd be glad to take care of her."

They discussed the price and it was quickly settled.

"I will bring her, beginning Monday," he said then added, "I think she will be much happier here. She cries when I take her to the other woman."

His words were punctuated with the happy sound of his daughter shrieking in delight as they heard a pile of blocks falling across the floor. He decided not to mention his daughter feigning illness with a tummy ache.

Annalee laughed. "Bucky likes it when the blocks fall down."

"Sounds like a normal little boy to me," Jack replied.

He looked at this young widow. She was a fine looking woman, with her slim figure and black curling hair. He wondered what her life was like, living alone with little money and two children to care for and bring up.

He knew how it was for himself. He had a nice home, in a good part of town, but it was dark and lonely. There were no lights in the windows when he came home at night and no welcoming smile from his beloved wife. There was no welcoming odor of a supper meal on the stove to greet his nose after a long day at his desk, either.

And those were only a few of the things that he missed. He remembered his wife's sweet face, her bubbling laugh, the softness of her skin, the clean smell of her body, and the glow of love shared between them. But his aching loneliness lay carefully hidden behind his friendly smile.

His little girl was not happy these days and hadn't been since losing her mother. She missed that loving touch so much it hurt him to see it. Yes, being widowed as he was, or a widow like Annalee, was a tough thing to handle. Jack looked at this lovely young widow and wondered what her marriage was like. Not so many were as happy as he and Amelia had been.

Annalee certainly was a picture—tall and slender with thick, dark, curling hair and straight, narrow nose. After he finally caught the shades of her eyes, he was surprised to see several shades of lavender, even deepening into purple in their depths.

Just then the children rushed into the living room to interrupt his observance of Mrs. Lines. Jack saw his little girl flushed and giggling as she chased after young Buckley. He had a doll in his hands and she wanted it. He held it out and she cried, "My dolly—mine."

It was probably Sarah's baby doll, but she was busy with another toy and didn't seem to care about it.

Annalee reached out to catch her son and caution him, "Bucky, what should you do about this?"

"Yeth, Momma, I know—she's a girl and I have to be nice and give her stuff."

He held the doll out and little Sissy took it. She didn't run, but held it in her chubby arms as she stood there gazing up at Buckley with a look of total adoration.

"That's right, Bucky Boy," Annalee said to her son. "You're going to be a fine young man someday—and a good one."

In her very soul, she'd prayed so often to raise a son with kindness in his heart, unlike that brutal father of his.

Jack felt his heart swell with relief. He had the feeling his daughter might be very happy in this household. It might be a shabby little home, but it was obvious to him that this young widow had a warm heart and would be good to his daughter. She needed the money, and he was glad to pay generously.

To see his daughter in a happy place meant a great deal to him. Cecelia had lost so much for such a tiny girl. And, unlike so many men in these depression years, as an engineer at a utility company he had a steady income.

He shook Annalee's hand. "She will be eating here, probably quite a bit, I'm sure. So if you don't mind, I'll bring a few things along when I bring her on Monday."

His hand was large, warm, and firm. Her own small hand was dwarfed in his as she noticed the clean nails and the solid, masculine way his hand looked and felt. His touch was, in some unconscious way, comforting. But feeling a flush of heat rising up her neck, she quickly snatched her hand away and moved back.

He called his little girl and, reaching down, caught her up in his arms to depart.

Annalee opened the door for him. "Good night, and thank you very much, Mr. Harrison."

Jack walked down the crumbling sidewalk to his shiny Oldsmobile sedan. He set his daughter on the front seat beside him and, as he drove away, asked her, "Did you like that lady, Sissy?"

"Yeth, Daddy, her little boy ith nice to me. He lets me touch his truck and his blocks, too."

"How about the lady?"

"She's nice, Daddy. She likths her kids, too." She giggled up at him. "Bucky likths me, Daddy."

Jack felt satisfied with the arrangement he'd made with the widow. His little one wouldn't cry if she had to go there and stay all day. He drove down the darkening street, seeing the few street lights come on. It was a small town, and he enjoyed working in the regional office the utility company kept there. Small towns made his life a bit easier in some ways.

His mind went back to the young widow. He'd never seen her around the little village, but imagined she moved in different social circles from the ones he and his wife had frequented. Her little house was poor, but she had kept it as clean and neat as if it were a more imposing home. Her children were clean and well groomed as well. He'd also seen that she had her share of pride. He'd have to be careful bringing things to that house. He didn't want to offend this woman. If his daughter was happy and safe there, that was all he asked.

Chapter 3

Annalee was up early, had her children dressed and eager to accept little Sissy for her first day. She had oatmeal on the stove for breakfast. At the sound of the knock on her door, she was ready.

She opened her door and bade the tall man who carried his daughter in his arms to enter. Sissy clung to him tightly this morning, and Annalee saw she was fearful of being left with strangers once again. She didn't blame the little girl one bit. She would have felt the same way.

Buckley came up to Mr. Harrison. "Hi, there. You got Thithy?"

Annalee hoped he'd lose his lisp pretty soon, it sounded so babyish.

Hearing Buckley's voice, Cecelia brightened and struggled to get down from her father's arms. "Daddy, I stay with Bucky?"

"Yes, my darling, this is where you will stay while Daddy works. You can play all day long." He patted her head. "But you must promise to be a good little girl for Mrs. Lines today."

"Yeth, Daddy," she called as she ran away to another room with Buckley.

Jack heaved a sigh of relief. "Thank God for your little boy. She cried every day when I left her with Mrs. Stark," he said. "I will give you my phone number in case you need to call me." He whipped out a small pad and wrote something on it.

"Excuse me, sir, I have no phone here. We never had one put in."

"Oh, I didn't know that." He thought a moment. "Ma'am, would you mind if I had one installed here? Cecelia has had a few episodes of stomach cramps. I worry about that and would want to be informed."

Annalee knew she couldn't refuse his request because of his concern for his child. But she also knew it would be another cost she couldn't afford.

Seeing her hesitation, Jack knew immediately that Mrs. Lines was worried about the cost. He held up his hand. "Please, ma'am, my daughter seems happy here, and I think this will work out well for her. I will take care of the cost of the phone." He didn't plan to take no for an answer on this subject. It was too important.

Annalee saw his determination and understood the reason for his concern. "I guess it'll be all right then," she said. "I know you are right to be worried if Cecelia might be taken ill. With three children here it might be hard to get to a phone in that case," she added. "Has she seen a doctor about these stomach cramps?"

"No, they only last a short while, so I haven't—not yet." He flung out his hands and grimaced, indicating his struggle to be a good father and the only parent. "But as for the phone, I'll have one put in this afternoon." Satisfied his child was in good hands, he asked Annalee, "Where is she, I'd like to say goodbye."

Annalee hurried to the kids' bedroom and brought Sissy out to say goodbye to her father. She was glad to see that the little girl didn't cry at being left. Instead, she kept her eyes on Buckley, who stood in the hallway, hands on his hips, waiting for her.

With the father gone, Annalee called them to have breakfast. It was oatmeal with brown sugar on it and they ate pretty well. Little Sarah needed some help, but Cecelia did a pretty good job of eating without making too big a mess.

❧❧❧

It had gone well for Annalee these past few weeks. She found she got along well with the sad little child who missed her mother so. Cecelia eagerly allowed Annalee to cuddle her for a few moments when she had a bump or fell down.

Two-year-old Sarah had taken exception to that interaction and was jealous. She would cry and hang on Annalee's skirt, crying. "No! My mommie."

Annalee made room for two of them.

Mr. Harrison had brought several bags of groceries, saying, "I have no idea what you use or need, but I want you to have enough to feed my little one."

Annalee had the idea he thought she had little enough and was trying to be tactful in what he brought. It was far more than she'd expected or needed, but Annalee wasn't sure how to put a damper on his giving. She said nothing to him outside of, "Thanks."

She had thought of inviting him for supper some night, but couldn't bring herself to ask him something so personal.

He arrived each night to take his child in his arms and head out the door. He always said, "Thanks for taking care of her. Cecelia has been much happier, lately, and it's because of being here in your home."

One time Annalee thought she saw the beginning of a tear in his eye, but Jack Harrison wasn't a man given to tears—she saw that about him, too.

୧୬୧୬

Annalee heard a knock, and answered her door to see her friend Carol standing there.

"Hey, come in," she cried, happy to see a friendly face. She ushered Carol to the sitting room and, with the children playing quietly in a bedroom, they sat down to talk. "I'm so glad to see you, Carol. It's been a while."

"I haven't been feeling too well, lately," Carol said, a sly smile on her lips. "What's going on in your life these days, An?" She leaned forward as though to hear Annalee's reply.

"I'm sorry if you are not up to your best, Carol. Want some coffee, or tea, maybe?"

Annalee got up to head for the kitchen to fix something for her guest. They had known each other since high school days.

"Anything new going on?" Carol asked, her tone probing and insistent.

"I have a little girl I'm taking care of now. She is the daughter of an engineer that Amy's husband knows—his three year old. I believe the mother has passed away. He said she was unhappy where he had her and needed to find different child care for her while he works," Annalee answered as she brought in a small plate of cookies. "The coffee's making."

"I hadn't heard of anyone like that. What does he look like?"

"Sort of tall and blonde. Seems like a really nice man. I'd say he is still mourning the loss of his wife." Annalee shrugged. "It's hard enough trying to a raise a child on your own as a woman. I can't imagine it would be so easy for a single man."

"You ought to know how it is well enough yourself," Carol said. She sat there, looking at Annalee, like she was trying to decide what she wanted to say. Finally she said, her voice quiet and low, "Uh, Annalee, you'll be the first to know, but the reason I don't feel so good is—well, I'm pregnant and several months along by now."

"How wonderful! Does Donald know?"

"Not yet. I don't know how to tell him, and I think I'm headed for trouble. A while back his doctor informed him he couldn't make babies—if you know what I mean by that." She hastened to add, "Not that he can't...uh, well, you know what I mean." Carol flushed red with that statement and had a strange, almost dreamy, look on her face.

Annalee wondered if it was partly guilt. If her husband was sterile, as she had just implied, Carol ought to be feeling quite a bit of fear over being pregnant.

"I don't know what he's going to say about me being

in the family way, An," Carol went on. "If what his doc says is true—I'm plenty scared to tell him." She flung out her hands in desperation, as though hoping Annalee had the answer to her situation.

"Man oh man, Carol! What are you trying to say? Are you telling me you have been unfaithful to Donald?"

"I guess that's what I'm saying, An.'' Carol wrung her hands. "If his doctor really told him that, he'll be looking daggers at me. He'll be mad as a hornet, about it. What'll I do if he kick's me out and divorces me?"

Annalee wondered about Carol and Don's marital relationship, especially if Carol was out looking around. "Would he do that?"

"If he thought the kid was his, he wouldn't divorce me. He'd be over the moon happy. Of course, doctors have been wrong before. Maybe I can convince him things have changed for him, and he'll be okay with it now," she said with a snide smile. "He'll likely believe almost anything I tell him because he wants to be a father in the worst way." Carol brightened, sat back, and crossed her short legs. "That's what I'll do. Feed him a line big enough to rope an elephant." She almost giggled in her relief. "Where's that coffee?"

"Coming up, dear, but is that healthy for an expectant mother?"

"Who cares, An?" Carol tossed her head. "I think you've helped me find a way to handle this. Thanks a million."

Annalee didn't think she had helped Carol at all, and she didn't like the secretive look in the woman's eyes. But she said nothing as she set the coffee cups out and poured them each one.

Carol took a sip then looked carefully at the contents of her cup. "Say, this isn't your usual coffee. What are you using?"

"Mr. Harrison brings groceries sometimes, and this coffee was in the bag. It's Maxwell House coffee. I usually buy Eight O'clock if I have the money. It's only nineteen cents a pound. This brand costs about thirty-six cents for a pound, and that's way too expensive for me." Annalee flushed with the reply. She didn't want Carol to get the wrong idea about her and Mr. Harrison.

Sipping the dark brew, Carol commented, "Seems like he's getting pretty cozy with you these days, An, buying your groceries and all."

"There is no 'and all,'" Annalee replied. "He said he knew I'd be feeding his daughter and didn't want me to run short. That's all there is to it."

"Humph. I'll just bet." Then Carol went on to ask, "Anything else new in your life, aside from a big handsome guy coming to your home every day around dinner time?"

"Didn't you already ask me that?" Annalee replied, puzzled and irritated, wondering what Carol was getting at.

"Well then, tell me more about this father. Good looking is he?"

"Good enough, I suppose."

"Tall, dark, and lonely, maybe?"

Carol was prying for some reason of her own. Annalee had vowed she'd never go down the marital road again, no matter what. But she didn't plan to ever release that bit of information.

She didn't want any gossip spread around about how

miserable her marriage to Gerald Lines had been. It was over and she was done with it.

She remembered Carol's question. "He's never let on about anything like that. Of course, I had never seen the man before, in any case. His big worry was his child and if she'd be happy here with us. She wasn't happy where he had her before." Annalee took a sip of the very good coffee. She didn't want to waste a drop of it. "And he said that she misses her mother very much." She chuckled softly. "She really likes my Bucky, and that helps."

They both heard the sounds of the children playing in one of the bedrooms and Buckley's voice giving orders to the little girls.

Carol sniffed. "Well, I hope it works out for you. I guess I'd better be going. Thanks for your help, dear." She rose from her seat on the couch. "Let me know if you need anything." She took up her purse and donned a short jacket.

Annalee led her to the door. "I'm so glad you came, Carol. It's lonely these days, being a widow."

Carol walked out the door without another word and made her way down the sidewalk to her car. Annalee stood looking after her. "Wonder what that visit was all about."

She had never let on about her abusive marriage to anyone but her parents and she hoped no one else had known about it. Having a husband treat her that way was a thing of shame to her.

Something about Carol kept bothering Annalee. From what she'd said, it sounded as if she had probably gotten herself pregnant by another man and planned to pass the baby off as her husband's. It wasn't right, but

Annalee had no thought of putting her two cents' worth in about that situation.

Somehow, she had the feeling that her conniving friend just might manage to fool her husband. Remembering some of the things she'd known Carol to do in the past, Annalee was sure the woman wouldn't mind stirring up a bit of trouble if she saw the chance. Newly aware of what underhanded tricks her friend was capable of, Annalee determined that Carol would never have the chance to hurt her that way. Sadly, it undermined the feeling of friendship and trust she'd always had for the woman.

For some reason, she felt she needed to be on her guard against Carol Woods. Too bad, but since living with that devil of a man, Gerald, Annalee had grown wary and much harder of thought somehow.

Chapter 4

On one particular day, when Carol had come to visit, it was rather late in the day. Annalee had the idea Carol wanted to get a glimpse of Cecelia's handsome father when he came to pick up his child. She said nothing on that subject, just waited to see if that was what Carol had on her mind. Annalee smiled to herself, remembering he wouldn't be here for another hour. He had called and said he would be a bit late today.

As she was busy brewing a pot of coffee for the two of them, Buckley came to her. "Sissy's sick, Momma."

Annalee, remembering what Jack Harrison had said about Cecelia's stomach cramps, hurried to the children's bedroom. She found Sissy curled up on Buckley's bed, her arms trying to hold her stomach

She put her hand on Sissy's brow and felt the warmth radiating from it. "Where do you hurt, honey?"

"It's my tummy again. It hurted me."

She gazed up at Annalee. Her eyes, glazed and shining with fever, reflected her misery. Annalee felt a touch of panic, remembering a friend she'd had in the eighth grade. He'd often had the same complaint. She'd seen him bending over from his pain and feeling warm at those times, too. His complaints had been ignored. Their teacher at the time paid little attention to him, thinking it was merely a stomach ache like many children have. It was felt that he'd get over it as he always did. She also remembered he had died later of a burst appendix after one of those episodes. Her parents had gone to his funereal and taken her along.

She ran to the phone and called Mr. Harrison. "Sir, Sissy is having one of those attacks. I think you need to take her to a doctor. It's pretty bad this time, much worse than what you had described to me."

Annalee hung up the phone.

Carol had followed her every step and overheard every word. "What are you getting all excited about? Kids complain of bellyaches all the time. You're letting that kid make a fool of you."

"I'd rather that than have him lose this child. It might be something much worse than a little bellyache, Carol."

"I'll just bet it isn't. I know kids, An. They love play acting. I'll bet she's just doing that to get more attention."

"Not so likely with this child. Her forehead is warm, Carol. She's only three years old—a bit young to pretend an illness," Annalee retorted, her voice sharper than usual in her disgust at Carol's unfeeling attitude. "Will you please let her father in when he gets here?"

Annalee went back into the bedroom, but she hadn't missed the excitement in Carol's eyes at her request. She shook her head at the woman's eagerness to get a look at this man. No surprise there—Annalee had suspected all along that was her friend's reason for the late afternoon visit.

Annalee's worry over the little girl took precedence in her mind. She sat beside the child and stroked her hair. It was slightly damp from perspiration by now. Seeing the intensity of Cecelia's discomfort, Annalee's worry increased. Could she have the same thing as her friend from the eighth grade?

Annalee heard a car drive up and the sound of voices as Carol answered the door. As she stepped out of the bedroom to greet Mr. Harrison and bring him to his daughter, she heard Carol going on about Cecelia.

She stood in front of a very worried Jack Harrison, batting her eyes, and letting her hips sway in an overtly sexual motion. Annalee found her behavior completely disgusting, especially as she heard Carol telling him, "She's in here, Mr. Harrison." Her voice was low and filled with concern. "I worry she has something very serious. Please, you must take her to the doctor."

He hurried into the room and squatted beside the bed to feel his daughter's heated brow. "My goodness, honey, I think we will go and see Doctor Gleeson. He can make you all better." He looked at Annalee with utter gratitude in his eyes. "Thanks for calling me. I've been worried about this happening again—just like it has before." He picked his daughter up in his arms and headed for the door. "I'll let you know what we find out."

Without a glance in Carol's direction, he made his way out the door and down the sidewalk with his daughter in his arms. He gently placed his child in the front seat and soon roared away in his car.

Obviously miffed at Jack's disregard of her, Carol said, "Well, he was sure in a hurry to get out of here, wasn't he?"

"This wasn't exactly a social call, Carol. His little girl might well die from a thing like this."

Carol sniffed and plunked herself down solidly on the couch. "That's ridiculous, and you know it. She'll be running around as soon as they get home."

Annalee sat down too and put her head in her hands. "I hope you're right, Carol. But I wonder—why did you tell the father you were so worried and that he should take Cecelia to the doctor? I had planned to tell him that."

Carol made no effort to answer that question, but merely shrugged with a sly smile on her lips.

Annalee got up and changed the pot on the stove to the tea kettle. "Whew! I could use a cup of tea—how about you?"

She was angry that Carol had tried to take over the care and concern of Cecelia. *What has that sneaky woman got in mind, pulling a stunt like that?*

Carol finally spotted the phone, though Annalee had called on it moments before. "Hum, I see you have a phone now, too. So how did you manage that?"

"Mr. Harrison wanted it in case his daughter got sick. I can't tell you how glad I was to have it handy today, for exactly what just happened. He's been worried about her stomach pains, too. They've happened a few times before."

"He put it in for you?" Carol snickered a bit. "And you're still calling him, mister?"

"Of course. There is nothing going on with that man or any other man. It is strictly a business deal, me taking care of his daughter." Annalee was sick of Carol's snide innuendos. "Like some tea?"

"Sure, I'll have a cup. Sorry, Annalee, I didn't mean anything by what I said. I suppose you need all the income you can get. I think you're lucky. It's a nice little kid to play along with yours."

"Cecelia is a nice child. She still misses her momma a lot, I can tell you. Her father said the same thing." Annalee poured the hot water over the tea leaves and dug about in a drawer. "I have a strainer somewhere."

"Why don't you get those nice tea bags, like everybody else?"

"I would but they are more expensive. I have to be careful these days. My husband left me nothing but the children. No insurance or anything. I am trying to keep a roof over our heads, and paying for bulk tea is about all I can manage these days."

"It must be tough on you. Maybe you could take in more kids?"

"I'm making out all right, Carol. Mr. Harrison brings extra food over to be sure his daughter has enough to eat."

"Really? How nice for you, my dear. Are you sure he isn't interested in more than child care?'

Annalee had started wondering when this busybody, so-called friend of hers was going to leave the house. "Carol, there's never been one word that way. He is an honorable man and still in mourning for his wife."

In her own heart, she'd vowed never to get entangled with any man again—ever! She'd had enough of that to last her a lifetime. But Carol Woods was the last person in the world she'd ever let on to about that subject.

It was way after dark and Carol was about to leave when the telephone rang. Annalee answered it. She looked at Carol. "It's Mr. Harrison," she mouthed with her hand over the receiver.

She listened intently for a few moments and then hung up. She turned to Carol. "He said Sissy is in surgery right now, and they hope they will be in time to save her life." She felt her tears burning her eyes. "He called to say thanks."

Carol looked pale and her hands shook like leaves blowing in the wind. "Oh, my gosh, what if you hadn't done anything? She might have died." She paced about the kitchen. "Did he say what was wrong?"

"No, but he was very upset and sounded scared to death for his daughter. I think I'll call Amy and tell her. Her husband works with Mr. Harrison." After Annalee made that call, she asked Carol, "How about your husband? Is he at home waiting for you?"

"Yes, I almost forgot I was supposed to be home earlier than this." Carol glanced at the wall clock. "With all the excitement around here, I just forgot."

She left the house after that, and Annalee realized they hadn't had time to discuss her pregnancy and how she was doing with it. She shrugged. Her own two little ones were clamoring for her attention right now.

Chapter 5

It was ten days later when Mr. Harrison knocked on her door. Annalee opened it and bade him enter. "How is Cecelia?" she asked.

"She is coming along just fine." He grimaced a bit. "That's what I need to speak to you about. She will be discharged tomorrow and, I wonder, will you be up to taking care of her if she needs a lot of special attention?"

"I'm sure I can take care of her just fine. Can you tell me what kind of special care does she need?"

"Just that she is very tender in the abdomen. They put in a lot of rather large stitches. They said it was very close, and they got it just in time. The doctor said it was her appendix."

She could see him struggle to fight his tears. "Mr. Harrison, please don't worry about feeling like you do. You have the right, if anyone does. Of course, it was close for her, but you got her there in time. We are all terribly grateful she made it through."

"Thanks, Annalee." He manfully tried to hide his emotions. "You are one fine woman, ma'am. My little girl has been calling you Momma and asking for you. I hope that's all right. It seems she may have transferred her love for her own mother to you." He flung out his hands and flushed a ruddy color at the admission. "I don't know what to do about that."

"No need to do anything. I am quite honored she thinks of me that way. When she's older, she'll know better. You'll be there to teach her about her own mother, and you should," Annalee told him. "I'll take care of whatever she needs. I'd love to."

"She may need to spend the night here for a week or so. I don't want to haul her around too much at first. Is that possible?"

"I think so, yes. Is it all right if I put her in with me? I can make sure she is all right during the night that way."

For Annalee, the solution was simple but for Jack, it was a downright imposition. It was way too much to ask of any casual baby sitter. His daughter had become attached to this lovely young mother, even to calling her Momma. He felt trapped by it and embarrassed as well.

Annalee saw his frustration with the situation. "I know you think it's too much, but if my little girl was in the same situation as yours, I would do it this way. It's for the best and I don't mind it. It's not an imposition at all Mr. Harrison, not to me." Annalee smiled at him. "She calls me Momma? I think that's just fine."

"I'm afraid she does, ma'am."

"You may call me Annalee if you like and, no, I won't mind the extra trouble. I won't, really. I'm just thankful she will be all right. I was so afraid. I have seen this very situation before, and it didn't turn out for the good."

"I'd say you have saved my daughter's life, ma'am. And in that case, you must call me Jack. All my friends do, and you have certainly earned the right to be called a friend of mine." He took her hand in his for a long moment and then headed for the door. "Good night, Annalee, and I thank you, more than I can say." His voice was low and softer than usual.

ↀↄↀↄ

Cecelia came to stay for almost two weeks. She blended with Annalee's children well enough, in spite of some jealousy on Sarah's part. Her youngest child remained possessive of her mother's lap and so did Buckley, but little Cecelia managed to enjoy that spot quite often as she moved about slowly because of her incision. It remained tender for a long time, and Annalee checked it often. The rather large and ugly cut slowly lost its redness and discomfort. Bucky was very curious about the scar, and Cecelia was always eager to show it off. Sarah looked and had big eyes when she saw it.

At night, Cecelia cuddled in bed with Annalee and called her, "Momma." The sound of it nearly broke Annalee's heart, but if thinking that, gave the little child a lot of comfort, Annalee was happy about it. Worried it would cause some trouble later on, she mentioned it to Jack.

"What can I do about it?" Annalee asked. "What will happen when you take her home at night again?"

"She has a lot of things to play with at home, but the

warmth and comfort she finds here can't compete with a room full of toys," he replied.

Jack had a deep look of gratitude on his face and that tore Annalee apart.

"Buckley and Sarah keep her busy," she said. "And I hold her when she needs it. I think she is happy with us. Of course, no one could ever fully make up for what she's lost, but we try."

"We never had the chance to have any more children before…"

He couldn't go on and Annalee saw the gleam of moisture fill his eyes.

She felt badly for Jack. He still mourned his lost wife terribly. For herself, Annalee hadn't mourned the loss of her husband at all. If feeling that way made her a cold-hearted woman, she couldn't help it. She breathed a long sigh of relief. Life was so much more peaceful without him.

When Jack came to the house, Cecelia would go to him with joy in her eyes, but Annalee saw that the little girl didn't want to leave her either. When she was well enough to go home with her father for the night, it was a gut-wrenching experience for all of them. Shrugging, he picked her up and carried her, crying, to his car, and carefully deposited her on the front seat.

Annalee wondered how Cecelia had spent the night, when she was so used to being cuddled against a warm body. She guessed Jack would tell her how it went when he brought her again next Monday morning.

That night, it was a Saturday, a large storm came roaring across central Wisconsin. Annalee heard her little home tremble and shake as the howling winds swirled

around it. Things cracked against the windows, and the
roof rattled until she feared the house could not withstand
it and remain erect. They had no basement to run down
into and, terrified, Annalee huddled in the living room
with her children.

It finally died down to a gusty, swirling wind and
slightly softer, though still heavy rainfall, and Annalee
relaxed. Her children were ready for bed when her phone
rang. "Yes, Annalee here," she answered.

"Mrs. Lines, this is Jack Harrison. Would it be all
right if I brought my daughter over? The storm has done
so much damage I have to go to work. Lines are down all
over, the roads are full of wreckage, and transformers are
blown."

"Why of course. You'd best plan on leaving her for
the night then. She'll be fine here with us."

She hung up and waited for his arrival. It still
dripped rain outside. She could see that through the windows. A fallen tree lay across the grass in the front yard,
and the wind still howled like a thousand devils.

Annalee put her children to bed and sat down on her
couch, shivering in fear of the storm as she waited for
Jack to bring his daughter.

At a soft knock, she opened her door and Jack carried in his warmly wrapped daughter, sleeping in his
arms. Annalee led him into her bedroom and had him lay
Cecelia down.

"Thanks, Annalee. You have no idea how much I
appreciate having a safe place for Sissy, and even more,
that she's very happy here." He headed for the door. "I'll
come and get her when we get this tornado mess straightened out. I'm afraid it may be a while. I hear everything

is down, except a few places here in town, and it's not over yet."

"It's not?" Annalee exclaimed. "A tornado, you say? I thought our roof was going to go, but I didn't know it was that bad." Seeing he wore rain gear, and rubber boots, she warned, "Be careful out there, Jack."

He left and, shortly after that, another knock came. Annalee opened her door to Carol. "What are you doing out on a nasty night like this?"

"My husband kicked me out, An, right out into this horrible pouring rain," she sobbed. "He's found out this is not his child. He was ready to lay hands on me, and I do mean hands. He was madder than a hornet."

"What made him so upset? How did he find out?" Annalee asked. "I thought you had things under control in that department."

"He found some note or other from a certain person. Like a dummy, I had left it lying around." Carol shook with terror. Her hair was awry and damp from the rain that still came down outside. "He shook it in my face with one hand, and I saw a clenched fist in the other." She sank onto the couch. "Can I stay here tonight?"

"Why, of course. Join the club. I've just gotten Jack's little girl, too. He said he had to go out and tend to all the downed power lines." Annalee added, voicing her thoughts, "Why would you leave an incriminating thing like a note around for him to find, anyway, Carol? You ought to know better than that."

"Oh, so your new man was here tonight, too, huh?"

"He's no man of mine, Carol. I take care of his child and that's all."

Carol had immediately forgotten Annalee's question

in her curiosity over that big, handsome father of Cecelia's.

Annalee reminded her. "Why leave a note or letter for your husband to find? Why do that?"

"I really don't know, An. Sometimes I just forget things."

Carol slumped into a ball of misery and wiped her eyes, partly from tears and partly from the moisture of rain. But Annalee held her sympathy. Already curious about her friend's machinations before this, she wondered about that business again tonight. Something didn't make sense. *What is this woman working up to*?

"You'll have to make do with this couch. I have little Cecelia in with me," Annalee explained. "Since she's lost her mother, she has taken to calling me 'Mommy,' and I haven't the heart to tell her I'm not her mother. She is just getting over her operation, you know."

"What do your own kids think of that?" Carol asked, her eyes squinting.

"I doubt if they've even noticed it," Annalee replied.

Was Carol looking for a way to put a wedge between her children and Jack's little girl? Annalee tossed that thought out. It was too ridiculous.

"How long are you going to keep her here?"

"As long as she needs me, I guess. Unless he finds another woman to be her stepmom."

"Hey, girl, if you played your cards right, it could be you." Carol had her eyebrows arched along with a little snicker at her comment.

"Marriage is out as far as I am concerned. I've had enough of that business to last me a lifetime." Annalee shivered as she spoke.

Carol looked surprised at this bit of news. "Are you kidding me?" She got off the couch and stared at Annalee. "All these years, and you never said a word that things weren't right between you and Gerald."

"I'm sorry I brought it up. I never meant to let that bit of information out. I never did—sorry." Annalee worried that with Carol's trouble-making mind set, this news would soon be spread all over town. "If I ever hear of this business being passed around, you'll be hearing from me. Pregnant or not, and I don't care who the father is, I mean what I say!"

"Whew, girl, go easy. It's not the kind of happy news anyone wants to hear. Are you saying your husband was less than perfect? Was he mean, An? Cruel in bed or what?"

"I'm not speaking another word about it. He's dead and gone, isn't he?" Annalee folded her hands and sat there, saying nothing more.

Carol tossed in another bit of information. "Oh well, An, let's face it. Most men have a lot to learn about the bedroom," she said with a smug sort of look on her face, which Annalee found puzzling.

She didn't feel like answering that comment. If Carol had spread herself around the country, it was no wonder her husband had kicked her out.

Annalee found it difficult to rake up a lot of pity for a woman who played fast and loose with someone else's husband. And she had the feeling that was exactly the case. Some other family out there would soon have a half-brother or sister to another man's children one day and never know about it.

Annalee looked out the window into the darkness.

"It's suddenly gone quiet out there now. We may as well turn in. I'll find some blankets for you." She left Carol and rummaged through the hall closet for the few things it held. She found an old pillow and a faded blanket and took them to her friend. "This is all I have, Carol—not much is it?"

"I'll make do. Don't worry. Thanks for letting me stay tonight, An." Carol took the bedding and, holding it in her arms, asked, "What was your husband like, then? He always seemed a decent sort to me."

"He always was—to everyone else." Annalee didn't plan to elaborate on her husband's cruelty, especially not to a blather mouth like Carol.

Carol asked nothing more about Gerald. She turned to make up a bed of sorts on the living room couch. Annalee headed to her bedroom to lie in her bed and cuddle next to Cecelia.

Chapter 6

I t was two days later when a grimy, red-eyed Jack came to collect his child. Annalee ushered him into her home and bade him have a seat. "It must have been bad out there by the looks of you."

"Everything was down—twisted and damaged. There were three people we know of who lost their lives in that storm. We aren't sure yet if there are any more." He wiped his face with a grimy handkerchief. "How's Sissy?"

"She's been just fine," Annalee said as all three little ones came running into the room.

Sissy spotted her father. She stood before him, gazing up at him. "Daddy, you all dirty."

"Yes, honey, I am." He grabbed her up gently and planted a kiss right on her cheek.

"Oh, Daddy, you scatched on me." She giggled, wriggled down, and turned to Buckley. "Look, Bucky, Daddy all scatchy."

Carol had remained at Annalee's home, afraid to chance going home to her husband's wrath. She had come into the room and stood watching the children with Jack.

Annalee saw her preen and let her eyes flutter as she asked him, her voice artificially high, "Was it really so awfully bad out there, Mr. Harrison?"

He looked up in surprise at her question. He hadn't noticed her entrance into the room. "Why yes, quite severe, like any storm, but a tornado is far more intense. There is an extreme amount of damage."

"And people were killed, didn't I hear you say?" Carol affected alarm with widened eyes along with her question.

"Yes, but that hasn't been announced on the radio as yet. Families will have to be notified, if they haven't been so far." He was puzzled by Carol's presence, and apparently didn't remember who she was or why she was there.

Annalee introduced Carol to Jack. At hearing her name, his face grew pale as he rose up to stand before her.

"Is your husband named, Donald Woods, a big, red-headed man?"

"Why yes, he is." Carol turned white as a sheet. "Why do you ask?"

"I'm not sure it is within my area to tell you this, but since you are with friends, I'll go ahead." He took a deep breath. "Mrs. Woods, it seems your husband has been one of the casualties of this storm."

Carol let out a long wailing moan, "Oh, my God, no!" she gasped and slumped down on the couch, clutching her enlarged belly around the middle. "It can't be him. Are you sure of it?" She got up and paced about the room, her head in her hands. "Why was he out in that storm? How did it happen?"

"They found him out near the street. A tree limb had blown down and must have struck him. That's where he was found, laying beneath that large limb," Jack said then added, "What on earth could have made that man go running out in the storm like that?"

But Carol knew exactly why Donald had run out into the street. Her husband had come to his senses after kicking his pregnant wife out of her home in the midst of a raging storm. He had gone out to look for her and bring her back inside, right during the worst of it, just as it had reached its most violent.

Annalee saw the look of comprehension on Carol's face. She went to her friend, took her in her arms, and patted her on the back as she helped her to a chair. "Oh, Carol, I'm so sorry to hear this. I'll help all I can, you know that."

Jack stood watching the two women. Worn to a frazzle though he was, he'd thought he ought to take his child home so as not to place too big a burden on Annalee.

Ma'am, I'll just take my daughter and go home. You have enough going on here," Jack said as he faced Annalee. He turned to Carol. "Mrs. Woods I am very sorry to bring you news like this, but it had to be done." He reached down and patted her on the shoulder. "Luckily, you have a good friend here to help you along."

Carol felt the touch of his hand and turned her tear-stained eyes to catch a glimpse of this good man's face. "Thanks," she murmured, positive he had given her a look that meant far more than mere condolences. The thought of this handsome male putting a hand on her sent her blood racing. He was single—and now, so was she.

"Mr. Harrison, by the looks of you, you need several hours of sleep before you take Sissy home," Annalee said. "Why not do that and come back later for her? She's just fine here."

He glanced at the fine-looking young widow standing before him and, knowing she made sense, nodded and turned to go. Sissy was running after Bucky and waved to him as he left.

Seeing how happy his daughter was in this shabby little home, a swell of utter gratitude to the Annalee rose inside him. He walked out of her door a satisfied man.

Carol left shortly thereafter to return to her own home. She was a widow now with many things to attend to in order to lay her husband to rest. She no longer had to answer to him. It wouldn't matter at all anymore who's child she carried. Everyone would automatically believe it was Donald's. She hugged her middle and smiled to herself—if *she* only knew…

She felt little sorrow toward the husband she'd lost. He hadn't been all that smart in the first place and, to say the least, she'd found married life with Donald Woods a crashing bore. He'd been a good-looking man, but a thing like that soon wore out. He couldn't even give her babies, and that was the main reason she wanted marriage in the first place.

She'd always wanted a baby. Someone to raise and train the way a child ought to be brought up—not the way she'd been "jerked" up. That was how she'd always thought of the way her parents had raised her. They'd loved her brother far more than her and had doted on his every move. It had always been that way and the mere memory of it made her burn inside.

She kept remembering that fine, handsome blond man who came to Annalee's home every blessed day— now there was a real man! He was really something, a man who wouldn't be boring in the least. Jack Harrison, being an engineer, must make a good living, too. Better than the paltry income Donald Woods had brought home. He'd been a lousy clerk in the grocery store—big whoo-pee!

Carol remembered bitterly how they'd barely made ends meet. They had a nicer home than many, but it had been her parents' home and already paid for. They were gone now and had left their nice home to her, so it wasn't like she had no place to go.

That home was all hers now. Her brother be damned, the spoiled brat!

In many ways, she wished she wasn't pregnant. Yet the secret she carried about who the father was made it almost more important to her than the forthcoming child itself. Wouldn't it be a real feather in her cap to let that nasty little cat out of the bag? And she would, when the time was right.

She smiled to herself, seeing a youthful, slim Carol getting things going with that handsome Jack Harrison. Those deep gray eyes of his had a way of going right through a girl. Oh yes, he was far more exciting than Donald had been and made more money in the bargain. She let her imagination run wild, seeing herself in his arms and on his arm at social occasions, too. How proud she'd be walking into a nice fancy-dancy place on that handsome Jack's arm. She'd be the envy of every woman there.

Already, her house seemed so much lonelier now that Donald was gone. She paced through the rooms, and they almost echoed. In the bedroom, she smiled as she saw again the wrinkled note her husband had read, crushed into a ball, and thrown on the floor. She retrieved it, smoothed out the crinkles, and re-read the heated message.

> *Darling Carol: I'm awaiting tonight with all I have to give you. And by now you know that's a plenty, don't you my dearest hot-hot sweetheart? Meet me in the usual place. The weather is fine tonight. We can be together once more. I have got a big heat on for you.*
> *U Know Who.*

Carol waved the wrinkled note in the air. *I know I should get rid of this, but what if a certain saintly woman just happened to find it sort of lying around somewhere? Wouldn't that be a real kick in the teeth for Miss Goody Two Shoes?* A malignant grin spread across her face as she thought of how delicious a thing like that would be. She could see it now—the shocked look, the tears, the feeling of being betrayed and having been cheated on. And best of all, this wonderful paragon of womanhood would know that she hadn't been woman enough to keep her man at home.

Carol brought out a clean white shirt, a suit, and necktie for her husband's burial and laid them across the big, empty bed. There was only the one funeral parlor in this little berg for things like taking care of dead people. Her Donald had been a good man, she guessed, but nothing to equal the good looks she'd seen on that tall, blond widower, Jack Harrison. And oh, those deep gray eyes. Oh God! How they just went through a girl like lightening.

She felt her pulse rise, imagining him bringing his little girl to *her* home and how cozy it would be after he got to know her. He'd see what a fine, sexy woman she was and how much she had to offer a big handsome man like him, so tall, and oh so sexy. He'd know how to take care of a hot little woman like her. She smiled to herself, knowing she'd always been good with men and knew how to handle them.

Alone now with a baby on the way, she might need some extra money, though Donald had left her a nice life insurance policy. She remembered the day that nice insurance man had come to their home and signed him up. She also remembered how his eyes had followed her every move. Maybe she'd take in some kids like Annalee. But her mind had already settled on only one child in particular. She could see it now. That handsome blond male driving up to her door every evening, lonely and needing what a woman like her had to give.

She hummed as she went about setting out the things needed to bury her husband in proper style. She wondered if he needed shoes and found herself giggling about seeing him wearing shoes while lying in that big box. She decided she might look foolish if she brought them to the funeral home.

She tossed them back into the closet, wondering what to do with his things. "Give them to charity, I suppose. I don't think that handsome Jack would want to wear them."

People had been coming to her door, off and on all day long, bringing food and flowers, doing what they could to console the new widow in their midst. Her dining room table was nearly full of casseroles, pies, and plates of cookies, and in her refrigerator, sat a meat loaf, sausages, and another casserole or two. She'd never be able to eat a particle of it.

The thought of it set her to wondering if she could find a way to share some of it with that good-looking Jack Harrison. Lost in thoughts about the man and how he would take her into his arms and into his bed and the hot things he'd do to her, she heard her doorbell ring.

The doorbell sounded yet again. Carol opened her door to see Annalee standing there with her two children. Surprised, Carol opened the door wider for them to enter. "Why, An, I didn't expect you to come visit me with all these kids to watch."

"I don't have Sissy today," Annalee said. "Mr. Harrison is taking time off. I guess he needed to rest up after all the time he spent taking care of the storm damage."

"Oh," Carol said. "I suppose so."

She beckoned Annalee into her living room. It was modest, but definitely larger than Annalee's shabby little one. Carol swelled with pride hoping she would notice and be jealous of how much nicer her furnishings were than Annalee's. That included a nice thick rug on her floor.

Carol thought of the cracked linoleum flooring Annalee had in her home and smiled to herself about how much better her home would be for Jack's little girl.

It would be a real improvement over Annalee's miserable shack.

Carol indicated the heavily laden table in the dining room. "How about a snack or something? People have been bringing food all morning."

Many dishes, covered and uncovered, sat about on the dining room table.

"Well, we might have a bite of something. What do you have that the kids would like?"

Carol waved her hand at the table. "Take a look. Lots of cookies and a couple of casseroles so far. I put them in my refrigerator, though." She looked down at Buckley. "Want a cookie, kid?"

At his eagerness for a handful of sweets, Annalee cautioned, "Just one Bucky—just one, now."

She let him select a large sugar cookie from the plateful Carol held in front of him. He nodded his thanks to her.

Sarah quickly took one for herself and lisped, "Fank you." She sat down on the carpeting and began to eat it.

Carol, seeing the crumbs falling into her carpet, snatched up the little girl and moved her to the bare floor. "Over here, sweetheart, so I can sweep up after you." She placed Buckley beside Sarah. "You too, Bucky." She handed each child a small glass of milk. "Careful not to spill it, now. I don't need any messy spills to clean up."

Annalee felt uncomfortable, sitting in Carol's home. Somehow, it was the first time over the years she had felt that way. It seemed odd to her how Carol worried about a few crumbs getting on her carpet, but didn't seem to care if she hurt the little ones' feelings. Annalee didn't plan to spend a lot of time visiting Carol, when she obviously felt the children were more of a nuisance than anything else.

As far as being a brand new widow, she saw no tears of devastation on her friend's face. Annalee had begun to wonder if her friend even gave a damn that she'd lost her husband. "Carol, are you all right? Is there anything I can do to help you?"

"No, not really," Carol replied. "I was in the process of putting some clothes together to take over to Crossly's Funeral Home. Donald needs something to be laid away in."

Feeling shock and disappointment in her friend, Annalee thought if there was ever a time a woman would shed a tear or two, this would be it. But she saw nothing like that—nothing at all.

Annalee rose to take her leave after a few more moments. Suddenly, at the sight of crumbs and a bit of milk spilled on the floor, Carol shrieked, "Look at that mess!"

Furious at Carol's incivility toward her little ones, Annalee went to the kitchen, got a dish cloth, and cleaned up the crumbs and milk. "Sorry, Carol. I guess visiting with children was not the best idea."

She took both her children by the hand and left the home, waving a short goodbye as they walked out the door.

ᏋᏗᏋᏗ

Carol's husband was laid to rest in the same cemetery as Gerald. Annalee and Carol sat side by side during the service. Annalee offered what support she could, but anymore, she felt a growing coolness between herself and Carol. She didn't understand why. They'd been friends for more than seven years, before high school graduation, and during the time of Annalee's marriage.

Annalee was busy these days with care of her own children, as well as little Cecelia. Carol frequently came over, usually around the time Jack came to claim his daughter. Annalee noted this situation with a growing sense of embarrassment. Carol would be overly friendly with Jack if she happened to be there when he came for his daughter. And she frequently made sure she *was* there—often enough to be obvious about her interest in the man.

Annalee had caught her friend speaking quietly to him whenever she left the room. She frequently returned to see Carol close to him, her lips moving. Her furtive look toward Annalee at those times made her wonder what Carol was saying to him.

Her behavior had become obvious to Annalee's thinking. But if Carol was trying to attract Jack, Annalee could see no sign of success in that department. She'd seen no interest displayed on Jack's face, but she *had* seen moments of disbelief and confusion cross his features, enough to know he disliked being stalked by Carol. And to Annalee's consternation, she realized he was being stalked.

One evening, after Jack left with Cecelia, she asked Carol, "Are you trying to attract Mr. Harrison?"

"Well, I could be," replied Carol. "I see the way he looks at me. Of course, I'm not my usual self with this kid I'm carrying, but I get the feeling he's looking me over."

Carol was short, almost chubby, with the few extra pounds she carried normally. But now, with the advancing state of her pregnancy, her burgeoning belly had added substantially to her stubby appearance. Annalee smiled at her own uncharitable thoughts, but Carol was no raving beauty to begin with.

Annalee hoped to dispel any fanciful ideas Carol had formed in her mind about Jack. "I think he still mourns the loss of his wife. I had the idea they were very much in love with each other and so far, he hasn't been able to get over it. He just can't forget her."

She'd also seen his look of disdain at Carol's forwardness toward him. A feeling of pity for Carol rose within Annalee to see that kind of sad disillusionment in her friend.

But Carol went blithely on with her own idea. "I think he's getting lonely for some company and is looking my way. My goodness, An, haven't you seen the way he looks at me?" She uttered a silly giggle, sounding like a girl of sixteen, instead of an overweight, pregnant widow—no longer a young girl.

Annalee shook her head at the ridiculousness of Carol's statement but decided to drop the subject. "How are you doing with your pregnancy? Feeling all right, are you?"

"Oh yeah. I don't spend a lot of time worrying about it. It ought to be a nice looking baby though. No doubt it will have dark hair and eyes—uh, sort of like his daddy did."

"Have you told the real father about this child?"

"Well, that would be pretty hard to do. He's not around anymore." Carol let out a silly giggle. "I don't think I could get through to him."

Annalee wondered if Carol was all right in the head,

making statements like that. Something didn't sound right. She seemed to be hinting at something, and it wasn't the first time—but what?

Carol got up and walked toward the door. Her gait had become a bit lumbering with her increased girth. "Well, An, I'd better get going. I get real tired these days," she said then added with a secretive smile, "I think this will be a big boy, just like his daddy."

Annalee didn't know why but she felt uncomfortable with Carol these days. And she had noticed that if Cecelia was there, Carol played with her to the exclusion of Annalee's two children. It wasn't fair to her children or anyone else's, and Annalee had asked her about it a few days ago. "Carol, why do you show favoritism to Sissy? You leave my kids out completely. They see it and feel it. Things like that hurt a child. You ought to know that."

"Oh, dear, am I? How forgetful of me. I'll try to do better from now on." Carol laughed and threw her hands in the air. "I forget myself sometimes. Sissy is very adorable though, isn't she? What do your kids say when she calls you 'Momma' the way she always does?" Her tone had turned cool with her question.

Annalee finally realized the truth of things. In disbelief she understood—Carol was jealous of her taking care of Jack's little girl. That had to be it.

Annalee thought back over the times Jack had come for his child and how Carol had managed to be present. All too often it had happened. It appeared calculated to Annalee and rather pathetic for a woman in Carol's condition.

Any time Jack entered the modest little home, his big male presence seemed to excite Carol. As soon as he appeared, she did overt things—talking silly nonsense, flip-ping her hair, playing with little Sissy, all to make her presence known to him. How she looked these days in her advancing state of pregnancy never seemed to bother her at all.

Annalee had begun to wonder if Carol was becoming confused with such obviously unrealistic hopes and ideas. With a quiet smile to herself, Annalee realized Carol would love to take Cecelia's care away from her. She wanted Jack to come to *her* house for his child each even-ing. Annalee worried about the child Carol carried and wondered if she cared at all about it.

Just then Jack knocked on the door and Carol, al-ready near it, hurried as fast as her condition allowed to open it.

"Why, if it isn't Mr. Harrison, as I live and breathe. Do come in." Carol acted as though it was her home and she was the hostess.

Annalee, seeing the wondering look on Jack's face, found she pitied the woman.

Annalee stepped into the room and smiled at him. "How was your day, Jack?" She exaggerated the friendli-ness between herself and Jack, letting Carol know she wasn't the only woman in the room.

Jack's friendly smile at her question didn't help Car-ol's mood at all, and right now, Annalee didn't care a bit. She'd become sick to death of the woman's machina-tions. It was hard to understand, but she now believed her friend, if that was the proper word for what Carol was, would happily undermine the only decent income An-nalee had.

"Well, Annalee, it was the usual day for me. Things

are back to normal after that big storm." He looked about for his daughter. "How's my girl today?"

Carol jumped into the conversation. "Oh, she's just fine Mr. Harrison. We get along very well—just like she was my own child."

Cecelia came running in. Spotting her daddy, she ran into his arms. "My daddy," she cooed to him and reached her tiny face up to plant a kiss on his cheek.

"Say bye-bye now, sweetheart. We have to go home," he told his child.

Sissy ran into Annalee's arms, held her little face up, and kissed her cheek. "Bye-bye, Momma, 'til amarro." Then she wriggled down and went to her daddy without giving Carol a glance.

Carol rushed over to her. "Bye-bye, little Sissy."

Sissy looked at her and mumbled, "Bye Carol." She made no move to reach out to her or give her a kiss, just snuggled against her father's chest.

With the father and daughter gone, Carol said, "Well, I'd better get on home."

Her tone was flat and her face had gone white. Annalee sensed a slow burning rage just beneath the surface in Carol as she left.

She heaved a sigh of relief watching Carol walk down the sidewalk. Annalee, glad to see her leave, had a sick feeling inside. Things hadn't gone Carol's way, and Annalee wondered what would come next.

She turned to making supper for herself and her children. She had plenty to work with these days as Jack was more than generous with what he brought to her home. Tonight, it would be pork chops. She felt some guilt about it, but he had a way of making her think it was all right for him to keep bringing so much. She didn't know how to argue with him about it.

She used the kerosene burners in the warmer months to avoid making the house too warm. The big iron cook stove was the best in winter as it warmed the house nicely while she baked and cooked. She knew some of the more modern homes had very nice gas cook stoves and central heating from a coal-fired furnace in the basement, but she'd never had anything like that.

While she cooked, she watched her two children playing blocks on the floor. They liked to be where she was, where they could see her, but not as much when Sissy was with them. Then they played in the bedrooms with Buckley calling the shots as much as he could.

Annalee felt badly for Carol. The woman had a completely unrealistic view of things to Annalee's way of thinking. Imagine thinking a man like Jack Harrison would take an interest in Carol in the way she hoped. If he should become interested in finding another wife— and it was way too soon after the loss of his first—it wouldn't be a calculating woman like Carol. Annalee was sure of that.

She believed he found it disgusting to be approached in the way Carol constantly did. The look of disdain on his face when she neared him was tell-tale enough. Annalee shook her head as she turned the pork chops and set their places at the small kitchen table.

Chapter 7

Carol fumed as she drove home in her nice, dark green Ford sedan. At least her Donald had had brains enough to get them a decent ride before he'd died, and one she definitely deserved. She thought of their intimate times together, but she'd found his performance rather lack-luster, compared to some she'd had. She smiled, remembering that handsome devil who'd fathered the child she carried.

But that was over now, too, and the heated memory of him had quickly faded once she'd seen someone new. Jack Harrison was alive and handsome. She had never thought a blond man looked especially virile, but she'd now seen the long, flat planes of his muscles and those dark gray eyes. She imagined what a man like him could do with a sensual woman like her. Yes, she couldn't get her mind off of that handsome Jack Harrison.

Her eyes narrowed. By some of the clever things Annalee had done, Carol believed she was trying, in her sneaky way, to keep him from becoming interested in Carol. And now, being in the family way as she was, she needed a husband. That handsome hunk of male was about the best thing she'd ever seen. She imagined his big body covering hers in the heat of passion and shivered in delight as she entered her driveway.

"If I could get the care of his little girl away from that snotty, goody-two-shoes, bitch, Annalee, he would be coming to *me* every day for his kid." She rambled on in the confines of her car as she opened the door. "I hope he doesn't think that scrawny Annalee is woman enough for a big dude like him." She snorted aloud at that. "That scared titmouse hadn't been woman enough for the man she had. If she had been, he'd never have come looking at me."

She felt her chest swell, knowing she had it all over Annalee in that department, oh yes, she did.

"There ought to be a way I could fix her wagon so she wouldn't be able to take care of his kid like she does." An idea began forming in Carol's head. "She uses that smoky old kerosene cook stove in summer." She grinned to herself in the rear view mirror before she left the car. "Those things can be dangerous, especially with a bunch of careless little kids around."

಄಄಄

Jack sat at his desk, frowning in concentration as he worked on the planning necessary for future installation of power lines farther out than ever before. The Rural Electrification Act had not been passed as yet, but it was being discussed and readied in the nation's capital. There were arguments for and against the feasibility of putting power out to farms. Jack's part was to study the future costs, potential benefits, and the needed planning required for such activity.

It was a huge undertaking. All those lines had to be laid out, surveyed, planned, and programmed in preparation. At this point in the nation, about ninety percent of urban dwellers had access to electricity. It was for the outlying farms and dwellings that the initial costs needed to be configured and laid out. He felt honored to be given this work and needed to get it done.

A shadow passed his desk and he looked up to see Derrick Lassen come walking toward him. He stopped for a moment. "How're things going for you, Jack? Getting that stuff laid out, are you?" He stood there for a moment, seeming to await a reply. "And how's that child care business? Is that working out?"

"Oh, yes, it sure is," Jack answered. "That little woman is wonderful with my Sissy. She is happy while she stays there during the day, and I swear if I don't hear her cry for that woman at night—calls her Momma, too." Jack shrugged, unsure what to think about that himself. "Of course, sometime in the future she'll have to be told different. But right now that woman is a godsend as far as I'm concerned." He felt a flush come over his face. He hadn't meant to go on so much about Annalee and how his daughter had come to love her as a mother.

Derrick patted him on the shoulder. "Annalee Lines is a real good woman. We've known her a long time. She and my wife have been friends since high school," he added. "Sure too bad about her husband—freak accident like that."

Jack had a question for Derrick. "What do you know about that other friend of hers?" he asked. "Carol Woods, I believe, is her name. She's expecting, too, unless I miss my guess."

"I don't know her that well, but my wife does. I'll check it out with her. Why do you ask?"

"She seems to be over at Mrs. Lines's home almost every night when I come to pick up my daughter. If I'm not mistaken, she's playing up to me, Derrick. She's swaying her hips around and making eyes. Makes me wonder if the woman has set her mind to cornering me for her next husband." Jack shivered a bit and looked up at Derrick. "I could be wrong, of course, but I get that feeling." He uttered a slight chuckle. "The woman has just lost the husband she had. He got caught out in that storm last month. Tree limb got him." He shoved a hand through his hair. "Hell's bells, Derrick, the man is hardly cold in the ground. There's no way I'd be interested in any woman—not now, maybe not ever. To tell the truth, I don't think I'll ever get over losing my wife. Things were very good between us, more than for most couples, I'd say. I doubt if I'd ever be lucky enough to find what Amelia and I had together again. Lightning couldn't strike twice, Derrick." His eyes clouded up. "I was lucky to find a woman like her the first time around."

"Amelia was a fine woman, all right. Amy and I miss her very much, too." Derrick sighed. "She was one heck of a great bridge player, I'll tell you that." He was ready to get on with his own business. "I'll check with Amy about that other question."

Derrick left and Jack went back to work, but he couldn't get past the sick feeling that he was heading for trouble with a woman he could barely tolerate. He shook his head in frustration and tried to concentrate on his work.

❧❧❧

Carol had come to visit again at about four in the afternoon. Annalee was sure by now that she'd set predatory sights on Jack. This situation had continued to the point it made Annalee feel uncomfortable having Carol at the house when Jack came for little Sissy each evening. She wanted to speak to Jack about it and tried to find a way to do that. She had to get Carol away from him long enough for the opportunity.

When Jack knocked on the door, Annalee was quick to answer it and open it for him to enter. She turned to Carol with a sweet smile. "Dear, will you go find Cecelia for her daddy?"

Carol had no choice but to comply with the request. When she left the room, Annalee said to the man, her voice hushed and her face reddened with embarrassment, "I'm sorry for what's going on with my friend Carol, but I don't know what to do about it, outside of kicking her out of my home."

Jack smiled down at her. "I can handle it. Don't worry about it."

But he didn't feel as confident as he'd portrayed to Annalee. However, he was glad that she understood what Carol was up to and, with that, knew he had an ally in what was shaping up to be an uncomfortable situation. He had no ready plan how to defuse Carol's overt sexual advances toward him.

Jack found it difficult to be rude to any woman and had to leave the situation as it was for the present.

Carol came flouncing her rotund little body into the room pulling Cecilia by her little hand. The child kept looking back and crying. "I want Bucky."

Luckily, Bucky, who had followed them out of the bedroom, said, "Aw, Sissy, yer daddy needs you to go home and you have to go. We can build that ol' fort tomorrow."

Sissy stood and looked at him. "Awight, Bucky. Tommowo." She giggled at him, twisted her hand away from Carol, and ran to her daddy.

He reached down, tossed her high in the air, and heard her cries of excitement.

"Whee, Daddy, we going to make a fort tommowo!"

Completely ignoring Carol, Jack turned to Annalee. "Thanks again for the care you give her." Then he nodded at Buckley. "What's this fort you're making?" He squatted down to face the boy, holding a fascinated Sissy in his arms. "Tell me about this fort business. Is it to fight off the enemy?"

"Yes, sir, we need to fight the wild Indians that sneak around behind the bed." Bucky stuck out his little chest. "We're all cowboys and have to 'tect our stuff. We need a fort."

"I see." Jack replied. "And Sissy gets to help you, does she?'"

"Yep, she's pretty good for a girl." Buckley stated with his hands on his little hips, looking at Sissy. "She can climb real good, too. We got a real nice tree outside."

Carol stood watching him with her hands on her hips, which she'd jutted out in an overtly suggestive manner. She smiled at Jack, but he didn't seem to notice that, or anything else she did. He just kept talking to that bossy little brat, Bucky, and ignoring her. This time, Carol felt it was deliberate and seeing that, she wondered if Annalee had said something to make him look away from her. The thought of her friend's treachery made her blood boil. She narrowed her eyes at Annalee, but she just stood there smiling at Jack and ignoring Carol, too.

His attitude had seemed far different this evening. Instead of his usual reserved self, he seemed downright standoffish toward her. It seemed even more so this time. Her eyes squeezed shut, and her lips tightened. She again wondered if Annalee had said something against her to Jack, trying to undermine Carol's efforts to attract the man.

Her heart fluttered as she looked at him. He was the picture of masculine beauty—tall, handsome, and blond with those wonderful dark gray eyes. It was an unusual combination for anyone and, on Jack, it was downright sexy. He was more than handsome in her eyes. All in all, he was a big, classy-looking gent. She had already spent hours imagining herself in his arms, wriggling in heated passion beneath that big body, and him doing secret, intimate things to her that set her heart on fire. God in heaven, she wanted him!

After Jack left with his daughter held high in his arms, Carol stood watching him out the window. Her attention was riveted on that tall form as he put his child into his car.

Annalee went to stand beside her. "Carol, you're not interested in Jack Harrison are you?"

"Who wouldn't be? I can't believe you haven't set

your cap for him, Annalee—a devilish handsome hunk of man like that."

"I haven't given it a thought, Carol. I believe I've mentioned once or twice before that that part of my life is over and done with. Being married holds no attraction for me." She shivered with her statement.

Carol noticed the shiver and her brow wrinkled in confusion. "An, it couldn't have been that bad. Your Gerald seemed like such a great guy."

"Maybe he was—to some." Annalee didn't want to say anything more. She'd said too much already and regretted the sparkle it put in Carol's eyes.

"Well, nobody knows what goes on in any home, especially in their bedrooms." Carol shrugged. "But as far as I can see, it would be a lucky woman who *was* able to attract that Jack. She'd need to be a real somebody and a woman who knows how to please a man." She chuckled to herself, knowing she was just that kind of woman. She patted her burgeoning belly, as proof enough of her feminine prowess.

Carol smiled. In spite of trying to keep her secret, she'd never burned that damning note. She had often envisioned the great emotional impact it would create inside the heart of a certain person when the truth about the father of her impending child came out. She turned to Annalee. "Well, I'd better get myself on home. I rattle around in that big empty house with Donald gone."

She loved to mention how much nicer and bigger her home was than Annalee's. Living in a nice home like that made her feel a bit above a lot of people in this podunk little town.

With her head held high, she left for her house in her

nice car, proud that Donald had made sure she had that, too.

Her biggest problem right now was how to attract the attention of that big, handsome man who came every night to Annalee's door. She felt sorry for Annalee. The woman was too stupid, or scared of a man, to take advantage of someone like that Jack.

If Annalee had no way to take care of little Cecelia, Jack would have to look elsewhere. And wouldn't she be just the right person to handle that situation? She felt her pulses race at the thought of it.

She remembered about the kerosene stove. She had even warned Annalee about how dangerous it might be with little ones around. You never knew if those little hands might turn on the kerosene jets when Annalee wasn't looking. You never knew, did you? Carol lay awake, trying to sleep but thinking of how easily she could do a thing she knew was terribly wrong. It kept her wide awake.

こうこう

It was long after midnight, nearly five o'clock in the morning, when a furtive figure slipped quietly inside Annalee's small home. No one locked their doors in this small town as far as Carol knew. There had never been a problem of people sneaking in and stealing things while you slept. Not that Annalee had anything anyone would want, anyway. Seldom did anyone lock a door as it wasn't something that had ever been needed.

Once inside, Carol stood still a moment, listening intently for any sound of activity.

She slipped quietly across the kitchen floor, hoping the small cracking sounds her steps made crossing the old linoleum flooring wouldn't wake Annalee. She reached the small kerosene stove and flipped on a burner. She struck a kitchen match to make sure it was lit and set it to a low flame. No curtains were handy, but she saw yesterday's newspapers scattered about on the kitchen table.

She grabbed the entire pile of them and laid them on the stove so near the flames they would soon catch and blaze up. She took a handy dishtowel and let it trail from the paper up across to a window curtain. Those curtains were of some cottony material with a long ago faded print. And all that dried old wallpaper on the walls would burn quickly, too. Carol turned her nose up at the sleazy curtains. "Flimsy worn-out things needed changing anyway," she murmured to herself as she waited until a near edge of a paper caught fire.

As it went from smoldering and burst into flames, she waited to see them lick upward toward the curtains. Then Carol made her way to the door and left. She reached her car parked across the street and climbed in. Smiling to herself in satisfaction, she finally saw the flames licking up the outside of the little home. It was taking hold on the kitchen side, right where she'd set it. In the early light of dawn, with the flames of Annalee's home flaring high, she drove away, laughing and crowing in glee, "Now, Mrs. Perfect Mother, I'd like to see you take care of Jack Harrison's kid tomorrow morning."

Tomorrow was Saturday, but that fact had escaped Carol completely as she'd sat in her car watching Annalee's home. She had driven farther away down the block so no one would connect her to the fire. She couldn't bear to have anyone thinking she had been guilty of a thing like that. It wasn't nice to burn down her friend's house, but she couldn't think of any other way she could get the care of that little girl. As long as Jack had her friend's place to go to, he wouldn't need to come to her. Parked, she waited to be sure it caught fire.

After this, little Cecelia would be looking for another loving home and Carol was just the woman who could provide that. With her home gone, Annalee would have to go and live with her parents in that other place they'd come from. Arnott, wasn't that what they'd said?

In Carol's mind, everything would work out so perfectly. Annalee and her two kids would be gone, and she would have an open field all to herself, as far as that handsome Jack Harrison was concerned.

Carol saw how the hungry flames quickly spread upward to the tinder-dry roof. Then thinking of the encroaching fire reaching the beds of those children, Carol choked up.

It hadn't rained for several days. She'd heard the forecast on the car radio, another little luxury Donald had given her. There was no rain in sight for tonight either. That little house would go up like a tinder box!

Realizing that, Carol suddenly understood that she might have just caused the death of Annalee and both her children. "Oh, no, oh God! I never meant it to go that far!"

She gasped for breath as she saw the flames spreading. She could hear the roaring of them now, as they engulfed that snug little home.

Carol began sobbing with fear and guilt. "I didn't mean it, Annalee, I didn't!"

Hands shaking so badly she could barely hold onto the steering wheel, she started her car and drove it home. It was way too late to do anything right now—and what could she do anyway? If she called the fire department, it would point a finger her way and make her look guilty, wouldn't it?

Carol walked into her home and slumped down in the living room. Her stomach had gone into a knot. She was far enough along in her pregnancy now that her stomach often tightened like that. Feeling guilty, she didn't know what to do. It was too late now. She'd just overstepped the bounds of human decency. If Annalee and her two children died tonight, Carol would be responsible for taking three lives—for murder!

She thought of brave little Bucky, trying to get away from the burning flames. She imagined little Sarah, crying in terror as the flames crept close. Was their tender, child's flesh on fire right now? She imagined them screaming out for their mother, frightened to death as the fire caught against their small bodies to end their young lives. Carol thought about her long-time friend, Annalee. What about her? Was she dead now? Had she burned to death, trying to save her little ones lives?

Carol shook her head in disbelief at what she'd done. Roused out of her guilty thoughts, she heard the clanging of bells that told her the fire engine was heading for the fire. Would they be in time? Carol went down on her knees in fear and prayed they would.

Chapter 8

Annalee woke up suddenly. Surprised and alarmed, she smelled smoke! Then she became aware of crackling sounds coming from the kitchen. Awake now, she saw by the faint glow of early morning light outside her window, smoke came pouring through her open bedroom door. When she heard the roar and the crackling of a roaring bonfire right inside the house, she knew something wasn't right. What was burning? Her sleep-fogged mind sprang fully alert and she coughed from the choking smoke as it rushed through the hallway into her room.

With her eyes burning from smoke, she leaped out of bed, pulled on her robe, and ran out of her room. Then she saw her living room engulfed in flames. She gasped at seeing the blazing fire running up the walls and across the ceiling. The way to the door was already burning, the linoleum flaming up, leaping, crackling, and creating thick, black smoke!

"Oh my God in heaven—the kids!" She ran into their room. They lay asleep as the smoke grew thicker, choking her and making her eyes water. She slammed their door shut to keep out some of the smoke. Then she grabbed Bucky and pulled him up. "Wake up, Bucky! Get up, the house is on fire!"

She grabbed Sarah in her arms and, touching the door, felt the burning heat of it.

There was no way out through there. The kids' little bedroom had already filled with smoke. Flames crept under the door and licked upward. She saw the window and knew it was their only hope.

She put Sarah on Bucky's bed. Then she grabbed a pillow, smashed it against the window, and broke the glass. With a few more blows, she made the hole big enough to put the children out. There was a three foot drop to the grass outside. She tossed their pillows outside and then grabbed Bucky. "I'm putting you out of this window first, then I will hand you Sarah." She faced him, looking into his frightened eyes. "You're my big man tonight, Bucky—out you go." She shoved him out, leaned out a ways, and dropped him. She heard him hit the ground and the pillows.

He turned around. "I'm okay, Momma. Hand me Sarah."

He held out his little boy hands and her heart went out to that brave young boy. Annalee grabbed Sarah off the bed and leaned out the window to drop her into his arms.

She was awake, clinging to her mother, and crying, but Annalee held her out and yelled to her, "Go to Bucky." She dropped Sarah into his arms.

Bucky fell to the ground with the burden of his sister, but he rolled away and got up, dragging her to her feet.

Annalee hissed at him, "Get away from this house—now!"

"But, Momma, aren't you coming?" Bucky cried up at her.

"You bet I am, darling. Here I come." She edged her body out the window. As she jumped to the ground, she felt a burning, searing pain as a sharp edge of glass ripped the skin of her right hip. It hurt and burned like crazy, but she got up and shepherded her little ones away from the blazing mess her home had become.

As they made it to the edge of the yard, she heard the rumble of a fire truck coming. Soon, a man rushed up to her and cried out, "Anyone else in there?"

Annalee couldn't speak, but she shook her head in the negative. He ran to shout orders to the men on his truck. The house was a mass of flames and, small as it was, she knew they would salvage nothing. Everything she'd ever owned was gone—burned into cinders. She hugged her babies close. They were safe, and that was what really mattered. Her right hip burned like crazy, but she realized she was alive to feel it. Shocked at the sudden loss of all she owned, she felt the cleansing tears rolling down her cheeks.

Mary Jensen, her close neighbor, the one she often left her children with, came running up. "My dear, are you all right?" She was an older lady, widowed, with a small pension. Annalee knew and trusted her.

"We got out just in time, Mary. It was so close." Annalee had dried her tears on the sleeve of her robe. "I've still got my babies and that's what counts. I don't know what I'll do now." She gasped for breath, clearing the residual smoke from her lungs. "We might have had insurance, but I doubt it."

"You poor dear, you must come to my home and rest. Time enough later on to figure things out." Mary was a good neighbor and generously offered what she had to give in Annalee's time of need.

"Thanks so much, Mary. I'll come after a bit. I need to speak to the firemen and make sure the fire's out before I come over."

"Let me take the little ones home with me, then," Mary said. "They must be very upset and afraid after what they've been through. They should be away from here." She put a hand on Annalee's shoulder. "I'm so sorry to see this has happened to you, my dear."

Annalee turned to Bucky. "Son, will you go with Mary right now, and take Sarah? I'll come along as soon as I can get away."

"Yes, Momma," he replied. "Is my truck all gone and my blocks, too?"

"Looks like they are, darling. But you're here and that's what is most important to me." She patted him on the head and hugged him hard. "I love you, Bucky Boy. Take care of your sister."

Sarah just stood there, staring, and sucking her thumb, something she had stopped doing a while back.

Mary left, carrying Sarah, with Buckley at her side. Annalee feared Sarah was in shock, but they'd be safe with Mary. Annalee turned toward the smoldering pile of wreckage that had been her home. She didn't know what to do next, but looked to the fireman who came up to her. He had a question.

"Ma'am, do you have any idea how this fire started?" He stood before her, smoke-smudged and waiting, hoping for an answer.

"No, sir, I woke up and saw the flames all over the kitchen area, going toward the front door. The linoleum floor was burning there too and we couldn't get out that way."

"You say, it was all over the kitchen area, first?"

"I think so." Annalee thought of her kerosene stove. "I always use the kerosene stove in the summer months, but I keep it turned off and clear of anything that might catch fire."

She shook her head at the thought of what might have happened, but couldn't think of any time she would have left anything near that stove. Carol had mentioned the same thing only recently.

"Thanks, ma'am. We'll make sure everything is completely out before we leave the area," he said then added, "It's certainly a complete loss. I hope you have some insurance on the place." He turned away and left her standing alone, looking at what she'd lost. She felt more alone right now than she ever had in her life. She didn't know where to turn or what to do. On top of all that, she felt weak and dizzy right now, too.

Another person came up to her. "Annalee, you are bleeding all down your right leg. Did you know that?"

She looked up to see Jack standing there. "Uh, I am?" She looked down at her robe and saw the spreading red stain on her clothes. It had run down from the burning slash on her right hip. "Oh, I must have gotten cut by the glass when I came out of the window. No wonder I feel so…"

Jack caught Annalee in his arms as she fell. "Hey anybody got a stretcher?" he yelled.

One of the firemen came close and took a look at Annalee. Jack laid her down in the grass.

"Passed out huh? What did she say?"

"She cut herself getting out of the window. That's all she said before she passed out," Jack nearly snarled. "No damned stretchers around here?"

"We got one. Ain't much, though."

Another fireman came with a folding, rickety-looking thing and opened it.

Jack wanted to see how bad the cut was, but he could tell by the blood it was on her hip and he wasn't about to pull her clothes up out here in public. He'd noticed a crowd gathering, but he didn't see anything of her children. A terrible fear took hold of him. "Where are her little ones?"

"Some lady came and took 'em across the street. They're okay, the lady said."

Satisfied about Annalee's children, Jack looked about. "She needs to see a doctor. Look at all this blood." He reached down and picked her up in his arms. "I'll take her to the clinic myself."

For this Saturday morning, he had no worries about Sissy. She had spent the night with Amy Lassen's two girls. He'd gone out to make a short run to an all-night gas station, but instead had followed the scream of the sirens and the column of smoke. Seeing the ruins of Annalee's home, he knew this fire would affect him, too. How much, he didn't know, but his daughter thought of this woman as her mother.

Right now, the poor soul needed the services of a

doctor and he could do that much for her. He sat Annalee in his car and let her lay against the door. He reached across her, locked it from the driver's side, and drove away. The small hospital, usually referred to as The Delano Clinic, was a ways off, near the west side of the small town. He hurried along. It was very early and the streets were empty. "Thank God," he murmured.

Annalee struggled awake. Finding herself in a car and moving, she felt a rise of panic. She opened her eyes to see she was in Jack Harrison's nice Oldsmobile, and he was driving. She was surprised, but not afraid. "What's happening? Where are we going?"

"I'm sorry, Annalee, but you were cut and bleeding all over the place. I'm just taking you to the clinic so they can take care of it." He soon parked his car, reached across her, and unlocked her door. He came around to open it, scooped her up in his arms, and walked into the clinic.

Annalee couldn't believe this was happening, but she did remember getting quite a painful gash as she came through the bedroom window. Her gown and robe felt sticky. She had the presence of mind to worry if she had gotten blood in his car. "Did I bleed in your car?"

"Never you mind about a little thing like that, my dear," Jack told her.

Inside, a nurse ran up to receive her and whipped out a gurney for Jack to lay his burden down. "We'll take care of her. You may register your wife at the desk there, sir," she told him as she wheeled Annalee away.

Annalee felt dirty, smelled of smoke, and had grass stains on what was left of her night gown and robe. In an exam room, the nurse pulled the blood-stained clothes away from her and clipped them off. She washed away the blood and smoke smudges, giving Annalee nearly a complete bath, except for her hair.

As the nurse put a clean hospital gown on her, she questioned Annalee about how she'd been wounded.

Annalee told the nurse about her home burning, escaping with her children through the window, and getting cut that way. "And I'm sure I don't know how I'll pay for this," she finished.

"My goodness, ma'am, you were lucky to get out alive, and with your little ones!" the nurse muttered as she cleaned the long gash on Annalee's right hip. "It's not so deep, but it's about ten inches long. It'll need closing."

A large soft dressing was applied to the wound, then, Annalee was covered with a thick white blanket. "The doctor will be in to do the stitches," the nurse told her. "You'll need quite a few stitches to pull things back together." Then she remembered Annalee speaking of payment. "Well, as far as payment is concerned, you can take it up with them out at the desk. But what about your husband? Didn't I hear the lady at the desk say he could handle your registration and things?"

Annalee, upset at the nurse's inference about Jack, declared, "You might have heard something like that, but that man is not my husband. I am a widow and take care of his child during the week. That's all there is to that." She held her chin firm, fighting tears, feeling embarrassed at her helpless situation.

With her home lost in the fire, she wouldn't be doing anymore child care anyway. That's the last she would ever see of Jack. She felt sad for little Sissy. The child had grown so dependent on her, even to calling her Momma. Annalee even felt sad for Jack, since he would have to start looking all over again. And, she had to admit to herself, she would miss seeing that handsome, friendly face every day.

For herself, she could always go live with her folks in Arnott. That would be the bottom of the well as far as Annalee was concerned. But she had to face facts. Her kids needed a roof over their head. Her thoughts were interrupted when the doctor came in.

The nurse introduced him. "This is Dr. Andrew Childs, ma'am. He is on staff this morning. He'll take care of you."

"So you've had a narrow escape, it seems. Let's have a look at your injury." Dr. Childs helped her to her left side and drew the sheet and blanket away to remove the dressing. He uncovered the long shallow gash she'd sustained. "Hum, not so bad. It should heal rather quickly. Let's just numb it up for you and we'll get this taken care of." He ordered the nurse to get certain supplies and Annalee soon felt the tiny needle sticks as he sent Novocain into her wound's edges. She thought she smelled alcohol, wondered about it and why they'd used it.

"Your husband is waiting out there," Dr. Childs said. "You'll be able to return home when we are through here." He hesitated. "If your home has burned, where will you folks live?" he asked, his voice puzzled.

"Doctor, that man out there is not my husband," Annalee said. "He is the father of a child I take care of during the day while he works. He has his own home. I've just lost mine and my child care job, too."

"I'm very sorry to hear that, Mrs. Lines."

Dr. Childs bent to his task and said nothing more. Annalee listened to them speaking together, but only about her wound and the stitches.

Dr. Childs finished his work. "Mrs. Lines, come back in about ten days and I will remove these stitches for you," he instructed. "Keep the area very clean to avoid infection if you can." He smiled down at her. "You should be able to be up and around without too much discomfort, although there may be a slight limp for a while."

"Sitting in a wheelchair might be very painful. Would you like to try walking out of here?" the nurse asked. "You should be able to."

She encouraged Annalee to get to her feet. Annalee took a few steps with the nurse holding her arm until she felt steady enough to walk on her own.

She looked at the gown and robe she wore. "What about these things I'm wearing? I have nothing else. I've lost everything I own."

The nurse smiled at her. "Just wear these things from here and return them when you come back in ten days, dear," she said. "This happens sometimes and we do what we can to help." The nurse also handed Annalee her soiled and cut nightwear in a paper bag.

Annalee stepped out into the waiting room and Jack leaped up from his chair to come to her. "How are you, Annalee? You look a little pale, that's for sure." He took her arm to head out the door.

"What about the bill for this?" Annalee asked.

"It's all taken care of. Don't give it another thought."

Her embarrassment caused a ruddy flush to rise up her neck, and she felt it burning. "That's not right and you know it isn't," she protested.

"Maybe not, but you've got bigger problems than worrying about a little hospital bill."

He looked over at her, wrapped in hospital garb, hair mussed and tangled. She looked so young and lost that his heart went out to her. The poor girl was alone with two children to raise, and now not even a home to go to.

It hurt him inside to see how alone this little woman was. Her heart was as big as all outdoors and what did she get for it? Not much besides two babies and no money to care for them. The pain of her situation bothered Jack. And almost against his will, an idea began to form in his head.

As he ushered her gently out to his car and helped her in, the idea had grown stronger in only a few moments. She wouldn't like it, being as straight-laced as they come, if he knew her at all. But his plan would answer a lot of problems for them both. He wisely didn't voice his thoughts for now. He had to do a lot more thinking about it himself.

He drove her to the house across the street from the smoldering pile of wreckage that had been her home. A few fine trails of smoke slowly twisted upward in the soft, early morning breeze.

"Here we are at your neighbor's home, Annalee. I will come to see you in another day or two. We need to talk." He got out and put his arm around her to help her up the steps to Mrs. Jensen's home.

Chapter 9

Carol sat at her small kitchen table, trying to eat breakfast. She had heard the sirens and wondered if they'd gotten there in time to save Annalee and her little ones. Carol's bread had no taste, her eggs were off, and even the strawberry jam had no flavor. Nothing was right this morning. Desperate to know what had happened, and terrified that she had committed murder, she snapped on her radio.

The news came blaring on, and she waited until she heard them talk about a sudden fire on Culver Street. "That's Annalee's street! Oh please God, let her be all right!"

The announcer proclaimed: "The home was a total loss, but the inhabitants were saved by the mother in a dramatic rescue. She sustained injuries which were treated at the local clinic…"

He went on with other news, but Carol had heard all she needed to know and heaved a huge sigh of relief. She hadn't committed murder. A great load of guilt had been lifted from her at the news that no one had died. She smiled to herself in exaltation. It had worked! Now homeless, little Annalee would soon pack her kids into that Model A coupe of Gerald's and drive away to Arnott to live with her parents.

"She will have to go and live with her folks now and I will go into the child care business," she gloated to herself as she decided to head over and see where Annalee had spent the rest of the night.

Carol dressed carefully, went to her car, and drove over to see what had taken place at Annalee's home. She saw the flattened, smoking mess and knew it had been a total loss.

There were no fire trucks, as they had all gone by this time. She felt the guilt of it, but no one had died, so it wasn't that bad after all, and Carol's sense of guilt disappeared as if up in smoke, just like Annalee's home.

At first, Carol parked her car below the burned out wreckage of Annalee's home and sat there for a while looking at it. Her head snapped up in surprise, when she saw Jack's car sitting across the street, right in front of Mrs. Jensen's home. He came out just then, got in his car, and drove away.

Carol heaved a sigh, seeing that he was no longer around. But he must have been in that house to see Annalee. Why, for heaven's sake? She couldn't figure it out. *Probably to tell her he won't be bringing Cecelia to her anymore as she has no place for her now.* She smiled to herself. Things were working out.

👄👄

Mrs. Jensen answered Carol's knock on the door.

"Could I see Annalee," Carol asked. "I want to see if she's all right. I see she's had some trouble."

"Why, certainly. She's right in here." The kind-hearted lady led Carol into her modest living room and waved her small hand toward the couch. "Here she is. She just got back from The Delano Clinic."

Carol gasped. "The Clinic! My goodness, Annalee. Were you hurt? I can't believe what must have happened last night after seeing the ruins of your house. I heard the sirens, way early this morning. They woke me up, but I had no idea it was your place." She sat on the edge of the couch near Annalee. "How did you get hurt? How badly are you injured then?"

"I have a long gash on my right hip from crawling out the window. I guess I didn't get all the glass knocked out. It was so smoke-filled, I couldn't really see or even breathe by that time," Annalee replied.

"Who took you to the Clinic? The firemen?"

"No, it was Mr. Harrison. He heard the sirens, saw the smoke, and came to investigate. He must have gotten here just as I fainted. I woke up in his car while he was driving me to the clinic."

Annalee wondered at the strange expression that came over Carol's face. It had rapidly tightened into a white mask of fury, though Carol did her best to hide it. She held her clenched fists in her lap. Annalee saw that, too, and frowned, wondering what had upset Carol all of a sudden.

"He brought me back here a little while ago," Annalee continued. "After the doctor sewed me back together. Mrs. Jensen took my kids home with her right after we got out of that burning house." She shuddered. "We were almost too late, Carol."

She let a few tears fall then and sank back on the couch, exhausted. The room swirled and she felt like passing out again.

Mary, seeing Annalee's white face and glazed eyes, said, "I think we should let this poor little lady get some sleep. She's at the end of her rope after all that's happened. I'll put her in my bed." She led Annalee down a short hall and into a room. "You go to sleep, my child. I will watch over your babies, dear. There'll be time enough to sort things out when you're rested."

Mary returned to Carol. "She is completely exhausted. I've put her to bed. I hope she will be in better shape to have company tomorrow."

With that subtle hint, Carol decided she'd better leave. As Mary walked her to the door, Carol said, "Tomorrow is another day, isn't it?" Her eyes narrowed. She wasn't through yet—not by a long shot.

Mary looked at Carol's car, a newer model dark green Ford sedan. It sat there, parked out it front. She frowned. "Is that your car, dear?"

"Why, yes it is. I just love driving it. It's nice, isn't it?" Carol said with her chin in the air as she went out to her car and climbed in. She drove away, musing to herself, "Wonder what Jack was doing over here so early in the morning. And where was his kid?"

She knew he worked some Saturdays, but today, Annalee wouldn't be watching little Sissy. Carol drove home to her lonely house and slumped down on the couch.

She was alone, pregnant, and wondering what she

ought to do. She also wondered whether or not something was going on between Jack and that sneaky Annalee?

∞∞∞

Several hours later, Mary heard the doorbell ring again. "My gracious, this is a busy place this morning." She opened to see a nicely dressed young woman standing there. "Yes?" she questioned.

"I am Amy Lassen, a friend of Annalee's. I understand she is here since that terrible fire."

"Why, she certainly is. Please come on in." Mary ushered the young woman into her house. "The poor dear is asleep right now. I have the children eating lunch at the moment." She motioned for Amy to have a seat on the couch.

"How is she then?" Amy asked. "She's had so much happen to her lately. I'm worried about her." She indicated the large bag she carried. "I've brought her some clothes. We are the same size, so it was easy enough to find something for her."

"Oh, my goodness, that was so thoughtful of you. The poor girl only has something from the clinic. She brought her clothes back from the Clinic, a torn messy robe and the ripped nightie she was wearing when she crawled out that window. It's no longer fit to wear. She saved her children and then barely got out herself."

"The clinic?" Amy gasped. "Was she injured?"

"She had a gash from the window glass, I believe it was." Mary said. "That nice man who leaves his daughter with her came out from of nowhere just in time to take her to the clinic for her injury."

"My goodness, ma'am, that was nice of him." Amy looked down the hallway to see Annalee come limping out. She jumped up from the couch and went to her. "An, how are you?" She took Annalee in her arms for a snug embrace. "This kind lady tells me you were injured getting out of that burning house."

"I'm okay, it's all sewn up." Annalee looked at Mary. "My children, where are they?"

"Can't you hear them, my dear? They are having a bite to eat. Sarah wouldn't eat a thing this morning, and young Bucky is trying to get her to take something, now." Mary shook her head. "Last night was terrifying for them. They might do better if you go to them." She pointed to the kitchen where Annalee heard Bucky's voice.

Annalee and Amy went to the kitchen. Annalee saw her children. Their faces were clean but they were still dressed in their smoke-scented, filthy night clothes. To her they seemed overly subdued, which made her wonder if they were still in shock from last night. She stood in the doorway and waited for them to see her.

Bucky spotted his mother and rushed into her arms. Sarah climbed down from her chair and came to her also. Annalee crooned to them and hugged them. "Are you two okay today?"

"I'm okay, Momma," Bucky said. "But Sarah's still scared." He looked at his sister. "She won't even eat. Mrs. Jensen made us pancakes for breakfast, and she wouldn't eat any."

"I know it was terrible last night, but you two are safe and that's all that matters, isn't it?"

"My truck and blocks—are they all gone, Momma?"

"I'm afraid they are, Bucky. We were lucky to get

ourselves out and couldn't worry about things like that."
She hugged him a little harder. "There's time to find
some nicer ones, and a new truck for you, too."

Bucky went back to the table and hauled Sarah with
him. "Now you'd better eat Sarah, so you can get strong
again. We got new toys to get."

Annalee and Amy went back to the couch and sat
down. Amy brought out the bag of clothes. "I brought
you a few things until you get back on your feet. I even
put in a hairbrush. Looks like you could use one about
now."

Annalee looked down at the way she was dressed. "I
guess you're right, Amy. I haven't had time to think
about anything yet."

"Well, as you know, I can spare a few things. Take
them and enjoy them. I did and hope you will, too."

Annalee took the bag. "Thanks Amy. You've always
been a good friend. I would do the same for you, but my
stuff wouldn't hold a candle to the good clothes you
wear." She laughed. "I wonder how I'll look in these
things of yours?"

"Wonderful, as always, girl. You were always the
best looking of the bunch, you know that. There's nothing that can beat those purple eyes and long, black curling hair." Amy laughed as Annalee flushed. "Well, I'd
best get going as I've lots to do yet today." She hugged
Annalee. "You just rest yourself and we'll see if there
was any insurance on the home. If you had to make pay-
ments, Derrick says there usually is an insurance policy
to protect the mortgage holder."

Annalee couldn't bring herself to say the words. The
home was only rented, and she had no claim on anything.

She'd faced the fact that she was completely and totally destitute. Going to live with her parents was the only alternative she had left. She dreaded the thought of living in that grim home again, but she had to consider it. She'd write the letter in another day or two.

After Amy left, Annalee crawled back in that soft little bed of Mary's and let herself go. She was exhausted and reached out for the oblivion of sleep.

c/ɔc/ɔ

Annalee knew nothing more until she woke up about eight the next morning.

She staggered out of the bedroom, stiff and limping, to see her little ones sitting at the table eating a nice breakfast Mary had fixed for them.

"Momma, you awake now?" Bucky asked, glad to see he still had a momma after all the uncertainty they both had faced since yesterday morning.

He had begun to wonder. Sarah merely looked at her and put her thumb in her mouth again. Annalee couldn't say anything to her about sucking her thumb as the child needed the comfort it gave her.

Seeing Mary, Annalee asked if she could wash her hair. It felt so grimy and smoke-scented. In spite of the cleansing she'd had at The Delano Clinic, her hair was still a filthy, smoke-smelling mess. It made her feel grimy all over.

Mary led her to the small bathroom and handed her a thick towel. She dug about in a drawer and handed Annalee a bottle. "Here is some shampoo. Use all you need, but be careful of your stitches for the rest of your bath," she said then added, "The children are fine, so take your time."

Annalee bathed from the sink, being careful of her dressing. She washed her hair three times before it felt clean enough. It curled enough on its own. She'd never had to have one of those permanents she'd heard about.

With her hair drying and feeling cleaner, Annalee turned her attention to the bag of clothing Amy had left for her. She pulled out a softly worn nightgown, a pair of tan slacks, a soft green shirt, under things, all slightly worn and holding the faint scent of her friend Amy's favorite perfume. There was a pair of shoes in the bottom, and she knew they would fit. She and Amy wore the same size. Annalee dressed and everything fit.

She looked in a mirror and barely recognized herself. Who was this tall, slim girl, wearing a green blouse tucked into slim fitting pants? To Annalee's surprise, she found some make-up items in the bag too. To amaze her kind host, Mary, she touched her lips with a pale rose color.

She walked out to see Mary, who stood there just staring, until finally she commented, "My land sakes alive, Annalee, you look just lovely!"

"Thanks." Annalee looked at this little woman, busy at the stove. "Oh, Mary, how can I ever repay you for all you've done?"

"Just sit here and wake up. It's a nice morning outside, and here's a cup of coffee." Mary sat beside her and put food on her plate. "Here, eat a bite. You need it to keep up your strength."

An hour later, Annalee brushed her hair to a lovely sheen. Looking in the mirror, she noticed her eyes were clear of the redness she'd gotten from the smoke. Satisfied with her appearance, she re-touched the lipstick to finish off her look. Just then, there was a knock on her door and Mary exclaimed, "My goodness this has been such a busy place in the past two days."

She opened the door to Jack. "Won't you come in, sir?" Puzzled, she said nothing more.

Jack's big form nearly filled the modest living. When he spotted Annalee, a slight gasp escaped his lips. He hesitated for a moment, as though he'd lost his breath. "Annalee, I believe I mentioned yesterday that we needed to have a chat. If you would come out with me, we could have a bite to eat and discuss some things."

Puzzled, Annalee stammered, "W—we do?" She knew it was about Cecelia and that her father would have to find someone else for her now.

"Yes, I believe so." He nodded at her and looked to the lady of the house. "If Mrs. Jensen will kindly keep an eye on your children, could we go someplace and talk? Please?"

Annalee rose from the couch and went to him. "Yes, if you wish. I'll come with you."

She was mystified by his request, but he was an honorable man. In many ways, the loss of her home affected him as well since Cecelia now had to go elsewhere. Annalee knew that would be painful in the extreme for Jack and Cecelia. His girl had been very happy with her and the children.

Annalee wondered what he wanted to discuss with her. It had to be something about Cecelia's care, but she wouldn't think of asking.

Jack offered Annalee his arm and escorted her to his

car. She vaguely remembered the nice plushy Oldsmobile four door sedan from the trip to the clinic. He opened the passenger side for her and, as she got in, she looked but could see no sign that her wound had bled all over the upholstery. She still believed it had and that somehow he had erased all traces of it.

"Are you hungry this morning?" he asked.

It was late morning on Sunday by now, she thought, but she wasn't sure of that either. Annalee had learned that time had a way of getting lost in the trauma she'd suffered.

"I haven't had much of an appetite since this happened, but I should eat something, I suppose."

He drove nicely, Annalee thought. No jerking, swerving, or cursing at other drivers. Memories of how Gerald had driven—as though he'd had the entire world against him, and most of them were on the road—came home to her. She smiled to herself. Not a son-of-a-bitch or bastard on the road this morning.

Jack noticed her smile and wondered what prompted it. He also wondered what her expression would be when they had their talk. He should have taken her to his home, but that hadn't seemed right to him, not at this time. After leaving the town behind, he drove through a small wooded area and finally pulled up to a small out-of-the-way diner. Eddie s Eatery, the sign proclaimed.

He opened her door to help her out to escort her inside. "We eat here some times when we're out this way. It's a bit shabby, but the food's great."

Annalee felt more strung out by the moment, as she limped inside. Her hip wound was tender and stiff this morning. *What has this man got in his head?* She hoped he'd spit it out so they could discuss whatever it was. She hated tension, and she'd had a belly full of it in the past five years. She didn't plan to suffer it again.

Jack ushered her to a booth and sat across from her, his elbows on the table.

"I guess you are wondering what on earth I've got on my mind. I would, myself, if I were in your shoes, and in your present situation." Annalee opened her mouth to speak, but he held up his hand. "I'll come right out and say what I've been considering. You can tell me to go straight to hell or maybe take some time and think it over before you decide what you might want to do."

Jack was wound tight as a spring. Annalee could see that much about him. It had something to do with her and she felt her heart beating double time as she waited to hear him out.

"After bringing you back from the clinic," he stated, "I've been doing some heavy thinking. I've been in a stew all last night and this morning, too." He twisted a bit in his seat and clenched his hands together, obviously nervous. "My big worry is over Sissy. Of course, you must know that. She has suffered so much. I can't bear to see her go through any more changes, especially the trauma of finding someone new to watch her while I work. It's because of her that I've decided to make you an offer."

Chapter 10

Jack gave the approaching waitress an order for coffee for them both and waited until she left to begin again. "As I see it, with the loss of your little home, you are at a terrible disadvantage right now. I feel terrible about that. I've come to think you are one fine woman or I wouldn't even be considering what I am going to say."

He fiddled with the cutlery and glanced about the room. "I don't want you to think I'm the kind of man who would take advantage of any woman in your situation, or any other, not in any way. I know because of this unfortunate fire, you have no home to go to and, unless I miss my guess, you've lost everything, even the toys for your kids."

"Yes, Mr. Harrison, it's the truth. I've lost everything."

"It's Jack—please, call me Jack." He shifted in his seat and sweat broke out over his brow. "My idea is that you and your children could move into my home. It's big and there are lots of rooms with toys all over the place, well…girl toys. But I'd take Bucky shopping for whatever he wants or needs."

Annalee sat there in shock, trying to take in what Jack had just suggested. She nearly gasped as she uttered her angry reply, "Well, I should say not! There is no possible way I could live in your home, just like that. Whatever would people *say*? I'd never live it down. You know how cruel people are." She groped for words to explain her feelings. "It certainly wouldn't look right, not to anyone, now would it? There would be such terrible gossip about a thing like that and all aimed at me." She wrapped her arms about herself. "People can be so vicious about a thing like that. I couldn't allow something of that sort to hurt my children, Jack, and it certainly would. I just couldn't do a thing like that to them—or to myself either!" She wanted to burst into tears, but her anger had her so tied in knots, she could barely speak. "What kind of woman do you think I am, sir?"

"I know what kind of woman you are, Annalee, otherwise I would never have suggested it. Please don't be offended. I think you are one of the finest women I've ever had the privilege to know. But what bothers me the most is that my daughter calls you Mommy. It tears my heart out to think she will have to lose a mother all over again." At seeing the tightness of fear on her face, he suddenly realized what she was afraid of. "My God, woman, you don't think I meant—"

"And just what am I supposed to think? Good Lord, what would any woman think of an offer like that?"

Jack reached out to take her hand, but she quickly withdrew it. "I wasn't hinting at anything like intimate relations between us!" He flushed at using the word, and the disgusting way it must have sounded to her, and tried to explain. "I still love my wife, Annalee. I don't think I'll ever stop."

"I'm sorry about thinking about it that way," Annalee said. "But isn't that unspeakable business between a man and woman a part of living in the same house? And on top of that—not being married?" She flushed again. "Jack, I've been down that road once already. Since then, I've been totally and completely determined I will never be involved in that way again, married or not. I am no good at that sort of thing and can't even think of it!"

She felt herself getting heated and angry and, worse yet, she had told this man things she wouldn't have had the courage to tell her own mother. She felt her face flame up and begin to burn like the furies of hell.

Jack did some fast thinking. He'd said everything wrong as far as this young woman was concerned. And now, he saw this chance for his daughter's happiness slipping away like water into arid desert sands. He was desperate. He didn't want to face losing this woman's care for his daughter. And he had not intended his offer as any sort of insult to her, either.

"Well then, would you consider it if you were married to me?" he asked then quickly added, "Of course, I don't mean in the full sense. I wouldn't ask that of you as we don't know each other well enough to ever consider such a thing." He flushed, imagining how she must see him right now, as some evil sexual predator rather than a worried father. Jack kept on persuading her. He had to. "But feeling as you do, and as I do about my late wife, you could live in my home without the stain of gossip. It would be legal that way. There'd be no reason for people to talk then, now would there?"

He had put himself out there. It was done, and he felt nervous as hell, waiting for what she might say. He could almost see the wheels turning in her pretty head. He also saw the way her hand clenched on her half-filled coffee cup and the embarrassed flush of her face.

Annalee had her head down, her face burning, unable to look him in the eye. She wanted to crawl under the table or run out of the place. "Oh, I'm so horribly ashamed for what I've said about my marriage. I never thought to let that out to anyone."

Jack reached across, caught her hand, and held on. "Annalee, I'm sorry you had that kind of marriage. I didn't know. In any case, I have no designs on you personally, though I must say, you are a very fine-looking woman. Any man with eyes would be mighty proud to have a wife like you on his arm." He smiled at her and gave her hand a squeeze. "Unspeakable business?" He couldn't hide the smile that tried to escape. "My God, woman, what kind of a man were you married to?" After saying that, he did his best to get back on track. "It's just that I'm very worried about my daughter. You've got to believe me about that."

He released her hand and sat back. The ice had now been broken and the topic broached. But Jack saw that she wasn't convinced—not at all. He felt he must persuade her or lose another mother for his child. An honorable offer was all he'd had in mind. How could he make this young woman believe it was just that and nothing more?

Jack looked her in the eye, when he could catch her with her head up. "Annalee, please don't be embarrassed to tell me anything. Things like a bad union in marriage happen. Believe me, I've heard of things like that," he stressed, hoping to get her to agree with his idea. "The fine heart you have and the loving way you have of caring for my daughter are the qualities in you that gave me the idea to ask you about this in the first place. I swear to you, I'm not looking for a wife in that way, Annalee—not at all."

He was embarrassed now and nearly reduced to begging. "But I will admit, aside from my daughter's happiness, there are some other things that would be nice, too. I would love to come home at night to see my little girl happy in her own home and playing with your children. To smell the wonderful odor of food cooking on the stove and seeing lights on in the house again would be wonderful beyond belief. You have no idea how lonely my life has been since I lost my wife—her name was Amelia." He looked like a man so completely lost, right then, that Annalee's heart went out to him.

She didn't know what to do as she mused aloud, hardly addressing him, "What it really comes down to, Jack, is a choice between going to live with my parents again—or your offer."

He waited for a moment as he saw Annalee sitting there, considering his idea. But then he went on, hoping to further influence her decision. "I would be a good father to your children and adopt them if you'd like. I would see to it that they go on to the Normal School when they are older." He tossed that bit about higher education in as an added benefit because, right now, he was afraid she was about to throw her coffee in his face.

Annalee knew she had to make a decision. He was a good man. She'd seen enough of him to know that. If he wouldn't ask for the intimate side of their marriage, she would have a decent home for herself and her children. She wouldn't have to suffer through that nasty business with an over-heated husband rutting about, hurting her, and mauling her about every night any more, either. She had to consider his offer.

She thought of the alternative: going to live with her parents. She shuddered. It was that or taking a chance on this man who sat before her. She knew him to be of good character, and he was handsome enough for any woman. Of course, she'd foolishly fallen into that trap once before. But right now, she didn't see any decent way out of the mess she was in.

She looked straight into his deep gray eyes. Could she trust him not to attack her in the night after she moved into his home? She had to decide. She had what he needed, too—so it wasn't a totally one-sided offer. If she allowed this to happen, it would solve all her problems, except for the possibility she might find herself in this man's bed somewhere down the road. She shivered again. That was a very real concern. Could she trust Jack to be the kind of man he claimed?

With her heart beating like a trip hammer, she made her decision, looked into his eyes, and nodded her head slightly. "I will do it, then." She couldn't bring herself to say the word, marriage, though—she just couldn't. It might look like a marriage to others, but thank you God, it wouldn't be one in reality.

"Thank you, Annalee, I swear, you won't be sorry. I

will make all the arrangements. We'll have to get the license. You'll need to come with me for that." He heaved a sigh and wiped his brow. "I am satisfied with this arrangement. My daughter will have a mother in the home, one she has already come to love." He smiled. "But I will admit I do like your company, my dear. I do."

Annalee felt her head spinning. She thought she might faint, until she heard him say, "Well as long as we're here, how about us having a bite to eat?" He signaled the waitress.

She'd heard him say, *us*, like they were a couple already. Just like that, her future was settled, and the man responsible for it sat across from her, hungry, and ready to eat. Annalee couldn't stop the smile from spreading across her face.

Jack looked up and saw her smile. "What? Why are you smiling like that?"

"Nothing really," Annalee replied. "It's just that you have just settled both our lives and our futures. Now, you are ready to have something to eat." She laughed. "Just like that, Jack."

"I'm very satisfied with our deal. We both have a lot to offer, and I think it's even, don't you?"

He laughed, too, and she heard the soft melody of it. He was a good decent sort of man and, suddenly, she realized she was actually hungry and ready to eat a bite herself.

"I believe I could eat something." She smiled at him and added, "After we eat, do you think we could go see your home?" She felt a bit forward asking, but if her children were to live there, she wanted, and needed, to see it.

"Why certainly. I'd be glad to show you your new

home." He had pride in his voice as he answered her.

The waitress appeared. Annalee ordered an egg salad sandwich. Jack ordered a hot beef plate.

They ate in near silence. Annalee couldn't decide what to say to this man. She had agreed to become his wife, yet there were no feelings between them to lead them along. She imagined Jack felt the same. To say the least, it was definitely awkward.

To her complete surprise, she realized she was happy. And she was excited to have him take her to the house that would become her home. This entire business had her in a state of disbelief. Yet, the idea of a fine decent home to manage and care for had her most anxious to see it.

She had no other place to go and no hope of anything else, in any case. She knew the dismal prospect of going to live with her parents had played a large part in her decision. The thought of a nice home for herself and her children and no doubt much nicer than she'd ever expected to have was mind boggling. After losing everything she had—and it wasn't that much in the first place—in that fire, she now faced having just about everything she would ever need. Truthfully, the whole arrangement had her nerves in an uproar. For now, she had just put her and her children's futures in the hands of a near stranger.

She believed she could trust him, or she would never have placed herself or her children in his care. He looked up at her several times as they ate and finally said, "Strange isn't it?" He uttered a half laugh. "It is for me, too, Annalee. I never thought this idea of mine would happen until you finally said yes. I only thought of it yesterday, when wondering what to do about Sissy. But I'll admit, just a bit ago, I was afraid you were thinking of tossing your coffee at me."

"It did enter my mind a time or two." She grinned a bit at her admission. "But if it goes as you say, I believe we can make it work. Like you, I believe our children are very important. I would do almost anything for them. I want so much to keep them safe. Your offer is a good one and, I confess, it's a life saver for me."

"Well, let's just be friends, then. And we have a good start on that already. I think you'll approve of my house, and your new home."

He dug into his plate again. His hot beef dinner was nearly gone. She watched this good man quietly devouring the food on his plate as she sat contemplating this new turn in her life and future.

Annalee finished off the sandwich she'd ordered. "That was very good. Thank you, Jack." She smiled at him. "And I drank my coffee, instead of throwing it at you."

They left the little diner—not arm in arm, but walking side by side. Annalee felt the feeling of companionship with him, something she had never felt with Gerald. She actually felt comfortable with Jack as he ushered her into his car. They drove away heading back to their little village of Delano. Jack said nothing and, as for herself, Annalee was deep in thought

As he drove, Annalee observed him as a driver. Again, she saw no cursing or snide remarks at other drivers and put that down to the kind of man he was. *Could this really be happening to me?* She was still in a state of disbelief. *Am I a crazy woman to do this?*

Jack pulled down a quiet street. It was pleasant with shady trees and filled with very nice homes. She saw big trees, well-kept yards, and kids playing—jumping rope, or hopping about playing hop-scotch. He pulled up to a large home, white with blue trim, two stories high, a balcony or two, with tall curtained and draped windows. He parked in the driveway, though she saw he also had a garage that looked big enough for two cars. Annalee's heart thumped wildly in her chest. Could she handle the care of a house this big?

He came to her door and helped her out. "Come inside and have a look."

He went to a side door and held it open for her. She came into a gleaming and spotless kitchen.

He waved his hand about. "I've had a woman come in and clean about twice a week, not being so good at it myself."

There was an electric range with coiled burners. She had seen them in stores, but never had the use of one. She saw a wall full of cupboards and opened one to see plates, cups, and another to see slender glasses of an amber shade she thought looked beautiful. "Oh, my, you have everything here, don't you?"

"Yes, it's all here, just like it was before I—" He turned to her. "Would it bother you if I mention my wife sometimes? I have the habit and it's not so easy to break."

Annalee shook her head. "No, it won't. It's an honor to her that you have these fine memories." Going to one cupboard after another, she looked through each one. "I must say, I think your wife had lovely taste." She turned to him. "I believe she and Amy were good friends. Amy is a good friend of mine, too. Yesterday, she brought me these clothes I'm wearing."

"That's good to hear. Derrick and I spend a lot of time together ourselves."

He urged her to see more of the house. The living room had thick, soft, dark-sandy shaded carpeting, finely crafted side tables, large soft chairs, and a long couch upholstered in deep-purple shaded velvet. Even the sheer curtains and thick draperies at the windows looked finer than anything Annalee had ever seen.

"Your home is wonderful, Jack," Annalee commented, her eyes aglow.

"Do you want to see upstairs, to know where to put your children?" He headed for the stairs located centrally off the kitchen and living area. Up the broad staircase, Annalee saw several doors along a hallway. She opened them one by one. She saw Cecelia's room, decorated for a little girl, and another that she took to be a guest room.

The bed was made up with a thick spread of a softly shaded pattern of roses and vines. The room looked very inviting with rugs and tiny rosebud wall paper. Annalee thought that would do for her. Sarah could sleep in it with her for the time being.

There were two more rooms with nothing in them. She turned to Jack. "Maybe one of these would do for Buckley."

Jack nodded. "We'll get some boy's furnishings for him." He laughed, obviously proud of what he had to offer her. "And a set of blocks and a truck or two, but what about little Sarah? Won't she want some nice girl's things, too?"

Annalee replied, nearly in tears, "Jack, this is so

much. I can't take it all in right now." She flushed. "And it's all so expensive for you!"

"I don't care about that, Annalee. If my little one is happy, that's all I want. I have a good salary, and as my wife, you can get whatever you need for yourself and any of your children. And that includes Sissy, too. She will be your daughter as well. For your children, right now, all they have are their lives—and you saved those for them the other night."

"You know, I love your little girl, anyway, so that won't be a big change for me, but everything else will be. There is no doubt of that." Annalee knew her life had just taken the biggest change imaginable.

He laughed as he led the way down the stairs and out to the car. "Well, we'd best get you back to your children. I'd have to say, this has been a very different day, hasn't it?"

She hadn't opened that last room off the upstairs hallway. Somehow she knew it would be his, and she didn't want to look in there, certainly not in his presence. It would have been embarrassing in the extreme. She flushed just thinking of a thing like that.

Annalee also wondered what her new address would be, but couldn't mention it right now. She'd had all the excitement she could handle for one day. Unable to fully grasp this unusual turn of events, she hoped she hadn't made the biggest mistake of her life.

Driving back to Mary's, she thought of Carol and wondered how she would take the news of her impending wedding. She'd had Jack all staked out for herself. It wouldn't be easy to tell her about the forthcoming wedding, but if she asked…

Chapter 11

J ack let her out at Mary's home. "I'll let you know what we need to do next. And don't you worry about a thing. It'll be all right. Thank you, Annalee." He drove away and she went into the house.

Mary met her in the living room. "Your friend Carol was here, but I told her you had gone out with Mr. Harrison. She went on home after that." She frowned. "She looked awfully funny to me. Is she sick, do you think?"

"Not that I know of," Annalee said. To herself, she said under her breath, "Not as sick as she's going to be." There'd be a storm coming from that direction. Annalee had thought of asking Carol to stand up with her, but she knew better and would ask Amy instead.

Buckley and Sarah came rushing up to her. Buckley demanded, "Where you go, Momma?"

Sarah stood quietly sucking her thumb. She hadn't done that for months, but she was doing it now. It had started right after the fire. Her little ones were so brave for all they'd been through. It had been too much lately with the death of their father and then that awful fire. Annalee still couldn't figure out how that could have happened. She'd always been so careful.

Annalee held her children close as she wondered how to tell them what was going to happen in a few more days. And how in the world was she going to tell Carol? Annalee was tired after the emotional day she'd had.

She needed to speak to Mary. They couldn't stay with her for so long and pay nothing. Annalee felt guilty about that, too.

She sent the children to the bedroom they occupied and found Mary. "I feel so badly putting you out like this. I have nothing to offer you for all you've done."

Mary smiled and nodded toward the dining room. "Annalee, you have a stack of letters lying in a pile on the table in there. When bad things like this happen, your friends, neighbors, and people you don't even know often step in with something to help out. Why not open some of them and see what's there?"

Annalee went to the dining room and found a small mound of mail, all of it addressed to her. Some of the envelopes were merely addressed to the woman whose home was burned. "My heavens, Mary, what's all this?" she exclaimed. Annalee opened one of the envelopes on top. "It says it's from a friend, and there is a five dollar bill inside. There's no return address. How can I thank someone who sends a letter like that?" She opened another and found ten dollars, and with another several ones poured out. "Mary, I can't believe what I'm seeing. Look at all this money. I can pay you for everything and I can buy my own wedding dress, too!" She stopped, realizing what she'd said aloud. "Oh my, I haven't told anyone yet."

Mary stood staring at her with astonishment on her face. Annalee knew she had to explain. But to this warm and friendly soul who'd opened her home in the time of need, she was eager to tell the good news. "Come, Mary, sit with me. I have something to tell you."

They sat together and Annalee explained to her about her marriage deal with Jack. "I wouldn't want the people around here to think it was such a cold-hearted business deal," she said. "But I think I can trust you, Mary. I wouldn't think of sharing this information with another soul."

Annalee knew Carol would never understand. To her and everyone but Mary, Annalee would have to put on like they had fallen in love. That would be a little hard to do when there had never been any sign of his interest in her, or hers in him. *Could she do it and make people believe it?*

There had been no sign of anything romantic between them before the fire—not one thing. During the wedding he would have to kiss her like it was the real thing. Annalee was sure of that. She shivered, thinking of having that man's fine, strong lips pressing down on hers. But of course it would only be a short peck, and she would be able to withstand that.

She wanted to talk to her friend, Amy, but Mary had no phone. Annalee would have to try and start that Model A of Gerald's. She had left the key in it. Everyone did the same, so it hadn't been lost in the fire. It was late afternoon now, and tomorrow was Monday.

She needed to speak to Amy, if she could find a

way—and what about Sissy? Things were piling up already, and Annalee felt the pressure.

"Is it all right to leave the children again?" she asked Mary. "I need to go see a friend."

"Why of course, dear. They are such darlings, I really don't mind. You must have a lot on your mind right now. Are you going to try and start that Model A? It's been sitting there for so long."

Annalee nodded. But at that moment, she saw Carol's car drive up. Her heart rate went soaring as she saw Carol get out and come walking up the front steps.

Annalee answered the door. "Hi, Carol, come on in. What brings you over so late in the day?" She had to say something. It was growing dark and her inane question was just the beginning.

Carol sniffed and tossed her head. "I had to see how you and the kids were doing. You could have come to stay at my house after the fire, you know."

"At the time, it wasn't up to me, Carol. Mary came across the street to see what she could do and my kids needed help right then. I was cut and bleeding, in a state of shock myself. Mary took them to her house, away from the fire, the smoke, and seeing their home turn into a pile of rubble. They are still pretty upset. Sarah is sucking her thumb again, and Bucky's very obedient and quiet—too quiet. He's hardly said anything at all about the fire. Yet, it must be on their minds, like an everlasting nightmare."

"Oh, I'm sorry to hear that," Carol exclaimed as Annalee led her to the living room sofa. She sat down and turned to face Annalee to comment on what was really on her mind. "I see you've been riding around in Jack Harrison's car again. What's going on?" Carol's eyes drilled right into her with the direct, almost angry questioning. "Why is he hanging around you like that?"

"Well, the first time, he took me to the clinic where I got these stitches." Annalee pointed to her upper right hip. "And, of course, he is very worried about finding care for his daughter. This fire has caused more changes than just for me and my kids," she said. "I still don't see how it ever could have started. I've always turned that kerosene stove off, and I never keep anything flammable near it—never!" She nearly gasped for breath and repeated, "I don't see how it could have started the way it did."

That mystery was ever on Annalee's mind. She still couldn't believe it happened.

Carol went quiet for a while. Her face had gone pale. But Annalee quickly saw it wasn't any loss of her own that lay on Carol's mind. Her attention was riveted on Jack.

"Well, have you learned what Jack is planning to do about his daughter's care? If you leave town to go live with your folks, he'll need someone else, won't he?"

"I suppose he would, but I won't be leaving town, Carol," Annalee said. She already knew what her friend had in mind.

She planned to have Jack's daughter at her house, so he would come there every night to get her. Annalee could just imagine how Carole would greet him at the door, too. Thinking of the way she would thrust her hips out at him and afford him the luxury of her slant-eyed, sexy looks, those thoughts made her far less reticent to tell Carol how greatly her options had changed.

"You won't?" Carol asked. "Well, just what are you

going to do, then? Where will you live? How will you live?"

"Carol, I can't believe this myself, but something has just happened." Annalee had to tell Carol about her engagement to Jack. She knew it would cause her friend to be upset, but Annalee had to let her know. She took a deep breath and began. "I imagine this will come as a surprise to you, but my future living arrangements have been decided. I'm going to live in Jack's home, Carol. He has asked me to marry him and I have accepted. We'll be married in a few days' time, or as soon as he can make the arrangements."

Annalee watched the unbelievable agony of desolation and fury mounting in Carol's eyes. Her face went as white as newly fallen snow. Her lips tightened and her fists clenched so tight, Annalee saw a few drops of blood on her long, sharp nails. She began to worry Carol was about to burst forth like an erupting volcano.

"How could this happen?" Carol barely gasped out her words of disbelief. Her throat seemed to have closed. "When did this happen?"

"I don't really know, Carol," Annalee said. "It must have been coming on between us gradually. And this morning, he asked me to drive out with him—he said we needed to talk," she went on, as though Carol didn't mind at all and was actually happy to hear the news, though Annalee knew better. "We stopped at a small diner he knew and, over coffee, he asked me." She threw out her hands in her most helpless, innocent gesture. "He apologized and said he knew it was very sudden." She watched the color draining from Carol's cheeks as she added, "He also said he thought I was a very fine young woman. But

I know what decided him is that little Sissy thinks of me as her mother and calls me Momma. It was more that than anything." She didn't stop there. "He promised to be a good father to my two, as well," she said. "He even offered to send them on to Normal School when they are older if they want to go. He's a real good man, Carol, and my kids need a father. I couldn't say no to him. I just couldn't."

"Oh, I'll just bet you just couldn't." Carol bit off the words, as she sprang up from the couch and declared through clenched lips, "I've got to go home. This is too much for me to handle right now."

"It's quite a bit for me to handle, too," Annalee said. "And Carol, he took me to his home. It was so lovely and big, with lots of bedrooms upstairs. Everything is there, all the things that were his and his wife's. He said the house and everything in it will be mine to care for and manage. He gave me a tour today so I could pick out the kids rooms." She knew she'd twisted the knife with that last bit, but she didn't feel very sorry for Carol. The woman had done nothing but throw herself at Jack, and Jack hadn't liked it or asked for it.

Annalee watched her friend turn away and walk out. Carol flounced to her car, threw herself in, and revved up the motor. Annalee heard the tires squealing as Carol roared away. She felt sorry for her, pregnant with some unknown man's child and all alone the way she was.

She herself, however, had a lot to face, too. Her hip wound was painful, and right now, she felt weak, nervous, and indecisive. She wanted nothing more than to go to that nice warm bed in Mary's room and sleep for a week. But that was not an option as she asked herself,

Can I do this? Can I manage a big house like that? God help me, I don't know."

Annalee walked back into Mary's warm living room and fell down on the couch.

Mary went to her. "My dear, are you all right?"

Annalee struggled to sit upright. "Yes. I'm all right, but I'm nervous and scared to death. Can I do this?"

"Annalee, are you afraid of this man?"

"No, not at all, I believe he is as good as any man alive, or I'd never allow my children to be put into a situation like this—marrying a man I hardly know." Annalee straightened herself up on the couch. "It's just that I was never going to ever allow myself to be involved with a man again, if you know what I mean by that."

"I think I understand." Mary frowned. "My dear, I was married for many years. And if it's being a wife to him that you fear, it doesn't always have to be a bad thing." She flushed and Annalee saw the red stain of it creep up her wrinkled neck and suffuse her withered cheeks. "I must say, I was very happy with my Lars," Mary went on, her voice becoming a dreamy whisper. "He was a gentle, understanding man. What I'm trying to tell you is that the way he was made everything all right."

Annalee knew what she meant and understood that Mary could not be more explicit than she had been. "Thank you, Mary. If it ever comes to that, I will try to remember your words." She hadn't wanted anyone to know what her bargain with Jack was to be, but again, she'd let some of that information out. "Please, Mary, you must never tell anyone how it's going to be with Jack and me. Please."

"No bother, dear. You have my word."

But by that certain look on her face, Annalee knew Mary believed she and Jack would definitely become a real husband and wife, and in the near future. Annalee shook her head at Mary because she knew better.

The doorbell sounded. Mary went to the door and came back with Amy Lassen. "You have more company, my dear. I'll go check on the children."

Mary walked away to see to the children, but her mind was in a turmoil about something else entirely. That friend of Annalee's—Carol—her dark green Ford sedan looked so familiar. She'd' seen it and something was not right about seeing it. She couldn't put her finger on it right now nor could she believe the passing thought that had crossed her mind. *For God's sake, it couldn't be*!

Annalee got off the couch and hugged Amy. "You have no idea how glad I am to see you," she said. "I have something to tell you."

Amy sat down and waited. "Yes?"

"Jack asked me to take a ride with him. He said we needed to talk." Annalee flushed and felt the burn right up to her hair roots. "Amy, he has asked me to marry him. I believe it was to give us a home and because his daughter calls me 'Momma,'" she admitted. "But I said I would."

"Well, I'm sure it wasn't just to give you a home, An. He has a very good opinion of you. Derrick and I both know that, but most likely his daughter *was* the bigger part of it. She is all he has left of his wife, aside from the fact that Jack is the loneliest soul I've ever seen."

Amy giggled a bit.

"You are a silly goose, An. Have you looked into a mirror lately? You are one beautiful woman. Yes, he loved his wife to distraction. He did, but with your looks and Sissy calling you 'Momma,' the idea to ask you to marry him must have hit him like a ton of bricks. That man was afraid you'd get away," she added. "You are great with your own kids and Sissy is happy with them, too. So why not?"

"Well, for whatever reason he asked me, Amy, I said yes. It was too good an offer to turn down, and I know him to be a good, decent man." Annalee took Amy's hand. "Dear friend, will you be my maid of honor?"

Amy gave Annalee a hug. "Yes, of course, I will."

Annalee frowned. "Carol was just here. You know she had her eye on Jack. She turned pale as death when I told her I was marrying him. I think she could have bitten through a box of nails when she heard the news. She rushed out to her car and I heard her tires squeal as she roared away."

"I heard all about that business from Derrick." Amy grinned. "Jack wasn't at all happy about the way the woman constantly threw herself at him."

"What's worrying me now is that I need to do some shopping. Mary will watch my kids, but who is watching Sissy?"

"Derrick and Jack both, right now. I'm sure they are hashing this business out between them."

Annalee wondered if Jack would tell his good friend what their relationship was going to be as she couldn't bring herself to mention it. It was enough that Mary knew the truth about it.

"Tomorrow, we will go shopping. I will manage Sissy's care for that day. I know someone. But, An, she cries for you at night. That's what Jack says."

"Oh, poor little thing," Annalee cried. "She was so sick when she had to have that operation, Amy."

"Jack told us how you took her in and took care of her after that. It's no wonder he's asked you to marry him. He couldn't let a woman like you get away, now could he?" Amy got up to leave. "Until tomorrow, then, and we'll get something for the little ones, too, while we're out."

Amy left and Annalee went to find her children. She took them into the bedroom where they slept together on a double bed.

It was time to tell them what was in their future.

"You both know Mr. Harrison and you like him, don't you?" she began. At their nodding yes, she asked them, "How would you like it if he becomes your daddy—every day, all the time?"

Buckley looked at her. "My daddy is all gone away, Momma. How can another man be my daddy?"

"He can be, if we get married—like I was married to your real daddy," she said. "Lots of times, people do that. If they lose a daddy or a momma, the parent that is left can marry another daddy or momma. If I marry Mr. Harrison, he will be your daddy, and I will be Sissy's momma."

"Oh, I'd like that," Bucky said. "She can climb real good, Momma." He was easy to convince, but Sarah only sucked her thumb.

"He has a nice big house," Annalee said. "There will be a room all your own, Bucky. Mr. Harrison said he will take you to a store to see if you can find some toys you like, a new truck, blocks, anything you might like."

Bucky jumped up and down. His big dark eyes shone

with excitement. "Oh boy, Momma, I really do need some more blocks."

Annalee took Sarah on her lap. "I think I will keep Sarah in with me when we move into his house, just until she gets used to everything." She squeezed Sarah. "Would you like that darling?"

Sarah snuggled her head into her mother's chest and said nothing. She would need more time. Annalee believed she was still in some sort of shock.

It was getting late by now and Annalee put the children to bed. They really had nothing to wear and wore old shirts of Mary's to sleep in. Tomorrow, she would get them everything they needed. She would use some of the money lying out on that dining room table. How kind people were, after that awful fire, to be so generous.

Chapter 12

Annalee was ready when Amy came to pick her up. She wore the same clothing as yesterday, since she had nothing else. She hopped into Amy's plushy Buick and, as they drove away, she said, "I am more excited by this buying trip than you could ever imagine, Amy. I have a pile of money people have sent to me here at Mary's home. Some of it came from people who put no return address on their envelope and I don't see how I can ever thank them properly."

Amy laughed as she drove into the middle of the small village. "People can be very generous, dear, and who needed it more than you? But think about it, An, maybe some people don't want a thank you for doing the right thing." She pulled into the best store available, Carlson's Mercantile. "Let's see what they have in here. If we don't like anything there, we can go to Wisconsin Rapids. That berg has everything."

Annalee felt nervous, excited, and eager to find

something for her children. They'd had little to nothing in the first place, so anything she found today would be a delight to them.

They walked through the aisles with Annalee choosing things for each child. She found shoes for each of them, several pairs of anklets for Sarah and four pairs of socks for Buckley. She picked out dresses for Sarah, pants and shirts for Buckley, and underwear for both, "I guess this is what those generous people had in mind, Amy. It's wonderful."

Amy spoke up. "You are being married, An, and that's what is wonderful. We need to find you an outfit for that." She pulled Annalee toward the clothing for women. "Let's have a look." She pulled one hanger after another, sliding them along the metal bar. "You're looking for something fit to be married in, but it doesn't look like they have a thing worth the bother in this store."

"Does it need to be so fancy?"

"Yes, it does. Jack is a special guy, An. You'll want to look your best and be a match for a man like that."

Annalee couldn't bring herself to say, *It's just a business deal*. She had to go along with Amy's idea of a proper wedding dress. She feared it would be too much in Jack's eyes, if she got herself decked out like a proper bride. "I wouldn't feel right, being married in a long white bridal gown, Amy," she protested. "Not in any way."

"No, of course not, it's too soon after his loss—and yours too, actually. A nice cream-colored dress ought to be the right thing for a small, informal occasion." She turned to Annalee. "We need to go to Wisconsin Rapids. I know a great store over there."

Annalee had to go along, but she only hoped she had enough money left to buy such a fancy dress. "Is it very expensive?"

"Not so very. Don't worry, An, when you are married to Jack, he has a decent income. You'll be able to get whatever you need when you need it."

At Annalee's worried look, Amy grinned. "Hey, this is a special occasion. You have to look the part."

Seeing the busy city of Wisconsin Rapids was very exciting to Annalee. Cars went buzzing past and people walked about everywhere. Everything seemed new and different in this city. They entered a store labeled The Bon Ton. Amy found a lovely creamy dress, with tiny violet dots sprinkled across the top, a dropped waistline, and an open neck Annalee worried was rather daring. It was also rather short on her tall, slim, body, but it did fit her very well.

"Quite a bit more of those good looking legs will be showing, but that's the style now, so may as well get used to it." Amy told her. "Better find you some great stockings. You certainly don't need a girdle, but do you have a garter belt?" She laughed. "No, of course you haven't. If you had one, it would be ashes now, wouldn't it?"

Annalee felt like she was in a dizzy whirl as Amy went about choosing accessories and jewelry. Soon, Annalee had in her hands, earrings, a bracelet, and make-up—none of which she had anymore. In most cases, she'd never had it in the first place. She realized she was entering a different world in marrying Jack. He was an educated man, a college graduate, and an engineer. Right now, she felt terribly inferior to a man like that.

Annalee tried to hide her fear, but she couldn't fend

off an overwhelming attack of cold feet. That little business deal with a nice home and a father for her children was rapidly becoming something else entirely.

"Amy, please stop!" Annalee gasped for breath. "This is all too much. I can't handle it."

Amy stopped and faced her. "What's wrong, An?"

"I'm suddenly scared to death with all this." Annalee flung out her hands in desperation. "I don't know how to handle what's happening."

"Okay, I've got it. Sorry, I got carried away, making so much of everything." Amy put her arm around Annalee and patted her back. "I think you are the bravest woman I've ever seen. So much has happened to you, and now this impromptu wedding on top of everything else." She grew serious. "It is a lot to handle, isn't it?" While Annalee just stood there in a state of confusion, Amy laughed. "Let's have lunch at the Woolworth's lunch counter. It's just around the corner. You need time to collect yourself. I'm sorry I got so carried away."

They went around the corner to enjoy a leisurely, relaxing lunch, which gave Annalee time to think. She had a lot to get used to in the new life that lay ahead for her. After that calming interlude, with quiet conversation enough to soothe her nerves, they finished buying the things they believed Annalee needed.

As they headed for the car to stow them, Amy said, "I'm happy for you, marrying Jack. It might be quite sudden, but you two need each other. That's the way it seems to me. I suppose it's a lot to take on with it happening so fast and right on top of the horrible fire in the bargain." Annalee's supply of money was gone for good now, but she had what was needed.

CRES

It was decided to hold a ten o'clock in the morning wedding at the little white Baptist Church. Annalee was a member and attended if she could. They had the license and the minister ready and had planned a very small ceremony, one pleasing to both Jack and Annalee. She had notified her parents, but they had sent notice that they could not come as their vehicle was broken down just now. Carol was invited, but Annalee hoped she would not attend.

Each of the children had new clothes and had been well groomed for the service. To the soft sounds of the organ, the two little girls wearing nearly matching finery, walked down the aisle with Amy, preceding the bride. Then to the wedding march, Annalee had Buckley walk her down the aisle. Jack had taken him out to buy him a new truck, a set of blocks, a new suit, and shining black shoes. His handsome little face beamed as he manfully walked beside his mother, walking her down to marry Jack Harrison.

To Annalee, the sight of that tall man in his dark suit, polished blond hair, and deep gray eyes sent a thrill zipping right through her all the way to her toes. She was worried though. Could she be a good enough wife for this fine, handsome man without the intimacies?

Amy had the two little girls beside her and Mary sat in the front row to take the children, if that was needed. Each child was dressed in lovely new clothing, new shoes, and had their shining hair curled. Annalee wore no veil. Her dark, curling hair trailed down her back. Her violet-shaded eyes were clear and shining, but they shone more with worry and apprehension than the joy of becoming Jack's bride. She carried a small bouquet of pale pink roses and, upon reaching the altar, handed them off to Amy. Then Jack took her hand in his warm, firm one. He smiled a slow, comforting smile at her and gave her hand a gentle squeeze.

They repeated their vows and, when all the words and promises had been said, Pastor Oliver Benson declared, "I now pronounce you man and wife. You may now kiss the bride."

Jack looked down into Annalee's pale face and saw the look of uncertainty on her beautiful features as she took this step into an unknown future. He wanted to assure her, but in a moment of unexpected excitement, he swept her backward in his arms as his lips claimed hers for a good, solid kiss. Startled, she clung to him for support until he set her upright again.

Annalee had feared this intimate kiss most of all and had carefully prepared herself to tolerate it, determined to keep the façade of their business-deal marriage intact. But when Jack's warm lips touched hers, she felt an instant jolt of electricity. The touch of them sent wild sensations zinging through her body like a sharp, almost painful surprise. The feel of his lips on hers hit her right below the belt, all the way through, down to her stomach and beyond. The force of it shocked her into a totally new kind of awareness.

She muffled a gasp as he let her up and felt the rush of a maddening, heated blush, staining and burning her cheeks. She'd never felt sensations like that in her life. The feelings that kiss had aroused within her body filled her with a fear of those intimate things that were not supposed to come from this marriage. And now, too late, she realized, she'd walked right into it with eyes blinded by her desperate need.

As they turned to make their way together back up the aisle, she caught a look from Mary and a very knowing nod. What she saw on that old woman's face made her blush even harder. She held onto Jack's arm as she walked, partly to keep from falling over. Then she caught the piercing glance of someone else. A nicely dressed man sat in the back pew, off in a corner—alone. His dark eyes swept over her as she walked past his pew on her new husband's arm.

He'd been there all along, sitting there quietly, watching everything. But what shocked Annalee, almost enough to make her faint, was that the man was nearly the spitting image of Gerald, her dead husband. She felt numb all over, but she kept walking somehow, automatically. She spoke to well-wishers along the way. Yet, inside, she was so completely stunned, upon seeing that man, that she barely knew what she was saying.

Amy announced to the crowd that there would be a wedding luncheon served in the adjoining building used for the many social occasions that happened among the church parishioners. Someone had been very busy, putting it all together. It was partly the ladies of the church— but a lot of it was Amy. Annalee was sure of that.

She looked about for the sight of Carol, wondering if she had come to the wedding. Annalee didn't see her, but she did see the dark-haired, dark-eyed man who resembled her dead husband again. He stood among the well-wishers, mingling, but not talking to anyone in particular.

When she had a chance, she sought him out as he

chatted amiably with a man he'd met in the small crowd. Up close, he seemed far more polished in appearance than Gerald ever had, but his face seemed almost exactly the same.

"Who are you, sir? Why—what are you doing here at our wedding?"

"I believe I am your brother-in-law, my dear." He had the same voice, though he spoke in the same tone, yet somehow his tone was warmer and more gentile. Annalee knew the man wasn't lying. He couldn't be. She remembered Gerald saying he had a brother, but no other relatives. He'd never told her a thing about the brother. She'd known nothing of his family, but had always wondered.

"Why are you just now showing up? Gerald's been dead for months."

"I thought I'd come and meet my nephew and niece, and you, too. It seems I'm a bit late meeting my sister-in-law." The sound of his voice echoed in her mind, bringing with it shards of fear and anxiety. Thank God, she no longer lived alone with her children—not now, with this man lurking around.

Jack walked up, introduced himself, and held out a hand in friendship. "I'm Jack Harrison, Annalee's husband. You are most welcome to join us at the reception if you care to." He took her by the arm. "Come, dear, we have people to meet." He urged her to come along with him, saying to the dark eyed man, "Excuse us, please."

Once away from the man, he whispered to her, "A ghost from the past?"

She nodded. "It seems so. I knew Gerald had a brother, but he never mentioned anything about his family in all the years we were married." She shivered as she said the words. "He looks just like Gerald—so much, in fact, he could be a twin, Jack."

"I imagine you'll know who he is, what he's after, and why he has just now put in an appearance, soon enough. But right now, we have a nice little wedding reception Amy put together for us, along with the good ladies of this church. Come with me, my dear, we need to mingle."

Annalee saw Amy had all the children with her and had taken them into the hall to find them something to eat. She looked back, but did not see that man again. The crowd was small and, thankfully, she had her duties to attend to. She was glad of it. On top of that, she realized how nice it had been to benefit from Jack's smooth intervention on her behalf. With him, Annalee felt protected and cared for. It was a good feeling and a very new one to her.

From then on she was so busy, she nearly forgot the dark-haired man. They cut the cake, fed each other a taste as tradition demanded, and opened a small pile of gifts. As the day wore on, Annalee was happy it had been a small wedding. She felt overwhelmed as it was. But she couldn't forget the stranger who looked just like Gerald, as much as she tried.

She felt a touch on her shoulder and turned to see Carol standing there. "Oh, Carol, I looked for you but didn't see you. Have you been here all the time?"

"Of course, I was. Think I would miss out on this little shindig?"

Annalee heard the icicles in Carol's voice. "It was pretty nice for being so hastily put together, wasn't it?" Annalee asked.

Carol ignored that question and got right onto the topic that interested her. "So, who on earth is that man you were talking to? My goodness, didn't he look just like you know who?"

She was curious, but Annalee couldn't have cared less if she was. Maybe Carol would set her sights on this new man—Annalee hoped so. She had no idea what his name was, either.

"He said he was my brother-in-law, if that answers your question. I had never heard of him and I don't even know his name."

Annalee saw her new husband laughing, talking, and being a terrific host to those who had attended their wedding. He was amazing as far as Annalee was concerned. She looked at him with pride—a wonderful feeling and very new to her.

The day had waned, people were leaving, and Annalee no longer saw the dark-eyed man. It was time to enter her new role as a married woman, and she was very nervous. His kiss at the altar had shaken her to the depths. By the mere force of it, she knew he could easily exert his masculine power over her if he chose to do it. And now she faced going home with him, to live with him, in the same house. Her hands shook like leaves in the wind.

She hurried about to find the children and saw Amy heading her way with the little girls. "Oh, I was looking for them." Annalee bent down to Sarah and Sissy. "How are you, little darlings?"

"I tired, Momma." Sissy had her fist in her eye and Sarah held onto Sissy's dress, "Sarah tired, too."

"Missed your naps today, poor babies. We'll go home soon and get you all set for beddie bye." Annalee turned to Amy. "Thanks for all you've done, Amy. It's been quite a day. I really can't believe this has happened."

"Are you nervous?" Amy asked quietly. She had that look in her eye, as if wondering how Annalee would handle the wedding night so soon at hand.

"I guess I'd have to say I was," Annalee replied.

She felt the heat of another disgusting blush, though she knew it was a great cover for hiding the truth of her relationship with Jack. Now she faced going home with him to that lovely house as his legal wife. Oh, yes, she was nervous.

Amy hugged her. "Don't worry about a thing, dear. Jack is a very kind man, and if you haven't noticed, he is one handsome, sexy guy."

"Oh, my God in heaven, Amy, stop!" Annalee thought she would faint just then, but Jack came up behind her and put his big warm hands on her shoulders. "I think we'd better get these kids home and to bed, my dear. They've had a very big day."

Annalee could only nod her head. She couldn't speak. She felt so dizzy with him touching her shoulders like that. His very words sounded, for all the world to hear, like an anxious bridegroom eager to get his bride off to himself, eager to get the honeymoon underway. Totally flustered, she turned away and let him lead her to his car. Inside, she noticed he had all three of the little ones in the back seat sitting together with Bucky in the middle, being the big brother. She looked at Jack in wonder. "How did you get them all together like this?" Sadly, she'd only had her dead husband to compare with Jack. Gerald fell way short in the fathering comparison.

"They're tired and ready for sleep, Annalee. It was easy, especially with Bucky to help me out. Wasn't it, Bucky?"

"Yep," came from the back seat. The males of the family had bonded already. She settled herself into the front seat with her new husband and they drove away.

❧❧

Carol seethed inside with jealously and hatred for Annalee. That little goody-two-shoes had plucked that handsome Jack Harrison right out from under her nose. Her feelings ran high, seeing them drive away like that, together as man and wife.

She kept up a running monolog with herself. "That skinny milk-sop bitch. What does she have to offer a man?" Carol snorted in disgust. "She wasn't woman enough to keep her first husband from straying and I ought to know." She patted her increasingly swollen belly. "He had to come looking for me to be with a real woman." She grinned with the memory of the many times she had welcomed Gerald Lines into her arms. "I wonder who that big, black-haired, black-eyed gent was? My God, he could be Gerald's twin brother, only so much better dressed." Her pulse rate jumped and raced at the thought of having a man like that after her again. Her eyes narrowed. "I wonder where he's staying?"

She vowed to find out what was going on in that area and if he was anything like his brother.

Chapter 13

Annalee entered that lovely big home with her new husband. Her name was now Annalee Harrison, another change to get used to. Together, they had three children.

Considering the children, she told Jack, "I'm not sure they have had enough to eat. I'll see about that first and then put them to bed if they'll go."

He merely nodded in reply, but she saw a speculative look in his eye that set her nerves on edge.

She took them to the kitchen. "Is anyone hungry?"

Their little faces looked a bit lost. They were not used to being in this home, and Sissy had not had them there before this afternoon. Her two had gotten quite comfortable with Mary and coming to this house meant another big change for all three of them—and for her, too.

"I'm hungry, Momma," Buckley said.

Annalee hunted about to see what she could feed

them. She opened the refrigerator and saw plenty there. Several quart jars of milk awaited her use. She guessed Jack had a milk man's daily morning service. She'd had that, too, at one time. That big block of cheese looked fresh to her. Jack had brought in supplies, along with all the other things he'd done to make the wedding ceremony as painless as possible.

She checked the bread box and found it well supplied, too.

She sat them at the table. They were too short, their little heads barely visible, but Sissy had a kind of booster seat in her chair. "Anyone want a peanut butter sandwich or a jelly one?" For this early evening, she hoped that would be enough with a glass of milk.

At their excited nods, she found what she needed to feed them. She mixed the peanut butter and jelly together. They happily ate the sandwiches and drank the milk. Her children hadn't had enough of that the past few months, and she saw by their happy looks and smears of jelly across their mouths, that the small meal had been welcome.

After that, she took them up the stairs, led them to a bathroom, and cleaned their faces. She hadn't made arrangements yet for sleeping. Sissy had a lovely room, all decked out in cherubs in a pink flouncy bedspread, a frilly white lamp, and several pictures of lambs, baby animals, and a fairy princess on the wall above her bed.

Sissy looked up at Annalee. "Are you my momma all the time now?"

"Yes, I am, darling. I am your mother now and forever. Is that all right with you?"

"Yeth, you can be my momma now." Sissy looked

down at her hands. "I know my other momma is gone away to Heaven."

Hearing that, Annalee realized the child did know Annalee wasn't her real mother, so they would never need to bother about explaining anything to Sissy.

She hugged the child. "Where is your nightie, Sissy?"

Sissy went to a drawer and pulled out her night clothing, then, she pulled out something for Sarah, too. "Can Sarah sleep in my bed with me? She is little and 'fraid."

"Why yes, if you don't mind sharing."

It was an answer to a prayer right now. Annalee only had to worry about where Buckley would sleep. She tucked the girls in and turned to find her son, but he was nowhere in sight. She went along the hall until she found an open door. Inside she saw her son curled up asleep in his own bed.

She also noticed a dresser and quite a few toys, including at least two trucks, many colored blocks, and a brightly colored paper kite leaning in a corner. She knew Jack had gotten a lot more than a new suit for her son. She felt utter gratitude to that generous man downstairs. But to keep to their bargain, she had to suppress any kind of emotion. And after that kiss at the altar, she had to be more than careful. With that one kiss, Jack had set a small fire inside her. One she didn't understand. And it worried her.

She went down the steps to enter the living room. He rose from his big leather chair and came to her. "How did it go up there?"

"Sissy and Sarah are sharing a bed tonight, and I see

Bucky is well fixed as well. You are a kind and generous man, Jack. Thank you so much." She wanted to cry with delight right now, but if she did, he'd take her into his arms to comfort her, and then...

Annalee was a very tired woman after the day she'd had, and she was wound as tight as a steel spring. But she knew he wanted to talk with her for a while. She sat in one of the soft, heavy, velvet-covered easy chairs scattered about the spacious sitting room and heaved a sigh.

He sat down again, but stayed across the room. "Are you all right, Annalee?"

His voice was soft and comforting, yet remembering his kiss at the altar, she still felt the heat of it inside her body. It had set her on edge, but he'd made no further move to disobey their secret contract and she appreciated that.

"Yes, I think so. This is a lovely home, Jack, and I will work very hard to keep it that way. With three little ones it might get a bit hectic at times, but they get along so well, I'm sure I'll be fine."

"I have no worries about your mothering skills, but I meant what I said about you living in my home and our agreement. I plan to honor it, but I have to say, Annalee, you are one drop-dead lovely young woman. Any man would be tempted by you." He uttered a slight chuckle. "Unless of course he was half dead."

Annalee fought the rising tide of another heated blush and thought to herself, as the heat rose in her neck and face, *Stop it, you fool! This is only your first night in this house!* "I'm very tired, Jack. If it's all right, I'd like to use that lovely room with the double bed and the rose-bud wallpaper. It looks like a woman's room."

"Yes, it is. We kept it for Amelia's mother's visits. My folks are gone, now, so you'll have no in-laws to contend with. Of course Amelia's mother comes to see Sissy at times, so she will be here, once in a while. It will be fine for you to use it." He laughed a bit, and she saw the crinkling around his eyes when he did so. "That room rather suits you, doesn't it?"

He truly was a handsome man, lanky and tall. She wanted to hastily bid him goodnight. But he had more to say. She wanted to escape, fearing what else he might say after the compliment he'd paid her.

He didn't let her go, just yet. He leaned forward and put his elbows on his knees. "What about that brother-in-law? He came out of nowhere, didn't he? Are you afraid of him, Annalee?"

"Yes. I believe I am to a certain extent. I don't know anything about him, nor had I ever heard anything of Gerald's family, aside from just the mention of a brother. Something dreadful must have happened to cause an estrangement like that. Gerald had a lot of violence in him. I haven't said much about it, but I can tell you, I didn't shed a lot of tears when he had that accident." She shuddered involuntarily. "I know that sounds harsh and uncaring, but how much abuse must any one person bear?" She felt the tears welling up in her eyes and was embarrassed she'd said so much. "I'm sorry I said all that. I didn't mean to. I—I got a bit carried away."

He came close, knelt down, and took her in his arms. "There'll never be any of that from me. You are a fine, decent woman, and I find it a shame you had to live with a man like that. Of course, I've known of men like that, and I have to say, I've never understood how a man could be that way. A woman is so much smaller—so helpless against a man's strength."

He gently stroked her back, and it felt so good she wanted to lean closer into him, but knowing where that could lead she forced herself to draw away from him.

"I'm sorry to be such a cry baby, Jack. Please forget what I said." She sat before him with her arms around her chest, a picture of a woman alone, fearful, and protecting herself.

Her words ignited a fire inside of Jack's mind, and he avowed, "Hell no, I won't forget a thing like that, and if that brother of his bothers you in any way like that, just give me a call. There *is* a phone in this house."

He moved away, knowing she feared closer contact. But to his personal chagrin, his own resolve was fast melting away. He had married a beautiful woman and a good, decent one, too. His little child already loved her. He smiled to himself, thinking that while she might be afraid of him as a man, she got the message at the altar when they kissed. And to his surprise, so did he. He already knew he'd never be able to keep the bargain he'd made with her. His mind had rapidly begun to devise a dozen ways to change her feelings about him and get close—real close. He felt himself responding to his thoughts about her and hoped she didn't notice.

Annalee rose from her chair. "Good night, Jack." She wanted to ask what time he needed his breakfast and what he liked to eat, but found she couldn't say the words. They had gotten too close already.

She turned away from him and climbed the stairs to enter that small, cozy bedroom. After doing her nightly bedtime ritual of cleaning, she crawled beneath the aged and softened sheets. She heard his heavy tread in the hall outside her door as he sought that room at the end of the hall. It was his room. One peek inside was enough to tell her that, and so far she had avoided going near it after that.

But hearing his firm, male-sounding tread down the hallway made her heart race, as she imagined that warm, heavy weight pressing her down beneath his body on his bed. Furious with herself, she pulled the covers over her head and curled her body into a tight little ball. But it was long before sleep claimed her.

❧❧❧

When Annalee awoke, it was very early. She heard nothing from the children and wondered if they had passed an uneventful night in a home so new to them. She slipped into the slacks and the green shirt she'd gotten from Amy just after the fire, and stepped quietly out of her room. Peeking into the girl's room, she saw two small bodies curled up together, still asleep. In Buckley's room, she saw him sitting in the middle of the room holding his new truck and admiring it.

Annalee entered Buckley's room. "Did you sleep well enough, Bucky dear?"

"Yep, Momma. But I had to get up and see my new stuff, Mr. Harrison got me." His eyes were shining as he held the new red truck out for her inspection.

Annalee heard no other noises in the house. Curious, she went down the steps to check out the kitchen. She found remnants of a hasty breakfast, cold on the stove. The dishes were carefully placed in the sink and the table cleaned. Of Jack, she saw nothing. She looked out the window, noticed that his car was gone, and heaved a sigh.

Knowing she had the children and the home to herself was a relief. She found Jack's presence far more disturbing than she had believed possible. And right now, she felt like an interloper in another woman's home.

Annalee helped herself to what coffee was left and sat down to read the paper, which she found lying on the kitchen table. It'd been a while since she'd had that privilege, too.

She heard the little ones waking up, giggling, and talking. She ran up the stairs to bring them all down for breakfast. She had few clothes for her own children and added the use of a few smaller, outgrown things of Sissy's for Sarah.

They had done well sleeping together, but there was one more room up there she planned to fix up for Sarah. It would be nice for each child to have a home territory they could call their own.

She realized by the way they stared about in wonder that her two children knew they had never been in as a fine kitchen as this one. Everything else in this lovely home was new to them, too. Annalee sat at the table spooning scrambled eggs, along with toast and jam out to all three of them while she talked about living together in this new home. She hoped to help them make the adjustment of living together.

Her two were still trying to get used to thinking of Jack as their daddy. She explained it all once again. "When two people get married, then their children become stepchildren, the same as in any family. Mr. Harrison is your stepdaddy, Buckley and Sarah, and it's all

right if you call him Daddy. He would like it if you do."
To Sissy, she said, "I am your stepmomma. You already
call me 'Momma' and I love that, Sissy."

Annalee didn't know how much of it they grasped,
but it was a start. Just then her head snapped up at the
sound of a knock on the front door. She went to the door,
unlocked, and opened it.

Carol stood on the small porch. It was sheltered by a
good-sized overhang. She also got a good glimpse of the
green lawn and vines trailing up the sides of the overhang, clinging to strings put there to guide them. Annalee
hadn't had time to see that before this moment herself.

"Well, my goodness, Carol, please come in."

Annalee felt the shock of seeing her friend standing
there and did her best to hide it. As she opened the rather
ornate paneled door wider for Carol's entrance, Annalee
realized she was seeing the outside of that lovely door
herself for the first time. It was one more very nice thing
about Jack's home.

"My, oh my, this *is* a very nice house, An," Carol
said.

She strutted about, looking at everything, touching a
statuette, or staring at a painting, even gazing up at the
chandelier. Annalee awaited the outpouring of Carol's
envy, but she decided to bide her time and see what this
wily friend of hers was after or where she was heading.
What did she want?

It didn't take long for Carol to voice what was on her
mind. "So have you seen that handsome brother-in law
again?" She stood waiting, hands on hips, for an answer.
She also noticed the children sitting at the table in the
kitchen, their eyes wide. They appeared to be quietly

wondering about Carol's visit. Annalee realized that children were quick to pick up on nervous tension.

"Not since that one time at the wedding," Annalee answered. "But I expect to see him again. He said he came here to see his niece and nephew and happened upon the wedding." She studied Carol. "Why do you want to know?"

"I have reason enough, An. If you knew the real truth of things, you'd know that." Carol was bragging. It was in her tone, and it sounded disgustingly brassy. "I want to meet that fellow," she said with a knowing chuckle. "He's one handsome stud—if you know what I mean."

"Hush, Carol! I won't have you speaking like that in front of the little ones."

Annalee was already sick of this intrusive visit. She realized that with her marriage to Jack, she had moved out of Carol's sphere and into one of another sort.

Annalee didn't really understand Jack's way of life yet, or who he socialized with, but she didn't think it included many of Carol's ilk. She was already eager for the woman's departure.

"Oh phish, An, they don't get what I'm saying and you know it. You're just getting all snooty and hi-toned now that you've married an engineer." Carol's tone was downright nasty and her sneer didn't help matters.

Annalee had quickly sickened of Carol's crude speech and threatening tone. "Why *have* you come to see me, Carol? If it was to get a look at the brother-in-law, he's not here and I don't know if he knows where I live, in any case."

"I just wanted to see your lovely new home, An. No need to get all huffy." Carol snorted and tossed her head.

"Why would I care anything about some wild-looking stranger? I did wonder why he's just now showing up, though. Where has he been?"

"If I ever find out, I'll let you know. I haven't seen him since the wedding." Then Annalee asked about Carol's pregnancy. "How are you feeling these days, anyway?"

Carol grinned. "Just fine, getting bigger every day. I'm glad my Donald left me a nice insurance policy. I have no worries at all that way, but I get a little lonely. Why don't you come visit me some day?"

She had a sly look in her eye that Annalee found unsettling. Somehow she knew Carol had something she wanted to let her know. She'd hinted at it for weeks now.

Chapter 14

Carol finally left after tossing a final comment over her shoulder. "Remember to come for a visit and bring all the darling little kiddies."

Annalee said she would and heaved a generous sigh of relief after she closed the door. She took another look at the fine home of which she had just become the mistress. She heard the children upstairs with Bucky's lower voice calling the shots as usual.

Annalee wandered about the downstairs, seeing it again with the eyes of a woman of the house, this lovely home that was now hers to love and care for. She had never had the responsibility of any house this nice and prayed she was up to it.

While roaming about the house, the doorbell rang. Yes, this house had one of those, also.

Puzzled, she opened it to find her hither-to-unknown brother-in-law standing there. Her heart raced in unease, as she opened the door to admit him.

Politeness demanded she let him in. "Come in, sir."

"Thank you, Annalee. I know my appearance has been rather shocking to you, but I wanted to meet my brother's children. He was all the family I had."

"Why have I never heard of you then? In all our five years together, Gerald only mentioned a brother, but never one that looked like him. Never a word about any others, but I have no doubt of what you say. You could be his twin, you look so like him."

"I am his twin," he said.

Though he dressed far better than her husband ever had, his black eyes and hair seemed the exact replica of her dead husband, Gerald. Annalee felt the shock of seeing that face again.

"My name is Harold Lines. Gerald and Harold. How about that?"

"My God in Heaven, I know you must be."

Annalee felt like fainting, but she didn't dare, not in front of this man. Oh, how she wished Jack was beside her right now. She stood facing a man who brought to the forefront of her mind all the horrors of her previous marriage.

Harold saw the sudden pallor of her face and wanted to reach out to her but, when he also saw the revulsion toward him on her face, he didn't. "My God, woman, what kind of man was my brother?"

"He's dead and gone now. I never wanted to see that devil's face again in my life. And yet here you are." Annalee slumped into a chair and faced him. "Where have you been? Why did he mention a brother and nothing else? I never knew a thing about your family, or you."

"There is a good reason for that. Gerald nearly killed

our parents in one of his rages. Before the police could arrest him, he disappeared. That was about six years ago." He smiled and shrugged. "Sorry to bring what appears to be a sort of an unpleasantness into your life this way, but if I could just see those two little ones, I'll leave."

"Why do you want to see them?" She knew why, of course, but couldn't help feeling a sense of fear from looking into those same eyes she'd seen filled with rage and anger for five miserable years of her life.

"They are a part of me and all I have left of my brother. You must try to understand that. I hope you can." He sensed her overwhelming fear of his departed brother and sought to put her mind at ease. "Please, ma'am, I am not a bit like my brother. And, of course, I had no idea what kind of man he'd turned out to be. But I'm beginning to suspect he wasn't a good man. If not, I'd still like to know how he turned out."

"You don't seem to be at all like him," Annalee said. "I'll admit that much."

He heard the indecision in her voice. Then, out of the blue, she asked, "Are you left-handed?"

"Strange you should ask," Harold said with a puzzled look on his face. "Gerald was, but I am right-handed. I have since learned that a thing like that is referred to as mirror twins." He regretted the fear he saw in her eyes and hoped she would realize they were just as opposite in every other way as well. "I assure you, I am not at all like my brother. By the fear I see in your eyes, ma'am, I can only imagine what kind of man he'd been to you. I will apologize for the way he was or for what he has done."

Right then, Annalee heard the ruckus coming down

the stairs. In her panic at seeing this man face to face, she had forgotten the children, who were playing up there. She smiled. "I think you are about to meet your brother's children." Annalee went to the stairs and came back with Buckley's hand in hers. The two girls came right behind her.

When Buckley saw the man, he drew back, his face went white, and he clutched his mother's skirts. "Momma! Is that my daddy?"

"No, Bucky, but this man *is* his brother and your Uncle Harold. They look just alike, but he is not your father."

Bucky shrunk back farther as Harold approached him.

"Son, I'm your Uncle Harold. Your father was my brother, my twin brother. Twins often look just alike, but they aren't just alike." He knelt down to Buckley's level and held out a hand.

Buckley buried his face in her skirt, and she felt his strong little fingers digging into her flesh. "Momma, I'm 'fraid."

Sarah stared at the man with tears of fear in her eyes. Even at her tender age, she remembered the screams and the heavy sounds of violence. She clung to Annalee's skirts along with Buckley. Sissy, unable to understand what was happening, began to cry. Annalee sat down and took as many of them in her arms as she could to soothe and comfort them.

"Looks like I've stirred up a hornet's nest, doesn't it?" Harold said.

She saw the regret on his face. Slowly, a liking for this man took hold within her. He really was different from his brother, or seemed to be. "How did you know about Gerald's death?" she asked.

"I live in Washington D C and work in the WPA Administration. By chance, I happened to see the notice of his accident and fatality. Until that time, I had no idea of his whereabouts—none at all." He shrugged. "When I saw that he left behind a wife and two children, I had to come and see about you."

Buckley peeked out from his mother's skirt, his face pale as he looked at the man. "Me and Sarah have an uncle?"

"Yes, son, I have been looking for you for a long time, now."

"You won't take us 'way?"

Annalee heard the tremor of fear in his voice.

"Of course not, but I wanted to meet your mother and see my brother's children—that would be you and this dark-haired, little angel." He knelt in front of them and reached out for Sarah.

She clung tightly to Annalee's skirts, her dark eyes huge. "No, Momma, no."

"Give her some time, Harold," Annalee said. "I'm afraid she has a few bad memories." She hated to have to say it, but it was true. His twin brother had been a brutal man, and his children, young though they were, had cruel and unhappy memories of that time.

"I can see that." He rose to go and took Annalee's hand, shaking his head. "Sadly, I have a good picture of what your life with my brother must have been. I am truly sorry for that." Before he left her door, he turned to her. "I'd like to meet and have a chat with your husband if that's possible in the near future."

"Why, I suppose it is. Why not come have dinner with us one night?" She thought a moment. "Why not this Thursday at seven? It will give me time to learn the ropes of this new kitchen and the rest of the house."

"I see your point on that. You have new things to deal with besides having a new husband. I'll be here with bells on then, Annalee."

She watched him walk down the sidewalk to his nice-looking vehicle. She didn't know what it was, but it seemed rather fine. She found the man a puzzle, but she no longer feared him. He was nothing at all like his abusive, rather uncouth brother, twin or not.

ೞ

Carol sat in her car, parked several houses down the block. She'd had the feeling this so called brother-in-law would show up at Annalee's door, and there he was. She had driven past it once to see that his shiny looking auto had plates that said Washington, DC.

Her eyebrows arched at seeing that. "He must be some kind of big shot if he lives in that place with all those senators and people like that. Must pull down a nice income to own a fancy-dancy car like he drives, too."

She wasn't sure what it was, but it wasn't some cheap old Model A. It looked like it must have cost some real dollars. Carol watched him walk out of Annalee's fancy new home, get into that black shiny vehicle, and drive away. She decided to follow him and see where that gorgeous hunk of male was staying. She wanted to meet him. If he was anything like his brother—wow, oh, the memories she had of that guy!

She followed him to The Village Green Rooms, the only rooming house in this crummy little berg. It was a small, clean inn, and the only place in town to find quarters available for a few days.

Delano was a small town, and that was the best it offered. She saw him walk inside. She drove slowly past his vehicle as she left the area and read the words *Phaeton* on the side. She'd never heard of a car like that, but to her it meant money. "He must be making a good salary. When he finds out what I have to tell him, he won't be able to leave me alone." The heat of her thoughts had her body burning inside, all the way down to her toes.

Crowing in delight, Carol drove back to her lonely home. As she walked into her house, she felt the baby growing inside her give a good strong kick. "Yes, my darling, you are strong and lusty—just like your daddy."

ೞ

A few days later, Harold drove to the only eatery he'd found in this small berg and went in. He was hungry this morning and looked forward to a great breakfast. Mary Ellen's was a small place, but he'd had some good meals there already. He'd done some checking about in the area.

His position in DC enabled him to remain in Delano for a while longer. He wanted to know his brother's children and awaited the promised dinner at Annalee's new home tomorrow night.

He was impressed with his brother's widow, but now, of course, married again. He wondered about that. It hadn't taken her long to tie up with a new husband.

Somehow she didn't seem the type, but he hadn't seen the last of Annalee Harrison. That was her new name. Maybe he would learn more about her situation. He'd already decided she was sure as hell one fine looker. He appreciated that about her, too.

He took a booth and surveyed the tattered menu. After he gave his order, he sipped his coffee and looked about the room. Only a few others were having breakfast this morning. One woman had come in after him, and he'd noticed she'd kept looking his way. Now that he'd met her eyes, she got up and sauntered over.

"Hello, Mr. Lines, I'm Carol Woods. I believe we are acquainted with a few of the same people." He knew she wanted to sit down and, to be polite, he nodded at the empty seat across from him. "Won't you sit down, ma'am?"

"Why, I sure will. If you are Mr. Lines?"

"How do you know my name?"

"I saw you at my good friend Annalee's wedding a few days ago." She fluttered her blue eyes in an attempt at flirting. "We spoke after she had seen you there that day." She giggled slightly. "I might say, I knew your brother pretty well too, Mr. Lines. You know, friends of the family, so to speak."

Harold had quickly gotten the feeling that something was in the wind from this person. She wanted something from him, or had something to say. He also began to feel a bit uncomfortable at her fluttering eyelashes.

"Is everything all right with you?" He shifted in his seat. "Was there something you had to say to me?"

"Oh, nothing at all, at least, for now." He caught that she was flustered at his question. "I just wanted to say hello. I'm widowed now and try to keep in touch with every one of my friends. I hope that includes you, too." Carol concluded that comment with a sly smile, aimed straight into his dark eyes.

Knowing his brother as he did, Harold wondered if this woman had been a hell of lot more than a friend to Gerald. By the eye-batting and butt-twisting in her seat, he decided she looked like she was on the make right now. That behavior from a bloated, overweight blonde didn't help his early morning appetite at all.

The waitress brought his plate of food and poured more coffee in his cup. He looked expectantly at Carol, hoping she'd take the hint and leave him to his breakfast. Or would she see that as an invitation to join him?

"Well, I see you are busy at the moment, Mr. Lines. I have things to do. Hopefully I'll see you around again while you're here." She gave him her best half-closed eye look as she rose from the seat.

As Carol walked away, aside from her sashaying bottom, he noticed her pregnant condition. That sight gave him cold chills and sent his imagination spinning in directions he didn't want to think of, or consider.

She departed, and he settled to his meal. But in trying to enjoy the good solid food in front of him, he discovered that the flirting blonde woman's visit to his table had almost destroyed his appetite.

Finally, he left his half-eaten meal lying on the table and went out to his car.

✑✑✑

Annalee heard the chugging sounds and the rattle of

a Model A pulling into the driveway. Those sounds had always made a good amount of fear rise within her. It came back to her now with such intensity she felt like time had gone backward.

She saw Bucky stiffen at those same sounds and cry out in a fear laden voice. "Daddy!"

She knew it couldn't be Gerald, but she saw how deeply her son was still affected by his father's cruelty. Worse yet, how his memories of it still lingered in his mind.

"It isn't your daddy, dear. You know that," she told Bucky, her heart beating double time, and ran out to see what had caused that sound.

Jack had driven up in her old coupe, the one that had been sitting beside her burned-out house. Puzzled, she stood there waiting for an explanation. Bucky stood beside her, his hands clutching her skirt and digging into her skin

Jack stopped the Model A and got out. "Say, Annalee, mind if I drive your car?"

He had a smile on his face. Any fear the sound of that vehicle had caused quickly vanished as she realized, all over again, this was her new husband and she definitely had no need to fear him.

She smiled at him and walked over to look inside. He had cleaned it up very nicely. The dust and ashes had been washed off, and the seats brushed clean before he drove it to her new home. "How did you get it started?"

"All it needed was a new battery and some cleaning up." He grinned and held the door open. "Want to drive it?"

"Not right now. The girls are upstairs playing dolls.

But I do need to go to the market later." She realized if the Model A was working, she'd have the freedom to go driving about town for the things she needed.

Jack leaned against the side of the newly cleaned vehicle and tousled Bucky's hair. "I think my car would do better for you with all three children along. There's more room. I'll use this for work, if it's all right with you." At her puzzled look, he added, "That way you'd have my car for your own use any time you needed it."

"You'll have to show me how to drive it then."

Annalee was delighted at the freedom a car for her own use would give her.

She still had things she needed. Personal supplies—things she couldn't bring herself to ask Jack to get for her. She felt her face flush, just thinking about it.

"What are you thinking, Annalee?"

When he laughed, she saw the flash of his eyes and how his throat looked just then with his head thrown back. Heat shot through her when that happened, and she felt her face burn.

She tried to answer him but fell short, unable to tell him why she needed to go shopping alone.

"Well, I—you wouldn't want to know, but sometimes a woman has to shop for a few things alone."

He nodded. As a previously married man, he knew all about those things and appreciated her sense of modesty.

"Derrick will be along in my car shortly. Which vehicle do you want me to leave you?"

"Looks like it will be the Model A for now. I know how to drive it. You can show me how to drive yours later."

He nodded and, as Derrick drove up, hopped in, waved goodbye, and they left. Now Annalee had a way to go shopping. She would pile the little ones in and get going. She went inside and called the kids.

છ૭છ૭

Derrick drove toward the office, but his mind was on his friend. He'd seen the blushing face of the new bride, and his curiosity ran rampant. "So, ah, how's it going?"

"Well enough." Jack didn't want to get into his personal life and took a different tack. "Her brother-in-law is in town. Did you happen to see him at the reception?"

"That dark-headed man I saw her talking to?"

"Sounds like the one. Annalee invited him to dinner, tomorrow night. She said he's not at all like her husband was. I take it her husband had been a mean bastard. She has tried to avoid admitting it, but it came out readily enough." Jack looked over at Derrick. "Her face went white as a sheet when she saw that man at the wedding."

"Amy had an idea Annalee's husband was like that. About the only one crying at his funeral was Carol Woods. Strange, huh?"

Jack laughed quietly. "There's plenty strange about that one."

"An said she was mad as hell when she found you two were tying the knot." Derrick laughed. "She stormed out and her tires squealed as she left. She really had plans for you, Jack."

"Not my idea. God help me."

The men laughed and as they returned to the office. Then they went their separate ways.

ℰᕲℰᕲ

Annalee put the children in the Model A with Sarah lying across the wide space above the seats. They giggled as she drove out onto the street. Annalee finally saw the name of her new street. *We live on Willow Street and our number is 34. What a lovely address.* She kept her thoughts to herself, but her heart was full, seeing her children well dressed, well fed, and liking very much the man who'd made it all possible. She counted herself a lucky woman.

Annalee felt happier now than she had in a long, long time. She hadn't known much of that feeling in her childhood and rarely after the first few days of her first marriage. She remembered being so in love with Gerald and how quickly that lovely feeling had become dampened. How easily she remembered the disgusting way her husband had taken her body with no warning or preparation. He'd taken her so fast, rough, and pain-filled, she'd never welcomed his embrace after that.

Her hands gripped the steering wheel as she remembered those painful thoughts. Could she ever forget the feelings of degradation she had suffered in her marriage to Gerald?

She realized the way she'd felt toward him may have caused some of his raging tempers, right from the beginning, making her first marriage one of pure torture and misery for her. She shuddered as she drove the small coupe down the streets to the store she sought and shook off her painful memories. *Those days are over for me. Jack would never be that way, but whoever knows about a man? It is a place I'll never be in again*!

Chapter 15

Annalee pulled up in front of Bartig's grocery store. She had shopped here many times, but never with enough money to buy all the things she really wanted and needed. She took the children inside and cautioned them. "Now I need to get a few things. You can walk around and look, but please do not touch anything. If you see something you want, come and tell me." She took her son by the shoulder. "Got that, Bucky?"

"Yep, Momma. I will watch out for them."

Annalee approached the counter, and a man wearing a slightly soiled white apron faced her. She handed him her list and he went over it carefully. He took up his long pole with the clamps on the end and carefully, one by one, selected the items she'd asked for and placed them on the counter. As he worked to fill her order, she checked on the little ones. Bucky and the girls stood in front of a cabinet looking at the candy inside.

"Momma, Sissy wants those, too," Bucky said.

He pointed to the pink wintergreen rounds with XXX stamped on them. Annalee remembered how good those had always tasted and nodded to Sissy that she could have some. Sarah only stared at the display, sucking her thumb.

"What would you like, Mr. Bucky?" she asked her son.

He pointed to the same ones. "Me, too, Momma."

"I will ask the nice man for some of those."

With her order complete, and a very nice roast in one of the boxes, Annalee asked the man for a bag of the pink candies. The grocer had a boy carry the food out to her vehicle, and she loaded the little ones in, all with a pink candy in their mouths. Sissy took the flat place above the seats, this time and giggled down at Bucky and Sarah as Annalee headed for her new home.

She decided she would like to have Amy and Derrick come to dinner also. They had two children, a bit older, about six and seven years old. When she arrived at home, she unloaded the groceries and then called Amy on the phone to ask her.

Amy suggested they set up a small table in the kitchen for the children and said she would bring an older neighbor girl to tend them while the adults had dinner in the dining room.

Annalee agreed. She knew Harold wanted to get acquainted with her husband, and she believed he would enjoy Derrick's company as well. It was shaping up to be quite a dinner party and Annalee felt her nerves getting the better of her.

Could she live up to the lovely new home and, even

more importantly, to the caliber of the husband she had married? He was a very fine man in every way. Annalee worried that being highly educated as he was, he might get tired of her ignorance, and things would not work out between them. And for that reason, above any other, she welcomed Amy's help.

The evening of the dinner, Jack came home with two small padded booster seats for Annalee's two children. "I hope Bucky won't think this is too babyish for a big guy like him."

He laughed in that easy way he had, and, at the sight of his head tossed back, Annalee felt that strange electric feeling go zinging through her body again. *You've got to stop feeling like this when Jack is around,* she warned herself, *or you'll find yourself between his sheets and wondering how on earth you got there.*

"Whatever you've got cooking smells like heaven, An," he said. "I think your dinner will come off just fine."

He stood there for a moment looking at her in her apron and slacks, flour on her arms, and a smudge of it on her nose. He tended to see his new bride all over again, every time he looked at her. She was far lovelier than he'd at first believed and a good part of it was that she had a loving heart and a generous soul. But he hadn't forgotten how her lips had felt beneath his at the altar, either.

He shook his head and headed up the stairs to shower and get ready for the dinner. His heart was racing in his chest, his mind in a turmoil with thoughts about that soft, slim body and how he'd come to feel about her. He imagined how she'd look in his bed, or how she'd look in his bathtub, any place at all. His new wife was on his mind constantly.

∞∞∞

Annalee welcomed Amy and her children, along with the older girl who was to be the caregiver for them during dinner. Her name was Marie Fancier, twelve, tiny with dark, curling hair.

"I'll go see what the little ones are up to, Amy, and get them ready for dinner," Marie said.

She took Amy's other two up the stairs and headed for the younger ones. Sissy knew her very well and, soon, so would Sarah and Bucky.

"Marie will get the kids lined up. She's a wonder with my two," Amy said. "It smells divine in here, An. How are you cooking that roast?"

"I put a few things around it and some inside it, too." Annalee smiled. "I hope everything comes out all right. It should be about done by now, and I hope everything else is, right along with it."

Amy looked into the dining room. "My, how nicely you've set the table, the glasses, everything. However did you manage to do all this?"

"As you can imagine, I never did any of these things with Gerald, but I confess I found a book Jack's wife had used. It was the biggest help imaginable." Annalee flushed. "I wanted things to be done right and to look right, Amy."

"Well, I'd say you've done just that. Now what can I do to help out?"

Annalee asked her to fix the kitchen table for the

young ones. Amy did and easily displayed her intimate knowledge of Jack's former wife's kitchen. She knew where things were and how to extend the small kitchen table. It was an intimacy born of long association, and one Annalee craved to have for herself.

She felt she had things as ready as she could. There was a cold green Jell-O/coconut concoction in the refrigerator, warm buns in the oven, and a finely cut cabbage slaw for the grown-ups. For the little ones, there were dishes such as macaroni and cheese, finger foods, and a plate of carrots, tiny tomatoes, and olives—things they most enjoyed.

"Could you keep an eye on things?" Annalee asked Amy. "I want to freshen up a bit before we call dinner."

She ran up the stairs and changed into a new lavender dress with tiny printed violets all across it. She had fallen in love with it at their only store in town. Buying a luxury like that had taken her by surprise, but it was something she could do, now that she had the means. The top had small flared sleeves and fit snugly. And the skirt had a flared hemline. The belt was a slim, violet-shaded sash tied in the back with the tails floating down.

She brushed her black curling hair and looked in the mirror to see all those tiny purple flowers sprinkled about on her dress reflected in her deep lavender-shaded eyes. *Can this be me?* She completed her make-up with a touch of rosy lipstick.

Feeling confident that she looked good enough to be the wife of a man like Jack, she went down to begin the dinner. By the look in Amy's eyes and the nodding of her head, Annalee knew she looked good. And that did a lot to bolster her uncertain confidence.

She took out the roast, and Amy looked it over. "My, oh my, An, that is lovely. Are you going to ask Jack to carve it for the diners?"

"Should I?" Annalee hadn't thought of it or had any idea of a thing like that. She greatly appreciated the hint Amy had tossed her way.

"Of course, An. He always does that if a roast is served and he'd be honored."

Amy was the most encouraging soul Annalee had ever known and, right now, the best help. Amy got out the proper carving set and took them to the head of the well-set-up dining table.

Annalee set the nicely browned roast on a delicate platter and put out the crockery dish of scalloped potatoes. The green beans, which she'd slowly simmered in a buttery sauce, were placed on the table. Then she added a dish of cranberry sauce, along with a plate of pickles, cheese squares, radishes, and a few olives for color. When all was ready, she rang the small silver bell she'd found in a drawer and watched the men come to dinner.

Jack came in along with Derrick and Harold. Annalee felt a tremor pass through her as she saw Harold. That dark man's features still had the power to strike fear into her soul.

Harold looked over the groaning table and nodded to Annalee. "Looks wonderful, my dear. I haven't sat down to a meal like this since I left DC."

Jack took his seat at the head of the table. Annalee sat to his right, and the others found their places. Amy had put the food on the children's table, while Annalee was putting her dinner on the dining-room table. In the kitchen, she heard Marie chatting with the little ones. Satisfied that the children were in hand, Annalee relaxed to watch how well the dinner proceeded.

As the men chatted around the table, Annalee noticed a growing comradery between Harold and the other two. This had the effect of helping her gain a beginning trust in the man—a hard thing for her when the sight of him reminded her all too well of the cruelty she'd suffered at the hands of his twin brother.

Before anyone touched as much as warm dinner roll, Jack held out a hand to each side and, as they all joined hands around the table, he beseeched God's blessing on the meal. Annalee burst with pride at how calmly and without fanfare he did it.

As the dishes were passed around, she watched with admiration as Jack deftly cut slices of juicy roasted meat for each plate given him.

"Just a small slice for me, Jack," she murmured.

The men discussed matters current in the government, including the implementation of electrification to outlying areas. "I wonder what sort of difference electricity will make to dairy farmers, living out so far as they do," Derrick asked.

Harold chuckled. "About the same as for the rest of us, I suppose. Better lighting, refrigeration for their milk products, and safer food maintenance in the home. Easier cooking for the ladies, too," he said, nodding at Annalee.

Amy and Annalee said little during the meal. Amy understood how it must be for her, unused to events of this nature, and gave her an encouraging wink a time or two.

Harold surreptitiously looked at his sister-in-law when he could. He had the idea his brother hadn't realized the fine quality of the woman he'd married. Harold heartily approved of her new husband, liked the man and his friends. He felt his niece and nephew were in a good home with a good stepfather to help her raise them.

He would go home to his own fine wife in DC and report to her. But in his heart, he'd hoped to find two little ones he could take home to his wife. She wanted children so badly yet had never conceived. They'd been heart-broken by that lack, but otherwise, she and Harold enjoyed a good solid marriage.

The dinner went on with the happy sounds of clinking dishes, glassware, and chatter. Annalee sat at Jack's table, full of pride in her surroundings. Seeing the evening going along so well, she felt special, almost like a queen.

Jack said little to her throughout the meal, but in his heart, he burst with pride in her. The way she'd risen to the challenge of putting together a fine dinner party like this one, in a kitchen so new to her, amazed him. He thought of how they had met at her poor shabby home. It'd been little more than a shack, yet how well she'd cared for it. Her children had always been clean, even dressed in their threadbare clothing. And best of all, he appreciated the love she had shown to his little Cecelia.

Though he was eating, his thoughts were on his new wife, and he shook his head. Her husband must have been a sorry bastard, treating a fine little woman in such a manner. Jack found himself thinking about later on in the evening, the time when the children were asleep in their beds, and he had time with her—alone. *I wonder…*

❧❦❧

Carol sat in her car a short way down the block. Curiosity had driven her to keep watch on Annalee's new home. The one she now shared with that handsome Jack Harrison. Seeing the activity around the place tonight, she seethed with jealousy, fury, and more than that—curiosity. And then there was that handsome looking Harold's fancy-looking car sitting in the driveway. "What is he doing there when Jack is home?"

When Carol saw Amy, her husband, and several children get out and go into the house too, she murmured to herself, "What is going on in there? I've got to know." She got out of her car and walked slowly toward the house. Her burgeoning condition allowed little more than that, as she made her way across the clipped, green lawn. Close to the house, Carol slipped up to the dining room window. The shades had been pulled, but there was a crack between them big enough to allow her a good view of the heavily laden table.

She got close enough to peer through into the dining room to get a look at Annalee sitting in the seat of honor, to the right of Jack. Amy sat across from her husband, Derrick. Carol's heart did flip-flops at seeing that fancy Harold Lines sitting at that table, chatting with the two other men as if they were old friends.

At the sight of the fancily set dining table and the happy group around it, Carol felt sick and betrayed. Bitterness engulfed her at seeing how Jack absolutely fawned over that treacherous bitch.

And she'd married him right out from under Carol's nose!

Carol saw how he kept looking at her, speaking to her, and she gnashed her teeth. "Why wasn't I invited?

I'm a friend of hers, every bit as much as that snooty bitch, Amy. She's gotten so damnable fancy she's gotten shut of the kids for this dinner, too. They're not allowed to eat with the snooty, uppity adults." Her fists clenched tightly and her jaw ached with the pressure as she'd clamped it down so hard.

Carol suddenly had the strong desire to burn this big fancy house down. Her anger had become a fearful obsession. She wanted that Harold Lines, too, and as she trudged back to her car, she determined to do something about it. She drove slowly, deep in thought, as she headed back to her own lonely home.

It was her dreadful loneliness that made her think of her brother, Henry. She hadn't seen him in several years. "I must drop him a line. I'll tell him how lonely I am these days, and how much I need him. If I was dying, I wonder if he'd even bother to come."

Her unborn infant kicked strongly inside her, and tonight it only made her curse him for making her look huge and ungainly. No wonder Harold Lines ignored her, she thought, feeling abandoned and alone. *If I was still married to Donald, would we have been invited?*

えつどめ

Dinner was over and Annalee asked young Marie to bring the young ones into the living room. The girl had washed their faces after their meal and led them in. Sarah drew away from her Uncle Harold, but Bucky just stood there looking at him.

Annalee watched Harold's ineffective attempts at interaction with his brother's children. He had a sadness about him as he tried to talk with them or hold little Sarah on his lap. He was a stranger to her and looked like the man who had terrorized her babyhood. She would have none of him and ran into Annalee's arms for security.

Annalee felt sorry about it and shrugged at Harold. "Harold, why not come during the day, maybe before lunch time. Sarah takes a nap after that and Bucky does sometimes as well. You might have a better chance to get close to them, if they see you a bit more." She saw his face brighten at her words and wondered at that. "Do you have any children of your own?"

"No, we don't. We haven't been lucky that way. It has been our hope that sometime in the future we will."

He smiled at her, and she felt a twinge of fear at a smile she remembered so well and trusted not at all. He was not in any way like his brother, she knew it, but it would take her some time to free herself of the fear she'd lived with for so long.

As the evening wound to a close, the company left, and goodbyes were said. Harold held her hand at the door and thanked her for a lovely dinner and the chance to get to know his niece and nephew a little better.

Annalee entered the kitchen and started to clean up after all the work of putting the dinner together. She felt happy and fulfilled. Overall, it had been a success. She found the dinner dishes stacked and ready to be washed and believed it had been that little Marie.

As she ran the sink full of warm water and poured the washing powder in, she sensed Jack's presence right behind her and whipped around. He stood close, way too close.

She could smell his masculine scent. Somehow, the

closeness of him made her feel dizzy, and she struggled to catch her breath. "Yes? Do you need something?"

"Annalee, are you afraid of me? Am I too close to you right now?"

"Uh—yes, you are. You are very close, Jack." She pressed backward into the sink, but had nowhere to go. "Do you want something?"

Jack wanted to smile. Standing so close, taking in the smell of her, and feeling her breath on his shirt, he did want something from her. Being around this lovely young woman these last few days of their marriage, he had finally realized he wanted everything she had to give. He knew he'd take even more than that, if he could.

She was scared to death of him making an advance on her like he was right now. He was in a great mood after the dinner and the few drinks he'd had along with it were enough to mellow him. He was happy and satisfied, and a heated glow had come over him at the sight of her. This lovely woman had the power to give him that feeling, and they had only been together as man and wife for a few days. He'd rapidly become aware of his awakening passion for her. But was it love? He didn't know, but he sure as hell wanted her.

He saw the fear in her eyes and had to back away, or she'd start screaming and upset the children. Jack thought they were asleep upstairs by now, but he wasn't sure about it. He moved away a bit. "Sorry, my dear, I sort of forgot. Tonight was wonderful. You're a fine cook, and everything was delicious. Do you know how alone and empty this house has been and for so long a time?"

He laughed with a kind of joy she hadn't ever heard before. Annalee heard the deep and happy sound coming from that solid masculine throat. He had the deepest, dark gray eyes, and she had already learned that if she looked into them, she'd get dizzy. She dropped her gaze to his feet.

He put his hand beneath her chin, raised her head, and looked into her eyes. "Annalee, you have made this house come alive and, like it or not, you've made me come alive along with it. I hurry home after work because I can't wait to see what you've discovered about the place or how the kids have been—all of it." He moved closer and his hand reached to encircle her waist.

Annalee twisted away. "I think I'll do these dishes up tomorrow, Jack." Her face flamed hot and had reddened. It let him know she was desperately eager to leave him standing alone in the kitchen.

He grabbed her and pulled her into his arms. "Not just yet, Annalee—not just yet."

He held her close against his body, and it felt like heaven. He bent his head down to find her soft, full lips and kissed her every bit as deeply and tenderly as he had at the altar on their wedding day. He felt her response, her soft whimper, and how her legs seemed to give way. It would be so good to keep going, to take her up to his room. Oh God, how he wanted that! But then, she tensed and began to struggle against him.

"Please, Jack! You promised me—remember that?"

He released her. "Sorry girl, I guess I had one too many and forgot that you were a wife in name only."

He couldn't keep the regret out of his voice, and it hurt her to hear it. He had done so much for her. But she reminded herself that wasn't why she'd married him. It all came roaring back, knowing what would have come next, if she hadn't stopped him. She'd find herself in his bed at the end of the hall, and all those terrible things men do to women would begin all over again. She couldn't face having a man do those unbearable, degrading, painful things again. She'd had enough of it!

"I'm so sorry, Jack," Annalee said. "But I just can't do those awful things again—I just can't."

She felt the damning tears begin and wanted to run upstairs to her room. He was hurt, she knew that. But what could she do? They had made a pact. What about that?

After Annalee made good her escape, Jack smiled at her departing back. She'd left him standing there and run up the stairs as though in fear for her life. Her fear of intimacy with him or any man was unreasonable, but he understood. She'd had a rough few years from her former husband, and that ugly memory lingered on. If a man was interested, it would take some well-spent time to change her mind about him, and all those "awful" things he might want to do with her. He couldn't help the chuckle that left his lips.

Jack believed himself to be a kind and gentle man. He'd grown up in a home where love between his parents had been visible, an everyday, ongoing loving climate. Nice surroundings for any child to grow up in. It hurt him inside that a woman, as loving and kind as Annalee, had had to suffer abuse at the hands of her husband. It infuriated him that a man who was supposed to protect and cherish a woman, did not. Knowing her as he did now, Jack felt the need to make it up to her and surround her with loving kindness where she'd know only cruelty before. Did he have what it took to heal her emotional wounds? He found himself aching with the desire to find out.

Yes, they had made a business deal out of this marriage, and he had planned to honor that. But he'd rapidly found his mind undergoing a revision. He felt himself attracted and entranced by this lovely young woman he had taken as a wife. The more he saw of her gentle violet-to-purple eyes and her soft curling black hair, the less he wanted to keep to their premarital agreement. Knowing that she was now his wife, yet unavailable to him while living under his very roof, had become a torture of wanting and a desperate need of her.

Was it seeing her, hearing her soft voice, watching her caress her children, as well as his child, and lavishing all her love and tenderness on them? Was it seeing these things daily in the intimate situation of marriage that had set a fire inside him? He felt his body singing, tight with desire for her. Surprised at himself, he faced it. He wanted her body, her love—all of her in every imaginable way.

He'd thought about this drastic reversal in his own feelings and wondered what had happened. She constantly rejected him, out of commitment to their pact and a fair amount of fear. He'd smiled about it, understanding her feelings. But he also remembered her response with that beginning kiss at the altar. He had planned to make it look like a real lover's kiss to honor their secret arrangement, but the touch of Annalee's soft, full lips had sent his body and mind a message he'd completely unexpected. In that moment, he'd become aware of her in a whole new dimension, of the woman she was. He now wanted her as his wife in every way.

He'd always believed himself to be a more-than-competent lover. He'd had a few good memories and believable compliments about it along the way and clung to that.

Her reluctance only made his resolve toughen. Annalee was a delightful young woman. Every move she made affected him. He felt the heat zing through him when she entered a room or he heard her soft voice calling as she attended to the little ones. He wanted those attentions for himself. He craved her hands stroking his hair or petting him in that same special way she had for their children.

Annalee often let her hair flow loose and free, hanging down her slender back. Her voice as she played with the children sounded like a small, musical trill, like water flowing over smooth rocks. Without conscious effort, her gentle presence in his home had caused the loving memories of his dead wife to slowly fade away.

Now, instead of Amelia's merry blue eyes and blonde hair, he saw deep lavender eyes, black curling tresses, and a tall, slender body moving about his home with the grace of a young doe.

Annalee was gentle, loving, and kind, but her stance against him, his touch, or his getting close, was firm. Jack smiled to himself. He had before him a pleasant and exciting mountain of fear to gently overcome. He was more than thrilled by the lovely task at hand.

Chapter 16

Harold had phoned and asked if he might come by and spend time with his brother's children. Annalee happily welcomed his visit and, in a few short moments, she opened her door to him.

The children were finished with breakfast, and Annalee had allowed Bucky to bring his toys downstairs. He was busily telling his uncle about his new train set, and Harold laughed. "This young man is a take-over sort of guy, isn't he?"

Annalee laughed, too. "He had no trouble taking over little Sissy. She follows him around like a puppy and does whatever he tells her." She was happy these days, seeing that her children had enough of everything. Just that knowledge alone made her feel safe and worry-free. And she no longer feared Harold, as he'd proven to be the exact opposite of his twin. She wouldn't have believed it possible, but the proof was there before her eyes.

He was on his knees with the boy, watching Bucky

put the tracks together and tell Sissy what cars to put on them. Sarah busily played with sections of track, and Annalee watched how cleverly Bucky worked to get the piece he wanted as he handed her a different one.

Sarah wouldn't allow Harold to pick her up, or get very close, but she no longer had the look of fear in her eyes when she saw him. Annalee sat in the living room, quietly watching this group at play. Bucky had many of the same features and characteristics of his uncle and, in addition, her son was also right-handed. Did this mean he would turn out like Harold and not like his father? She prayed that would be the way of it.

Sissy easily went into Harold's arms. He played with her, tossed her up a few times, and made her giggle, but Sarah hung back. She kept looking at him, while keeping a close eye on her mother.

Harold looked at Annalee sitting there, watching everything. "I think they are getting used to me, don't you?"

His voice held the wistfulness of a man who longed to be a father, but never would, if what she'd heard him say was true. His wife had been unable to conceive. A thing like that was always sad. She felt the sting of tears, but wouldn't allow them to fall.

Startled to hear the sound of her doorbell, she opened the door to find Carol, standing expectantly before the on the small vine-covered porch.

"Well, my goodness, Carol, won't you come in? I have some company at present, but please, do come in." Annalee took in the woman's heavily swollen belly, as Carol waddled inside her home, and ushered her to a seat.

"Well, if it isn't Mr. Lines?" Carol cooed the words

as she gave him her sexiest slant-eyed glance.

Annalee decided that Carol wasn't letting her advanced state of impending motherhood stop her from being a silly flirt and sat down to watch. "It seems you have met Mr. Lines before, is that right, Carol?"

"Oh, yes, we've met. We nearly shared breakfast the other morning, didn't we, Mr. Lines?" Her tone dripped with honey.

Harold managed to conceal his feelings of disgust. He really felt sorry for this poor, lonely woman. Looking at her swollen belly and, from the few hints Carol had dropped, he had a strong feeling she might be carrying his brother's child. But he smiled at her and replied in smooth tones, "Why, yes, I believe we did meet at the little breakfast place called Mary Ellen's. One day last week, wasn't it?"

"Oh how nice. You remembered me." Carol's voice deepened and she flushed with pleasure that he'd kept her in mind. She looked at the children—playing with the cars on the train track and Bucky running them off, causing a train wreck—and sniffed slightly at the mess the kids were making. "I see you are getting acquainted with Gerald's two, are you?"

Harold grabbed Sissy and tossed her into the air to make her squeal with delight. "And with this darling little three-year old, as well."

He felt elated that he had gotten closer with two of the children but knew he had a ways to go with little Sarah. What could a little child like that have seen to make her so fearful? Angry thoughts toward his dead brother made him forget where he was for a moment.

Carol wasn't through with him—not at all. She was

curious about this man and wondered why he continued to hang around that goody-goody, Annalee. "Well then, if I may ask, what are you doing around here for such a long while if you live in Washington, D C?"

"I have some work to do around here while I'm in the area. How much do you know about Rural Electrification?" He hoped an intricate subject like that that would stop her questioning.

"Oh, my goodness, Mr. Lines, that sounds so important."

Carol wiggled in her chair and crossed her ankles. Annalee, shocked at how swollen they were, missed seeing the eyes Carol had made at Harold.

My God, that pregnant woman is flirting with me! Harold couldn't believe the effrontery of the woman and decided that right now was a great time to take his leave. He got up from the floor and took Bucky's hand. "Young man, I think you will make a great engineer someday. Looks like you're already on your way by the way you make those trains run on time." He tried to pick Sarah up in his arms, but she ran to Annalee and clutched onto her mother's skirt. "Looks like I'll have to work a little harder on Sarah. She's a lovely little girl, Annalee, but why not? She looks a whole lot like her momma." He said goodbye and nodded to Carol as he left the house.

Annalee came back to Carol and sat down. "How are you these days?" she asked, hoping Carol would tell her the truth of things. She also wondered if Carol had let her doctor know about the swollen feet. "Does your doctor know about those puffy feet?"

"Oh, I'm doing just fine. The doctor says many women have their feet swell during pregnancy." She tossed her head. "I hope the guy's not a quack. He's all they have around here, but I don't want to leave this berg to see some other doc. It's too far to drive anymore."

Annalee indicated Carol's puffy feet. "He says that is okay, then?"

Annalee had carried two children with very little swelling of her feet. Carol was quite a bit shorter and a lot heavier normally and Annalee wondered if that made a difference.

She decided to speak to Mary about it. The woman had proven to be a font of knowledge about things you wouldn't expect her to know. Because of her surprise at the depth of the woman, Annalee often wondered about Mary's earlier life. Where had she come from and what had she experienced? She might look like just another old lady to some, but to Annalee she was an interesting and knowledgeable person. Mary was also someone Annalee could go to more intimate knowledge about certain things, like marital relations.

Carol broke into her thoughts. "What's that brother of Gerald's doing, sniffing around here?"

"Sniffing around? It's hardly that, Carol. He is an identical twin and wants to know his brother's children. That's the reason he came here. He hadn't known where his brother was for many years."

"Why is he staying so long if he works in Washington?"

Carol's questioning had turned serious and nosey. Annalee wondered what business it was of hers and why she wanted to know. "He wanted to meet Jack. They have quite a few things in common, I think. They spoke about putting power in the outlying areas."

Annalee realized it felt good to be able to say that about her husband. He was a man of importance and she appreciated the difference of being married to a man of substance, like Jack.

"Is that what the big dinner party was all about, then?" Carol's small upturned nose was up in the air, and her lips were pressed tight.

"How did you know about that?" Annalee figured she must have been skulking around this neighborhood to even know about the dinner. Was she angry about the dinner party? She was certainly upset about something.

"I had planned to pay you a nice visit. It's been a while, you know. But when I saw all the cars outside, Amy's and Derrick's too, I figured you were much too busy with them to bother about me."

"It was after six in the evening. Were you going to pay Jack and me a visit that late?"

Annalee remembered how many times Carol had been present when Jack had come to pick up his daughter. Had she done that so she could get a good look at him, or was it to try to take his child away from Annalee's care?

"Well, that's water over the dam or under the bridge, so what difference does it make now?" Carol shrugged and did her best to look lost and helpless all of a sudden. "I guess I'd better get going, but I do want you and the children to come visit me one day soon. If you can find the time, that is."

Annalee didn't miss Carol's "poor little me" tone. "How about day after tomorrow? I plan to visit Mary Jensen that day, too. She was so much help when I had that fire—a real life saver."

"Oh good. It will be so nice to have some company. I'll make lunch for us when you come. What do those kids like to eat?"

"How about peanut butter and jelly sandwiches? That's something that never fails with them."

Annalee had finally reached the point that she didn't care what Carol was saying and felt increasingly uncomfortable with her being here at all. Carol had not proven to be a friend of any kind. From now on, Annalee would be all politeness, conversing without emotion. Yet, she couldn't help feeling a sense of pity for this lonely, trouble-making soul.

Carol finally left, and Annalee had a few hours to straighten things up and start dinner for Jack. She wanted a meal ready when he came home. She remembered his saying how he longed for lights on and the smell of dinner when he came home after a long day at work. He'd missed that for so long. She wasn't sure what his favorite foods were and hadn't yet asked him about that. It was another thing she felt was too intimate.

Annalee had a plump chicken and decided to roast it with stuffing. She would make biscuits, too. That was one thing she knew Jack enjoyed. What man didn't? First, she checked on the children, playing railroad with Bucky up in his room after Harold's visit. She was continually amazed at how well those three got along, and she noticed that Sarah had stopped sucking her thumb.

❧❧❧

Jack walked into the kitchen, saw the table set with the three booster seats in place, and heard the hum of the little ones playing upstairs. His eyes sought Annalee, but she was nowhere in sight. At the sound of her light step on the stairs, he turned and smiled as she walked into the kitchen.

He had to stop himself from going to her and sweeping her into his arms. She had freshened her face, hair, and dress before she called everyone to dinner. She had on a slim-fitting skirt and a loose blouse with sleeves that belled out from her shoulders, rather like a buccaneer.

"You look lovely tonight, my dear."

"Thanks, Jack." She went to the oven and peeked in. "Should be ready in a few minutes."

She faced him, her cheeks flushed from the heat of the oven and her eyes deep lavender turning into purple. Jack stifled a gasp of delight at the sight of her. She had the table set up and the kid's booster seats in place. She went to the stairs and called them.

Hearing nothing, she ran up the stairs. It had been too quiet up there for a while. Her heart began hammering in her chest when she heard nothing from any of them. She peeked into Bucky's room, saw nothing, and ran into Sissy's room—again nothing.

"Bucky! Now what are you trying to pull on me?" She knew he had them hidden away to surprise her. But she didn't really know that for sure. "Bucky!" she called again.

Finally, she heard a tiny giggle coming from the empty bedroom. It remained bare as they hadn't gotten anything for Sarah's room yet. Annalee pulled open the closet door and the three of them let out a squeals of delight.

Annalee wanted to swat a bottom or two, but they

seemed so happy these days, she couldn't bring herself to do it. She firmed her face and tried to growl at them, "Shame on all of you! You scared me half to death. I thought some big bad burglar had come and stolen all of you away, and here I have supper ready and waiting."

"We didn't want to make you 'fraid, Momma. We wanted to s'prise you."

Bucky manfully led the two girls out and Annalee checked them over before they headed for the supper table. Sarah needed a clean face and Sissy needed the use of a hairbrush.

Jack stood outside his room, watching the whole affair. His heart was full seeing the happiness of his little daughter in this new family situation.

Annalee went down the stairs after the children and Jack quietly followed. Never in his life had he wanted a woman as badly as he wanted the one who walked before him. He'd thought of her soft lips, full bosom, and laughing violet eyes all day long, instead of working on the electrification projections.

He hoped what he'd done was correct, but he'd need to re-do them again tomorrow to be sure.

He quietly took his seat at the table. He looked at Bucky sitting in his chair on the new booster seat. He used it because Jack had assured him it was a big boy thing to do. "Say, Bucky, what was all that ruckus upstairs a minute ago?"

"We wanted to hide from momma and give her a s'prise."

"You made me think some bad burglar had stolen you away from me," Annalee said. "I was so scared, Bucky, I almost cried."

Bucky's little chest swelled with pride. "Aw, Momma, you know I wouldn't let that happen."

"I think you are going to be a real good man someday, Bucky," Jack told him. "And a brave one, too."

"His Uncle Harold came for a visit today," Annalee said. "He played trains with the children, all of them. Sarah isn't too sure about him, but he, Bucky, and Sissy get along very well."

She reached over to help Sarah with her meat, cutting it into small bits for her. As she reached to help her daughter, Jack caught a glimpse of a swelling breast when the neck of her blouse hung loose. He was very glad he sat at the table. He needed the coverage it provided down below, while his blood roared inside his head to the point it made him dizzy as hell.

The children ate well. His little Sissy chatted happily with Annalee and Bucky. For himself, Jack waited until she had them all in bed, asleep. He wanted time alone with her to help her understand that things between a man and a woman did not need to be the evil way she imagined.

Chapter 17

Annalee came down the stairs. It had been a long day with Harold coming and, worse yet, Carol's rather upsetting visit. Annalee had thought Carol was chasing after Harold the last time they'd met, and the woman appeared to have tried again today. She'd made a few moves, though she was hampered by her very pregnant condition. But there was something more in her attitude.

Somehow Annalee knew Carol had something on her mind. It seethed beneath the surface, fulminating there, ready to erupt.

It made Annalee more than a little apprehensive about her forthcoming visit to Carol's home.

She entered the kitchen, ready to clean up after dinner. Jack had the dishes stacked and ready to wash, but he had waited for her, lounging his rangy body against the sink.

"Like a bit of help getting these done?"

His tone was disarming, but Annalee immediately felt uncomfortable. He was edging close again, and she was wary.

"No thanks, Jack, I can get these." He didn't move from his stance in front of the sink, and she stood there, not knowing what to do. "Is there something you want, Jack?"

"Actually, Annalee, there is. I want to get something straight between us. I believe it's about time."

"Like what?"

"For one thing, I am not your enemy, girl. Every time I come close, you shrink away and run like a damned rabbit. Am I that frightening?"

She flushed, wanting to run again, but she couldn't. She'd have to have it out with him. "No, but—well, remember our agreement?"

"Hell yes, how could I ever forget that?" He stared directly into her eyes. "Annalee, I made a deal, yes. You know I would have done a lot to make life better for my daughter. But even then, I knew you to be one hell of a woman. What I didn't fully realize was the fact your husband had brutalized you to the point you were afraid to ever trust me or any other man again. That's a very big hurdle for anyone to handle."

"I thought we could work this out between us, Jack. You were still so much in love with your wife that I didn't think it would come to...that you would want..."

Annalee couldn't bring herself to say it outright. She felt weak and thought her knees would buckle. Watching the deepening shades of gray in Jack's eyes, she saw the tightness across his lips. He was angry with her and, from her past memories of abuse, she wondered what would come next. Her mouth went dry and her body began trembling, but she couldn't stop it. While she waited for the blows to fall, inside her mind, her anger grew. *Not again—never again*!

In amazement, Jack saw the changes cross her face. He saw her terror. He saw her body brace as she awaited for the heavy blows from his fists. It tore his heart out. "Annalee! What are you thinking?" He reached out to pull her frozen body into his arms. "Are you afraid of me?" His voice had gone higher in his frustration. He held her close against his body and stroked her hair, breathing in the fragrance of it. "Please, girl. Don't you know by now, I am not that kind of man?"

He held her ever closer and, though she still trembled, she seemed to relax a little. He nuzzled his nose into her hair. It smelled like heaven. He kissed her cheeks and moved down to her mouth.

"Oh, God, please. What are you doing? Is this some trick of yours?" She tried to pull away, to look into his face. "What are you doing?" she repeated.

"I'm just holding a very frightened young woman in my arms, one who has no need to be afraid of me." He held her out from his body. "My God, Annalee, don't you trust me at all?"

She thought his voice had gotten higher. "I am trying, Jack, but you seem to want to be more than what we agreed." She flushed crimson from her neck to her hairline and tried again to pull away.

He smiled down at her. "I'm afraid you're right about that, Annalee. It was that kiss at the altar that did in our agreement. I haven't been able to think straight since that moment."

He was a big man, and she felt the strength of him. She was reminded all over again that he could do anything he wanted with her, or to her, willing or not. She knew how that felt. "What are we to do, then?"

Her voice was tight with apprehension, and he heard it. "Well, we could just do up these dishes together, just like a real man and wife." He kissed her solidly and let her go. "Sorry, I had to do that." He had to let her go for now, but he'd had that heady feeling and already knew for certain that she would weaken one of these days. He turned around, let the hot water run into the sink, and poured in the soap powder. "Let's get these dishes done, then."

He made himself busy trying to quell his highly charged passion, so easily generated by the smell of her and how the touch of her slender body felt against his.

Annalee stood beside him in a state of shock. He had let her go so gently and, because of it, her trust in him increased. Maybe he wasn't like some other men. Yet, she knew he wanted her. She had no doubt of that at all. She had thought herself safe from his masculine desires when she married him. After all, he still loved his first wife. But she remembered, he was a man and they had their ways, their wants, and their needs. He would not be denied for much longer, and she had to face that fact. She was happy in this home, in this life, and for her children. She couldn't think of leaving or running from him. But knowing what he wanted of her sent chills of fear through her. Hot tingles and cold chills crept through her body.

Jack no longer thought about his dead wife, remembering his life with her. He was thinking of this lovely young woman who stood trembling beside him. It hurt him to think he had frightened her to the point she'd expected violence at his hands just a moment ago. And it sickened him that she had suffered and endured the horrors that created such thoughts.

Annalee stayed and braved it out. But she desperately wanted to run upstairs and crawl into the safety of her bed. She'd had to stand her ground or become a spineless figure of pity. And she possessed enough pride to detest that idea. Holding her head high, she began to dry the dishes he'd washed.

All was quiet for a while, until she spotted a bit of food on a plate. She handed the dish back to him. "You missed a spot, Jack."

"I did, did I?" He turned to her with a disarming smile. "Forgive me, Annalee?"

He couldn't keep the passion out of his glance as much as he tried. He wanted her to the point of distraction. If she had any idea of the wild thoughts in his head, she'd run up those stairs to her room and lock the damned door.

"There's nothing to forgive, Jack. I'm sorry, for the way I acted, as well. I guess I have a ways to go before I can forget certain things. I'm truly sorry about that and, of course, none of it is your fault."

She turned away, to hide the burning flush across her face, and grabbed another dish. He stifled his desire to reach for her again. He had some work to do before she truly became his wife.

After a few moments of silence, Jack quietly told her, "There is a dinner-dance in two weeks at the Twin Oaks Country Club. It's held twice a year to celebrate community events. This one is to announce the plans for the coming electrification to outlying areas." He nudged her side. "It's a Saturday evening, and I'd like us to attend as a married couple. Think we can manage that?"

She looked at him. "I've never done anything as fancy as that, Jack." Her trembling voice betrayed her fear of not being up to a social occasion like that. "Do you think I can manage to fit in?"

He smiled, thinking of holding her in his arms for a few spins around the floor. "These events are nothing to worry about—just a few speeches, eating, and some dancing. They usually have a great band at those things."

"I'll have to discuss this with Amy." Annalee knew she would get all the help she needed from her good friend.

Poor Carol, she would not be attending this event, either. For some reason, that gave Annalee a feeling of satisfaction.

When the dishes were done and put away, she took her leave of Jack and headed up to bed. He wanted a good night kiss, but knew better than to ask.

Yes, he had some work to do with that lovely little woman.

ഗ്രൗ

The next day, Annalee loaded the kids into Jack's nice Chrysler sedan and drove over to pay a visit to Mary. Later, she planned to see Carol, where they'd been invited for lunch.

She knocked on Mary's door and was soon ushered into her snug little home.

"My, oh my, don't you look nice these days," Mary

exclaimed, seeing a nicely dressed Annalee. "And look at these children. They're growing by leaps and bounds." She sat them down and gave each of them a small cookie. "So how are things going with you these days?"

Annalee knew she meant between herself and Jack. "Everything is fine. It is a lovely home and keeps me busy taking care of it, especially with the three children." She flushed a bit and looked Mary in the eyes. "I know you wonder about our arrangement. He is holding to it, but I already know he wants far more than that. I'm not sure what to do. The thought of...well, you know what I mean. I just can't imagine it, Mary. Thank God, I can talk to you about this. No one else even knows."

By her friend's quiet smile and understanding nod, Annalee knew she understood everything.

"My dear, he is a very good man. If you want to keep him, you might need to consider changing your thoughts on those things. I speak from long years of experience." Mary smiled at the young woman sitting before her. "You are a very beautiful girl, my dear. Jack Harrison is a nice fellow, but he *is* a man and, unless I miss my guess, he is a very good man, in *every* way. The right man can make those things you fear into something else entirely. For some lucky women, the right man can make their nightly needs seem quite wonderful." She laughed a bit. "You know, just about every young unmarried female in this town had her eyes on that man. He could have had his pick of any one of them."

Annalee didn't hear all Mary said before her ears started ringing and her cheeks burned like fire.

"Stop saying those things, Mary!" she gasped. "I'm scared to death of what you're saying. I'm sure you are right, but I can't—I just can't." Her hands twisted into a tight knot. "What am I to do?"

"Why not let him take the lead? I'm sure he'll be very considerate with you."

Mary's soothing, encouraging voice seemed a lot like a gentle shove, pushing Annalee farther down the road to intimacy with her new husband. Thoughts of those things he might do to her, disgusted her, froze her insides, and scared her beyond reason.

"I have to go, Mary," Annalee said. "I must visit my friend, Carol, too."

She wanted to get away from this knowing old woman who sensed her fears, yet led her toward them with every word she uttered. Annalee called the children, who were playing in one of the bedrooms with some old toys Mary had kept.

Mary ignored Annalee's plan to leave just yet. Instead she asked, "Is Carol a very close friend of yours?"

"Why, yes. She has been since high school."

"I shouldn't say this perhaps, not being completely sure, but I was up walking about my house the night your home burned down. I don't sleep so well now that I'm older." Mary shrugged. "I was up and it was coming on five o'clock in the morning, I think. And I swear, I thought I saw Carol's car drive away. I didn't see anything right then, but very shortly after, I saw the flames shooting up and ran next door to call the fire department." She looked down at the floor. "I feel terrible saying it, but is there any chance your friend Carol could have set that fire?"

"Oh, Mary! You don't think she could have done a terrible, deadly thing like that to me, do you?"

Annalee thought back over the many times Carol had come to visit right about the time Jack came to pick up his child. She also remembered clearly how Carol had flirted and had practically thrown herself at the man. Slowly, Annalee realized it could have been one of Carol's tricks. A poorly thought out trick, for certain.

If so, it would explain why she was so upset that Annalee wasn't leaving town to go live with her folks in Arnott and also why Carol had been so devastated to learn Jack had proposed marriage to Annalee. How well she remembered Carol storming from Mary's home with her tires smoking and squealing as she sped away.

Annalee grasped herself around the middle and slumped over. "Oh, Mary, I am going there next for lunch. I won't say a thing about this right now. How could I even mention a rotten thing like that? We might all have died that night."

Had Carol even considered that? Annalee imagined her two children burning to death in that poor little home. It was too much to take in, but she knew Mary just might be right in what she had said.

"Doesn't Carol drive a dark green Ford sedan?" Mary asked.

"Yes, she does."

At Mary's positive nod, Annalee knew for certain it had been Carol who had set her home ablaze. Maybe Carol hadn't planned to kill, but only to force Annalee to leave this small town and go live with her parents in Arnott.

This time, Annalee finally did leave. She hugged Mary and thanked her as she ushered her little flock to the car. "Sorry for such a short visit, Mary. Thanks for what you've told me. I can scarcely believe it, yet I'm sure it's true. I was so careful with that stove, always."

As she drove to Carol's home, Annalee compared Mary with her own parents. They would never have understood her deal with Jack. And they certainly could never have given her the understanding advice that Mary had.

But, knowing their hide-bound attitudes about marriage, Annalee would never have told then about the arrangement she'd made with Jack in the first place. She shook her head, feeling sorry for her parents. They'd missed out on so much of their daughter's life, due to their lack of real understanding and inability or unwillingness to provide help in her hour of need.

They arrived at Carol's home and went to her door. Carol met them with a smile on her face and bade them enter. She cooed and awed over the children and offered them each a small cookie to eat before she served lunch. Annalee, uneasy to say the least, watched her friend with new eyes. She couldn't stop thinking about what Mary had told her.

Could this so-called friend of hers have done such a thing? In her heart, Annalee realized Carol would go to any lengths to get what she wanted. She had cheated on her husband to have a child, and bragged about the man who had fathered her child. Annalee didn't care about that anymore. She had a different life now, a far better life, thanks to Jack. In a sickening turn of events, it was thanks to Carol. Knowing she could be having lunch with the very person who had burned her home and nearly killed all of them, Annalee decided to mention the dressy evening out with her handsome, new husband.

"I've been so very busy with the new house and all, you know, with three children now instead of two. And it's so large it takes all day to keep it clean enough. And on top of all that, I have to find a fancy dress for the dinner-dance at the Twin Oaks Country Club in two weeks." Annalee giggled a bit. "Jack insists on my going. He wants to show off his new wife, I suppose.

"Oh, my you have really hit the high life, haven't you, my dear?"

Carol kept her voice cool and even, but Annalee believed Carol was fighting the fires of jealousy—her own personal hell.

Annalee had indeed ignited murderous thoughts inside Carol's mind. *Oh, the nerve of this goody-two-shoes bitch telling me all this. She knew I wanted Jack Harrison for myself. But she jumped right in and took him right out from under my nose. I wish she'd have died in that damned fire!*

"Are we eating soon, dear? I must go hunting for new bedroom furniture for my Sarah. She needs a nice room all her own, even though she likes to sleep with her new stepsister, Sissy." Annalee grinned at Carol as she smoothed the fabric of her new print skirt. "They get along so well. Sarah already loves Jack and trusts him. She was scared to death of her own father and is still afraid of her Uncle Harold. But I must say he is really trying hard to get acquainted with both Sarah and Bucky."

Carol looked like she was ready to have a stroke, or deliver that unborn child, by the tightness across her features and the way she clenched and unclenched her hands.

"I guess I'd better put some lunch out. I made peanut butter and jelly sandwiches for the kids and a tuna salad for us. I hope that's all right with you—unless you have gotten so fancy you can't eat canned tuna anymore."

Her tone was cold and clipped, and Annalee also saw a gleam of fomenting hatred in Carol's eyes.

I'd better be on the look-out from now on, Annalee warned herself. *She's planning something.*

Chapter 13

Carol and Annalee set the kids in a circle on the floor and put the sandwiches in the center. Carol poured them each a small glass of milk. "There you are, kids. Go to it." She turned to Annalee. "Why not come into the bedroom a moment? I have something I think you need to see."

Annalee followed Carol, frowning. She wondered what new trick Carol had up her sneaky sleeve. She'd hinted at something for months, with that know-it-all look of smugness on her face. Maybe today, Annalee would have the answer.

In the bedroom, Carol swirled around as much as her rotund stomach would allow. "You think you're the cat's meow, don't you, Mrs. Annalee Harrison? Is that how it is now? Well, have I've got news for you, Miss Perfect-in-all-things? Take a peek at this if you will." Her venom-filled voice had become close to a snarl as she handed Annalee a slightly crumpled, yellowed bit of paper.

Annalee took the wrinkled paper only because it was handed to her. She spread it out to read it and recognized a familiar scrawl. She read a hastily written, impassioned note from her dead husband to her dear, long-time friend, Carol Woods. Annalee felt a cold sickness growing inside her as she stood there, looking at the hate-filled face of a woman she had thought of as a friend.

Carol stood gloating as Annalee read a note proving beyond a doubt Carol had slept Gerald and was carrying his child.

"So now what have you to say?" Carol sniffed, her nose in the air, proving her superiority as a woman who knew she had the sexual appeal to take a man's loving attention away from his wife and bestow it on herself. She waited.

Annalee held her bitter anger inside. "So this is what you've been hinting at all these months while pretending to be my friend?"

After her visit to Mary, Annalee already come to believe this so-called friend of hers had literally tried to kill her in a fire. Now, Carol had delivered her another stab in the back.

Carol's crumpled note only confirmed what her true friend, Mary, had told her. It was proof to Annalee that Carol was capable of murder to achieve her own ends. She had sneaked into the house in the wee hours of the morning and set it on fire while Annalee and her children lay asleep. And, if so, it was an act of murder, or attempted murder.

Annalee felt numb, almost nauseous. She threw the note to the floor and looked Carol in the eyes. "You allowed that ugly, evil man to paw you and do those nasty, cruel things to you, and you want me to feel upset about it?" She snorted. "I can only say thanks for taking him off of me for a while. I hope you enjoyed his ugliness because I can assure you, I never did!" She lowered her voice and continued. "Is this the way you felt after you set fire to my home and tried to kill me and my children?" she asked with a laugh. "It didn't turn out the way you'd hoped, did it? You did me the biggest favor I've ever had, Carol. Thanks for unwittingly giving me a completely wonderful husband, a lovely home, and a brand new life."

As Carol gasped, turned white and speechless, Annalee turned her back. "I'll be leaving now, Carol. I hated that rotten excuse of a man, and you have all my sympathy because you are carrying inside you all that remains of a cruel, filthy-minded monster. I hope you can live with that."

Looking at the mess her three had made on Carol's shining wooden floor, Annalee gave no thought to cleaning, that or anything else, and called her children. "Come on, kids, let's go for an ice cream."

They scrambled to their feet with shouts of joy.

"Oh boy!" Bucky exclaimed as Annalee wiped their mouths of the food they had tried to eat.

They left the mess on the floor for Carol and departed. Annalee wanted to cry and scream, partly at the betrayal of her husband, but more for the loss of someone she had always thought of as a friend. Along with that, she shuddered with the sick feeling that came to her as she imagined Gerald rutting with Carol and both of them laughing at his stupid, ignorant wife, sitting quietly at home, never suspecting a thing.

They stopped for ice cream and sat in the white-painted little room at the creamery store. The children made their usual mess of eating. Ice cream dripped off their cones down their clothes and hands, but the happy smiles across their faces let Annalee know it was worth the mess. Seeing them happy and knowing that she had the means to do this small thing for them gave her a glow of satisfaction.

Looking outside at the curb to see the nice Oldsmobile sedan she now drove and thinking of her lovely new home, she wondered if Carol saw everything as a contest she had to win. Annalee actually felt sorry for the poor lonely woman and pitied the conniving soul Carol had become.

Annalee had her new husband to thank for all of the good things she now had. Along with that, she saw him as a man any woman would be proud of. She had far warmer feelings for this very fine man than she'd imagined possible. She was most certainly aware that he saw her in this new way as well—she could see it in his eyes.

He wanted her—as his wife, a real wife, not some fearful shell of a woman. She shook inside, remembering how his hands on her shoulders had made her feel. She remembered, too, Mary's words. *'The right man can make those things you fear into something else entirely. For some lucky women, the right man can make their nightly needs seem quite wonderful.'*

Annalee had frozen inside at hearing what Mary had said, but she'd not forgotten the words. She found them hard to believe and impossible to imagine. And she understood those words had been difficult for a shy woman like Mary to say.

Were they the truth? Annalee wondered. *Could it be possible?*

She found napkins and cleaned the children enough to get them home. Bedroom furniture for Sarah could wait until another day. Annalee was shaken to her bones at Carol's evil trickery and the cruel way she'd shoved that note in Annalee's face. She didn't want to give into it. She just wanted to get home, give the kids a bath, and start Jack's supper. And right now, she had no idea what to prepare.

All the way back to the house, she fought tears, thinking of Carol's cruel treachery. *What did I ever do to make her hate me so?* Annalee couldn't imagine why a thing like that had happened. She believed Jack would know how to help her understand. When the children were in bed, she planned to tell him about Carol's treachery and ask him his opinion. Feeling better, she took her little brood upstairs and gave them all baths. She made them an early supper of scrambled eggs and toast with jam. Knowing none of them had taken a nap, she had them in bed before the sun went down.

Jack was late coming home this evening. He had called to let her know. Glad for the extra time, she decided to make him something special and searched through the refrigerator for the right thing. Finding only hamburger, she made a meat loaf. Hers were very good. That and baked a potato for each of them with a batch of biscuits, two ears of corn, and a salad of slaw, and dinner was ready. She set the table for two and right then she heard that Model A coupe pull into the drive. He was home.

Her heart rate rose in anticipation as she heard his

footsteps come through the door. She had the food ready to take from the oven and looked up as Jack entered the kitchen as he always did each evening. Tonight he looked bigger than he usually did. He was a tall slender man and his shoulders were wider than some men's, too. She'd always thought that looked good on a man.

Jack stopped in mid-stride. "What's going on, Annalee?"

She flushed right down to her toes. Blushing like a silly fool made her angry with herself. "Well, a few things happened today."

He looked around. "Where are the kids?"

"They didn't have naps and were so tired that I fed them, bathed them, and put them to bed early."

"What happened today? It's all over your face, Annalee. It's one of your best features. You have a face that never lies or keeps secrets." He stepped closer to her, but didn't touch her. That lost and confused look on her face made him want to take her into his arms. "Something has happened to get you all tied up in knots. What is it?"

"Let's eat dinner, and I'll tell you about it." She brought the meat loaf out of the oven along with the biscuits and baked potatoes. She took the slaw from the refrigerator and they sat across from each other.

As he ate, she nibbled her food and tried to begin what she had to say. "I hardly know where to begin, but I visited Carol today. She's been hinting at something for months, and today she let me have it—right in my face." Annalee tightened her grip on her fork handle until her fingers cramped. "She let me know that my husband had been seeing her whenever they could manage it." Feeling a sense of betrayal and shame, she gasped for breath.

"Jack, Gerald is the father of the child she carries!"

"Oh, my God, Annalee! She told you that?"

"Yes. She had a note he'd written to her, trying for another of their cozy little get-togethers. I know his handwriting and the note had definitely been written by him."

Annalee choked up. Her throat was tight and she couldn't go on. Nor could she tell him what she'd told Carol. How glad she was to have been relieved of the evils of his assault on her own body those many nights. She didn't know how to say a thing like that.

Jack stayed in his seat, but he wanted to gather her in his arms and soothe away the hurt she'd endured. "What a day you've had, you poor, dear girl. How did you handle that?"

"I let her know I really didn't care. But no matter how you felt about your husband, hearing a thing like that is a stab in the back from someone you'd always thought of as a friend." Then she remembered what Mary had told her. "There's more. You won't believe this, but Mary saw Carol's car across the street from my home about five o'clock the morning of the fire." She tried to take a bite of food, but found she couldn't. "It's entirely possible she set my home on fire. And if she did, it was so I would have to go live with my folks in Arnott, and you would bring Sissy to *her* house every day." Annalee suppressed a smile. "She had her eyes set firmly on you, Jack, right from the beginning. But to burn my house down and likely kill us all—how could she do that?" She shuddered. "We barely made it out alive."

He couldn't wait any longer. He got up, came around the table to her, pulled Annalee from her chair, and folded her into his arms, close against his chest. "Sorry, dear, I can't help it. I need to hold you. I can't believe the tough day you've had. I want to help—you know that."

Annalee felt so good standing against this man who had never done anything but change her life into one of fullness and comfort. In the beginning it might have been for the benefit of his child, but the way she felt when he held her, she knew things had changed between them. Now, she also felt the need and the urgency of his touch. He needed and wanted her terribly.

For a man who sat at a desk all day, he had long, strong muscles, and they gave her the feeling of safety and comfort. But she also knew they had the power to overcome her and to take her to his bedroom. She tried to imagine how having sex with this man would be. She couldn't—and imagining the worst, she stiffened and drew away.

He didn't try to hold her close against him but let her move away. Annalee found she felt the loss of his warmth and strength when he let her go. And it *was* a loss. She never thought she would ever think a thing like that, but right now, she wanted back in his arms. Only fear kept her at arm's length.

Upstairs, she heard a cry. Not knowing or caring which child it had been, Annalee turned and ran up the stairs. Jack was right behind her, although she didn't realize it. Outside the girl's room, she heard the sobbing of a small girl and went in. It was Sarah.

Annalee slipped onto the bed and took the little girl in her arms. "There, there, Sarah, what's wrong?" She snapped on the little bedside lamp, held the little girl out before her, and looked into her face.

"Mommy, I 'fraid."

"What are you afraid of, Sarah?"

"Is my other daddy taked me?"

"No, Sarah, he can never do that." Annalee didn't want to say he was dead.

Sarah clung to her mother. "But, Mommy, he comes here. He tries to take me. I 'fraid."

Annalee looked up to see Jack standing in the doorway. "That man is not your daddy, Sarah," she told her daughter. "The only daddy you have now is this man." She pointed to Jack and held her daughter close. "Jack is your daddy, now. Do you believe me?"

Sarah nodded her head and looked up at Jack. "Are you my daddy now, and not that dark man that comes?"

Jack came into the room and knelt beside the bed. He took Sarah into his arms and held her a while. "I am your daddy from now on, little darling, and I will always be your daddy. No one else can have you."

"Pwomise?"

"Yes, I promise." He hugged her little body. "You are safe in this house. Are you ready to sleep now?"

"Ah-huh"

He laid her down beside Sissy, smoothed her dark hair, and pulled up her covers. Annalee turned out the light, and they left the room.

Out in the hall she turned to him. "Her own father would never have done that for her. No wonder she loves and trusts you."

Jack gave her a sardonic smile. "If only her mother felt that way." He took her into his arms, kissed her on her forehead, and let her go. "Good night, my dear." He walked to his own room and shut the door.

She stood in the hallway, alone and vulnerable. Jack had been kind enough to let her go, knowing she didn't want him as a lover. Feeling lost and disappointed, she wanted to cry her eyes out. Her friend had tried to kill her by fire, and today, she had learned Carol was carrying her dead husband's child. Could things be any worse than this?

Annalee went into her bedroom, closed the door, and threw herself on the bed. She was surrounded with good things, yet she felt empty and lost. She crawled into her bed and hugged her pillow, hoping for the oblivion of sleep.

❧❧❧

Awakened in early dawn to a quiet home, Annalee checked the children and found them asleep. Downstairs, she found Jack had gone and heaved a sigh of relief. His presence kept her in a state of tension and her nerves were stretched to the max because of it. And now, she turned to the next big hurdle coming up. She needed a suitable dress for the dinner-dance at the Twin Oaks Country Club. *No quiet life for you*, she told herself, while wondering how that evening was going to go. Was she up to being the wife of an important man?

She waited until after eight o'clock in the morning to call Amy. They arranged for a shopping trip to "the Rapids" as Amy called Wisconsin Rapids. She would know the right thing to wear. The children were having oatmeal and toast and jelly. Then she would get them dressed for shopping with Amy.

Right then Annalee wished for a neighbor girl who

could watch them for a while. Shopping would be so much more fun that way.

At a knock on the back door, she opened it to find Amy standing there along with young Marie and Amy's two girls. "Hey, An, how about we leave the kids with Marie for our shopping spree?"

Annalee knew it was the right thing and nodded. She welcomed Marie into the house, and the girl immediately took all the children upstairs.

"Well, girl, let's get going," Amy said. "We'll have to do some hefty shopping for the right thing, An. Dress, shoes, silk stockings, and a nice little purse. There's nothing worthwhile in this little berg for what you need."

"Oh Lord, how fancy *is* this dinner?" Annalee had butterflies in her stomach worrying and thinking about it. Her biggest concern was, as always, not embarrassing her husband. "Amy, I need to know what will happen while we are there, and what I should do when we go. I've never been to a country club, either. You know that."

"Don't worry, An, you're so beautiful, no one will notice if you use the wrong fork." Amy laughed as she edged Annalee toward her car, and they were soon on the road. "Let's just have a fun day and not worry about anything."

"It sounds good, but wait until I tell you what Carol has done." Annalee went into what Mary suspected about the house fire.

"My Lord, An! I wouldn't have believed anyone could be so vindictive. And of course it has to be your fault in her messed up mind, don't you imagine?"

"I know it is, she said as much. I'm sure she burned my house down so she could take care of Sissy. That's what I believe. And I understand now why she nearly bust a gut when I told her Jack and I were getting married." Annalee found she could smile about it now, but she felt truly sorry for anyone so alone and messed up in her head. She'd already felt pity for the forthcoming baby, Gerald's child.

"Hey, let's forget about everything," Amy suggested. "We are going to make you the beauty of the evening when we go to that fancy country club dinner."

Annalee was glad she had omitted telling Amy about Carol's affair. She hadn't been able to tell that to anyone except Jack.

Amy drove rapidly toward the larger city of Wisconsin Rapids and soon came to a very nice looking women's clothing store, Le Paree'. She pulled into a parking space in front. "I shop here if I need something special."

Annalee allowed herself to be led about like a teenager through the store. She tried on several dresses, most of them long. She'd never worn a dress like this. "Is this the kind of dress I need?"

"That's what I'm wearing. You want to look your best out on the dance floor, so maybe something a bit flared around the bottom." Amy lit upon a deep lavender dress, a long, slim cut, except for the flared skirt.

It fit nicely on top, leaving a good glimpse of cleavage. And it was simple in design, with trimmings of small, darker purple buds and tiny leaves embroidered around the neckline. It was sleeveless, which made Annalee gasp. "It's so bare!"

"Not really, An. It's by far the best thing you've tried on, don't you think?" Amy was excited and babbled on about how nice the dress looked.

Annalee thought so too, but she had a hard time imagining herself out in public wearing a gorgeous thing like that.

"Well, let's find some shoes to match, a light stole, and a small bag to carry." Amy went about as though buying a dress like that was an everyday thing, and Annalee followed suit.

She wasn't at all sure of herself in wearing it and only had Amy to guide her.

After pirouetting before the three-way mirror, she kept wondering how Jack would see her, wearing a dress so fine. She already knew that his opinion and how he felt about things meant more than she'd ever thought it could.

Chapter 19

Tonight was the night, and Amy had suggested that all the children should spend the night at her home. They would be cared for by Marie again. They liked her. Annalee's children had never spent a night at some else's place and were excited about it. For Sissy, it was nothing new, but very exciting for Annalee's two. Sarah had a tiny suitcase with her things in it, and so did Bucky. They looked forward to the fun.

With the children in good hands, Annalee had showered and dressed. Her make-up was nearly done when she heard the doorbell ring. She thought it might be Harold as he was due to leave for his home in Washington, DC tomorrow. She ran down the stairs, and opened the door. There stood her parents on the sheltered stoop.

"My goodness, Mom and Dad. Won't you come in?"

Annalee hadn't had any word from them since they'd sent notice they couldn't come to the wedding but, suddenly, here they were. Annalee looked down at her almost bare feet. She hadn't thought to put on her shoes yet, which were upstairs in her room.

She shrugged and ushered them in. She had gotten some very sheer silk stockings and had taken the time to be sure the seams were straight up the back. Of course, with a long dress on, who would ever know about straight seams, but just the same, she wanted even a mundane thing like that to be correct.

"Well, Annalee, I see you've gotten yourself pretty well fixed by the look of things." Not only was her father looking at the home around her, but at Annalee in her new dress. She thought his look was one of approval.

Her mother was looking, too. "Annalee! You aren't going out anywhere in that dress, are you?" She had a look of shock on her wrinkled features. "My goodness girl, your bare arms are showing. You look half-naked in that skimpy dress you have on!" She walked around Annalee and checked the back of the dress. "Good Lord almighty, my girl! Not only is it too low in front, half of your naked back is showing!"

Annalee stood solidly in front of them and looked at them both. "We are going to a very nice dinner-dance at the Twin Oaks Country Club tonight, Mom. I needed a dress and things to wear with it, and my friend Amy helped me find the right thing." She twirled about and let the bottom of the dress flow outward. She saw an approving look on her father's face, even a look of pride.

Her mother sniffed, her chin firm, her mouth in a hard straight line. "You look like a street-walking harlot in that dress, Annalee."

Annalee felt anger rising within her. She faced her mother, hands on hips. "When I was married before, I came to you for help. You turned your back on me while I suffered the fires of hell married to that miserable fiend, Gerald Lines. All I ever got from you was, 'You've made your bed and now you must lie in it.'" She squared her shoulders and straightened her back. "Well, now I am married to a wonderful man, and I guess I'll have to lie in this new bed that I have made for myself, too. If you can't see me this way, then I'm sorry for you," she said and added, "The children won't be here until tomorrow if you want to see them."

Her mother's face went pale, but her father had nothing to say, as usual. Although, Annalee had seen his look of approval and it warmed her inside.

Just then Jack appeared wearing a fine silk suit, his blond hair slicked back, and his handsome face tanned and clean-shaven. He walked up to her father and held out a hand. "I'm Jack Harrison, Annalee's husband."

The men shook hands and Annalee introduced her parents to Jack. Her mother's mouth gaped a bit at first, but she quickly pressed her lips tightly together in her usual expression of disapproval.

Jack waved them to a seat and sat down across from them. "Sorry you were unable to attend our wedding."

Her mother appeared to ignore Annalee's remarks about her needing their help in her previous marriage and made no reply about that. But she did remember about the fire. "We were sorry to hear about your home burning down. It must have been terrible for you."

"Yes, we barely made it out alive. We lost everything. I had considered coming home to stay with you folks until Jack asked me to marry him."

"Your daughter was the heroic one that night, sir,"

Jack said. "She saved herself and her children in the nick of time."

Annalee saw her parents were impressed with her new husband and, most certainly, her new home.

"How are the children doing and where are they?" her mother asked.

"They're visiting friends tonight. They are quite well, Mom, and very happy these days. They love Jack and go to him for everything. He has gotten Bucky a boy's bedroom set and more than replaced all his lost toys." Annalee didn't mention how they still harbored a fear of their real father. It was evident by the way they'd looked at his twin. They'd been terrified of him, at first, but she didn't bring that up.

"Could you come by tomorrow, then? We will have the children home by noon, I'm sure." Annalee hoped they would take that as a hint to leave. She could see they were getting a bit late, and she still had to go up and get her shoes and bag.

Her father saw they needed to leave. "We'll come by tomorrow then, Annalee."

She walked them to the door and, all the while, her parents looked around at her home and at her and how she was dressed.

As she closed the door, Jack looked at her. "You handled that well enough, my dear. You mean to tell me, you went to them about how your husband was treating you and they did nothing?"

"Not a thing, Jack." Annalee fought the sting of tears as she remembered those horrible days. "They wouldn't lift a finger," she continued. "Now my mother looks at me as though I'm dressed like a harlot. She even said that. She nearly lost her mind when she saw my bare arms showing. Their visit was not what I needed to bolster my confidence to face this evening."

"You don't need anything but me beside you to face this evening, my dear. You'll be the best-looking woman in the entire place, and I'll be the lucky bastard that's got you on my arm." He stepped toward her and took her into his arms. "Every man there will be wondering how I got so damned lucky." He hugged her close then let her go. "Ready?"

"Not until I go up and find my shoes."

Annalee scurried up the steps to her room, and put her new shoes with slim high heels on. She held out her silk-clad leg and thought it looked just fine. Forgotten were her mother's dire comments and the perplexed frown on her father's face, though Annalee happily remembered seeing his look of approval.

Her husband's loving words had taken care of any worries she'd had about this evening. She grabbed her wrap and the little beaded handbag, with a hankie and some lipstick in it, then ran carefully down the stairs in those heels.

Jack helped her into the car and they sped away to the Twin Oaks Country Club. Annalee kept wondering what a place like that was like, inside and out, but to avoid a display of her ignorance, she didn't ask Jack anything about it.

෭෨෭

They arrived and Jack handed the keys to a young man at the front entrance. She watched as the car was taken away. Everything tonight would be new to her, and she was excited to see it through. She clung to Jack's arm. He pressed her hand close to his body and smiled down to her as they entered.

The place was ablaze with electric lights, and there were crowds of people standing about, some in smaller groups, chatting to each other. Annalee sought Amy and Derrick, but had yet to see them. Jack stopped and Annalee saw him shake hands with a tall, gray-haired man. Jack nudged her forward. "Delbert, I'd like you to meet my wife. Annalee, meet Delbert Black, our area supervisor for electrification for the Central Wisconsin Area."

The man bent his blue eyes on her and nodded. "I'm mighty pleased, ma'am."

Annalee gave a slight nod of her head. "And I am pleased to meet you, Mr. Black."

They moved on and she was introduced several times as they made their way to their designated table. There, she found Amy and Derrick, already seated. Annalee welcomed the warmth and comfort of seeing their familiar faces. They were unbelievably welcome to her in this sea of strangers. She took a seat next to Amy.

The table held eight so she would be meeting several more strangers. "I'm so glad to see you," she whispered to Amy. "I've already met more people than I'll ever remember."

"It's always like this at one of these regional meetings. There are lots of big wigs here tonight." Amy appeared completely at ease in these surroundings, and Annalee envied her.

"You look marvelous, Annalee," Derrick told her." His eyes held a look of approval, which helped her believe his words. "They have a great band set for tonight, and I'd love a dance with you if Jack will let you go for a round or two."

At that, she felt panic moving in. When had she danced last? She couldn't even remember.

"I'll let you know, Derrick, if you can have a turn around the floor with my lovely wife," Jack said. "If you do, I may have to claim Amy then."

He laughed and Annalee saw his head tilt back, displaying his muscular throat again. Her husband was all man. Slick and fancy he might be, but she knew the power behind those long, smooth muscles. She had caught glimpses of him with his shirt off a time or two. Remembering how he looked, she felt a slow, heated sensation slipping deep down inside her body and wondered...

Four more people joined them. Another couple and, to her surprise, Harold Lines took a seat opposite her. Another single man sat beside him. Introductions were made and dinner was announced.

In short order, waiters rushed forth with huge trays and, within moments, each table of eight was served with a salad, already dressed. They already had water in glasses with melting ice cubes floating in them.

Annalee looked at Harold in surprise. "I didn't know you would be here tonight."

"Neither did I, but since the topic of discussion tonight is in my area of interest, I was invited. You look absolutely lovely tonight, my dear."

She nodded her thanks and, smiling at Jack, nibbled at her salad. "This is delicious," she said to Amy. "I wonder what they put on it."

"I think it's a new Hollandaise or something. They

do try to keep up with what's new and fashionable these days. Amy smiled at her. "You are doing just fine, An. I'm terribly proud of you, and so is Jack."

Annalee ate little, but she enjoyed the delicate slivers of chicken served with a fine, creamy mashed-potato cup and freshly creamed baby peas. After the tiny dessert that followed, waiters removed dishes, refilled coffee cups and water glasses. Then the room was darkened slightly.

A man came to the podium and made a few announcements. There were to be several speakers. Annalee had scare understanding of what they spoke about and paid little attention, but her head snapped up when Jack rose from his seat to walk up and take the microphone.

Looking his handsome best, he casually launched into a speech discussing how rural electrification was slowly advancing. He promoted it as the wave of the future, for Wisconsin dairy farmers in particular, and outlined the benefits it would bring to them. He laid out enough facts and figures to confuse anyone, especially her. Her heart swelled with pride that the tall, polished man at the podium was her husband. Right now, Annalee could hardly believe she was married to a man like that. By the time he returned to the table, she was shaking like a leaf.

"You were wonderful up there, Jack," she told him.

The music began after the speeches, and Jack rose to stand beside her and hold out his hand. "Care to dance, my lovely Mrs. Harrison?"

His eyes narrowed as he said it, and she felt a thrill clear down to her toes. As though she were in a trance, she rose to take his hand. The soft strains of "Begin the Beguine" filled the room. Annalee had heard it on the radio many times and loved the song.

"I haven't danced since high school," she said as she slipped into his arms.

He smiled down at her. "Just yesterday, then."

His gray eyes seemed much darker, somehow, as he swept her away. He was strong and his arm held her close as he led her along to the music. He was easy to follow and she let herself go. Tonight was so unreal to her she couldn't believe this was happening. But it was, and all of it due to the man who held her so closely in his arms. She felt a rush of warmth toward him and wondered. *Am I falling in love with this man—my husband?*

She felt the sting of tears, but wasn't giving in to emotions like that, not now when she felt so wonderful. Glowing inside, Annalee was on top of the world as she laid her head on his chest and moved across the floor in his arms. Jack put his head down close to hers. "You are as graceful as you are beautiful, my wife."

As the song ended, he bent her in a deep dip that made her gasp and cling to him. Then he led her off the floor.

"Oh, Jack, that was wonderful!" she cried as she took her seat.

"Yes it was." He smiled into her eyes. "Shall I order you something to drink, Annalee?"

"Yes, I could use a drink."

She might have meant water, but he ordered something from a passing waiter. Soon a frosty glass was placed before her, with a bit of orange peel shredded on the top.

She sipped it. "It's nice Jack. What is it?"

"I believe it's called a Hanky-Panky. Rather mild if a person isn't used to spirits."

He smiled into her eyes in that way he had, and those sneaky, heated sensations went zinging through her all over again.

Right then, Amy and Derrick returned to the table as their dance had ended. Amy flopped down. "Whew, I think that was a Tango or something close to it. It was too much for me, Derrick." She wiped her brow and turned to Annalee. "How was *your* dance? And by the way, you looked wonderful out there. That Jack is a devil on the dance floor, isn't he?"

"Yes, he's very good. I hadn't danced for several years, and it didn't seem to matter at all."

Annalee took another sip of her drink and felt it burn all the way down. She found it delicious, however, and took another sip. She wondered what was in it to be called such a naughty name. She also smiled, wondering what dire, foreboding things her mother would say if she knew her daughter was out with sinful people, tasting the evils of alcoholic spirits.

Annalee danced with Harold next. She had the feeling she was dancing with Gerald, until he smiled down at her. "Annalee, I'll be heading back to DC in the morning," he said. "I want to thank you for giving me a chance to get to know my brother's children."

The scent of him gave her a haunting reminder or two, but his fine look and gentle touch tempered any feelings of aversion his similarity to Gerald might have caused her. He was a good dancer as well, but not as good as Jack.

"It was good to get to know you, Harold. It startled me at first, but Jack and I have a high regard for you. Please feel free to visit us anytime and bring your wife."

She uttered a giggle. "Maybe Sarah will let you pick her up by then."

"How lovely of you, my dear." He grew serious as he told her, "Gerald was an ignorant fool, Annalee. I'll always believe that."

After he returned her to her table, she saw no more of him and decided he'd left. Annalee danced with Jack again as the band played, "You Made Me Love You." It was slow, so smooth, and very romantic.

He held her very close against his broad chest, his head down near her cheek. "You did, you know, Annalee," he whispered in her ear. "You know you did, don't you?"

"What are you saying, Jack?" She buried her face in his shoulder, he smelled so good. "What did I do?"

"Just like this song says, my dearest girl. You've made me love you. I can't help how I feel. I never expected it and I never thought—" He kissed her cheek and pressed her closer as he swung her slowly around the dance floor.

Right now, Annalee felt as though they were the only two people in the universe, and her heart raced double time. She'd heard what he said. He'd had a few drinks, but not that many.

He meant it and she knew it. He was the best man she'd ever known, and if he wanted her, what could she do? Yes, they'd made a promise to each other, but she knew it no longer meant anything to him—not any more.

She wasn't sure herself what it meant to her now either. She was his wife and knew she would never turn him away again, not ever.

What would happen when they got home? No children to cry out in the night. It would be just the two of them.

Alone.

Jack had let her know how he felt and what he wanted of her. She trusted him and, remembering what Mary had been so sure of, Annalee wondered whether it could be something wonderful.

Chapter 20

Annalee sipped her drink. It had been renewed. Had he ordered her another? She felt like giggling right now and knew she wasn't really being herself, feeling silly that way. She tried to get a grip on her emotions, but she was soon in her husband's arms again for another gentle tune. "Night and Day," so smooth and haunting, had her thoughts in a whirl. Jack's lips came ever closer to hers as they moved together across the gleaming hardwood dance floor. He crooned softly into her ear, "Night and day, you are the one, and you are my darling, gentle, loving wife, aren't you?"

"What are you doing to me, Jack?"

She tried to be accusing with those words, but it wasn't working. He was so different tonight. Feeling slightly dizzy, she clung to him as they moved. His every touch thrilled her through and through, until she floated about the dance floor in a soft glow from head to toe.

He brought her back to their table, but before she sat

down, he whispered softly in her ear, "I think it's time we called it a night, my dear, don't you?"

He helped her into her thin, silky wrap—the one Amy had said she had to have—and they said their good nights. The crowd was thinning as they left the dance floor. Jack had ordered the car brought around. He ushered her into her seat, and they drove away.

Annalee sighed. She felt so dreamy. She curled up and put her head against Jack's shoulder as he drove. "It was a nice night, wasn't it, Jack?"

"Yes, my darling, lovely wife. You were the most beautiful lady at the ball tonight. I heard it said from quite a few. I was the lucky man who had you on his arm tonight and proud of you—all the way. You're a fine dancer, too. Another thing I'd never given thought to. You never stop surprising me, do you?"

She'd heard him call her "my darling, lovely wife" but, instead of alarm at his deeper meaning, she only felt a warm surge of happiness because of it. "I feel sort of dizzy, Jack. Do you think it's the drinks I had?"

"Maybe some of it was. But I believe there's something else making you dizzy, too. When we get to the house, we'll explore that a bit more."

"What are you saying? What else could it be?"

He didn't answer. "Here we are, home at last." He stopped, got out, and came around for her. Helping her out of the car, he held her close for a deep, lingering kiss and then led her in through the side door. "It's good to be home, isn't it, my wife?"

His voice was soft as feathers, and she felt the deep, velvet sound of it running all through her body. She couldn't stop the giggle that escaped. "I feel so good right now, Jack. I don't know what it is. You are quite a wonderful man. You know that?"

He caught her into his arms, brought her close, kissed her lips, and pressed ever so gently to make her open for him. She felt his tongue urging, but for some reason, she didn't feel afraid anymore. His thick, dark-blond hair and deep gray eyes seemed to mesmerize her.

Jack had become a wonder to her, and never more than right now. She felt herself slowly giving way to him and what he wanted of her. She had no further doubt of it, but she no longer felt the fear of what might happen. She had learned to trust this man—enough that the heated sensations burning inside her, those thrilling sensations he made her feel, no longer filled her with fear.

Annalee knew Jack would take over her body tonight and do those things she had learned to fear with good reason. But she felt so good right now she couldn't believe he would hurt her. Her knees were so wobbly, they were about to give way, as he gently explored the depths of her mouth. He drew her closer yet and stroked her back, kissed her neck, her eyes, all about her until his seeking mouth went deeper into her neckline, seeking the soft rounds of her breasts.

She struggled against him then, and he stopped. Holding her close against his body for a long moment, he whispered softly into her ear, "It'll be all right my darling wife. It'll be all right."

Nothing could have prepared her for what she'd found with this fine man. After the dinner-dance, she had planned to accommodate him in the bedroom, no matter how disgusting it would be. She wanted to give him that in return for all he'd done for her.

They were in the kitchen, a place familiar to her now, but she knew she needed to get up those steps and into her room. A place where she would feel safe from Jack's powerful male body and those intimate things she knew he was capable of doing to her. Yet, he felt so good against her, she couldn't run. How could she pull herself away from his warmth, strength, and that lovely glow he'd set softly burning within her? No, she couldn't leave the wonderful way his body felt against hers.

Something inside her cried out for what he had to give her. His masculine scent led her on, heating something deep inside of her. His strength gave her comfort, and his kisses had set her body on fire. She knew she was heading into an area so terribly familiar, something she had feared for so long, but, somehow, she didn't feel the same. Nothing was the same with this man.

She felt no feelings of disgust and fear, or the urge to fight him. Her strength had weakened, until she swayed. His arms swept her up and held her tight against his long, hard body.

Holding her close and softly crooning into her ear, he started up the stairs. Realizing what was happening, she stiffened in his arms.

He held her firm and kissed her deeply, as he reassured her once again. "It'll be all right, my darling, girl. Yes, it'll be all right."

Annalee remembered what Mary had tried to tell her. Jack had nearly repeated the same words, '*It'll be all right*' and in just the same soft way Mary had said it. Knowing what lay ahead, Annalee's heart hammered in her chest as he carried her. She felt the slight twist as he opened the door to a room she'd only peeked into. Now, she had entered that mysterious male place where Jack stayed and slept without her at his side, all those long lonely nights. The wide bed, where he laid his long male body down, where he slept, undressed, and waited for her to come and lay beside him. He gently laid her body down and soothed her as he began to remove his clothing.

Annalee heard his belt buckle click as it came loose. She'd heard that before, too, and it struck a pang of fear through her. But she couldn't move or try to escape. She was on fire now with those deep, insistent flames of need burning inside her that only he could extinguish. Somehow, she knew it had to do with him and the way he was with her. Things had never been like this before.

She felt him lay down beside her. His body pressed the mattress down to accommodate his larger weight. He held her against himself, kissed her ever deeper. His hands caressed her back, her hair, and went on to seek those other places she had feared. But, somehow, it was not the same, and she began to respond. Then his hands sought the slide fastener that held her dress together down the back.

She felt the cool air as he slipped her dress down her body. He pressed her against his chest as he slowly and carefully removed her underclothes. She shivered a bit, and he comforted her. He stroked her now in forbidden places that made her fires burn ever hotter.

Turning her to face him, he looked into her eyes. "Annalee, I have waited an eternity for this moment."

"Oh, Jack!" she cried.

No longer afraid, she reached for him, faced him, and began to return his kisses in ways she'd never imagined possible.

Had she become a wanton? She had a momentary, passing thought about that until she remembered she was married to this man who wanted her, body and soul. She was his, to do with as he wished. And he was hers.

His hands gently explored places she couldn't believe and soon she felt she would die if he didn't complete what he'd begun. She was ready to beg, but he took care of that, too, as he moved between her slender legs and took possession of all she was or ever would be.

Then momentarily lying quiet and still, he whispered, "Darling, are you all right?"

He didn't wait for an answer but began to move slowly, deeply, within her to an ancient rhythm as old as mankind. In surprise, she found there was no pain. She felt no shame. There was nothing to degrade her soul or to fear, and it seemed rather more like a sort of worship of each other.

Leaving all thought behind, she joyously joined him as he brought her to magical heights she'd had no idea existed. Annalee had never known anything like this being possible between a man and woman as he slowly brought her to the place that sent her cries of passion echoing through the dark, silent home.

The night went on for them, until all her barriers had been removed. Jack loved her, stroked her, and cuddled her in his arms. As the dawn came up, he looked into her eyes.

She blushed deeply but met his look. "Jack, I didn't know it could be this way." She giggled. "I never imagined this business could make you feel like you were out of your mind at times. Is that normal?"

"It's better than normal, dear. It's a kind of magic

some people are lucky to find, and not everyone does," he said to his blushing wife. "I don't think this lovely passion we have between us happens to people that much, Annalee. It could be that you and I have something very special, in spite of the strange way we started out."

He pulled her to his chest and kissed her over her face, neck, and lovely full breasts. "So how are we doing with our premarital deal, my dearest wonderful darling?" He laughed. "I admit it. I knew from that kiss at the altar that I wouldn't be able to keep my solemn promise to never try to get you where you are right now—in my bed."

"You are a naughty devil, Jack, and a handsome, fine one at that." Annalee looked at her husband. This stranger had come into her life almost by accident, yet here he was. She realized she was not only married to him, but in love with him, too. "I love you, Jack Harrison, completely," she murmured. "I think I am a very lucky woman, sir." She kissed him soundly. "I know now that I have never been in love, or ever loved before. Not even close." She kissed him again and jumped out of bed. "I need a bath and those kids will be showing up sometime today, or do we go get them?"

She giggled all the way to the bathroom, and Jack was right behind her. "Need some company in there?"

જીજીજી

Carol sat in her living room, feeling frustrated, defeated, and mad as hell. She had shown that damning note to Annalee, wanting to make her suffer. Annalee had stepped right in and stolen the man she'd wanted. Carol had long felt the need to let that goody-two-shoes know that she, Carol Woods, was way more woman than Annalee had ever been.

Gerald had come to Carol to satisfy his needs, and she had wanted to let Annalee know that. But thinking back, nothing she'd done had turned out right. Annalee had told Carol she knew it was her that had burned her home down, nearly killing her and her children. But though it had been done it in the heat of passion, Carol had to face the fact that she was guilty as hell. "I could go to prison for a thing like that if she ever tells on me."

Yes, she had done a terrible thing, but Carol didn't want to think about it right now, not when she as she was suffering so much. Life just wasn't fair. None of her plans had worked out. Yes, she had totally enjoyed her romps with Gerald. But now he was gone, and she was left carrying a dead man's child. With Donald dead, too, mostly because of finding that damnable note, she had no one to help her with this pregnancy.

She wondered if she would ever hear from her brother, Henry. She had written him, ages ago it seemed. "He doesn't give a damn about me either." She cried bitter tears as she realized another faint hope had become a dismal failure. Nothing had turned out right.

She'd stopped to look in her bedroom mirror this morning. She usually avoided seeing how she looked, feeling disfigured and swollen. Being pregnant like this was not her idea of having fun. But this morning, seeing her image staring back at her, she'd gotten the shock of her life. "Oh, my dear God in Heaven, this can't be me. I look like an elephant!"

She had finally gotten a real picture of herself, and it

shook her to the core. She was no longer the clever little blonde with those sparkling blue eyes that men just loved. Right now, she saw a fat, disfigured, bloated woman with swollen feet. And today, she noticed with a touch of alarm, her hands had become swollen as well. Her lips and nose looked puffy, too.

The doctor had cautioned Carol about her rising blood pressure. He'd warned her against salt and, because of his incessant nagging, she couldn't even have that anymore. And this morning, even her face was grossly disfigured with the extra water she had retained. "If I could just go to the toilet more often, it would all go away, wouldn't it?"

Should she worry about this, or let the doctor do it? That's what she paid him for, useless clod that he was. What a woman really needed at a time like this was the man who had fathered her child.

No other man would look fondly upon her as she was now, but she knew Gerald would. She was having his child and she knew he would love her all the more for that. Now her Donald was dead, along with Gerald. Gerald had been married, but Carol had never let that fact bother her, nor had she cared about it being wrong. He had wanted her, had left his wife at home and come to her to satisfy his needs. She was very proud of that. He had wanted her more than that insipid little ninny Annalee.

Now even that had been taken from her. Carol felt the tears flow as she held her middle the best she could. She was alone and lost. Sometimes, she wanted to curse the child she carried, although she knew it wasn't right. She missed Annalee's friendship now, too, which only added to her isolation.

"If only I could call her. Goody-two-shoes or not, I wish I could. I'm so alone." Carol slumped into a chair in her living room. Her mind was in a whirl. "What can I do? I have to make things right between us. Could she ever forgive me? She's a big time church goer and they're supposed to forgive, aren't they?"

She decided she would give Annalee a call, but not today. It was Sunday and Jack would be home. Maybe Annalee didn't need church anymore. Maybe she only needed to be home with her good-looking man and that bunch of brats she was so proud of. On the other hand, she might have gone to church this morning.

Carol felt a spurt of excitement. If she could meet Annalee face to face in a crowd, she might get her into a conversation where she could mend some fences. Carol felt more excitement than she had for days. "It's only nine in the morning. Maybe I will attend that cruddy little Baptist Church she loves so well."

It was nearing eleven in the morning by the time Carol got herself ready for the church service. "I guess I can stand to hear about burning in Hell another time or two," she sniffed as she drove the few blocks to the small white church.

"It's good the pastor doesn't know much about me or he'd be looking right at me with his burning in Hell stories." She giggled as she remembered some of her more delicious sins and found talking to herself very helpful.

It seemed to help a lot with the loneliness.

She looked about for Jack's nice Oldsmobile, but didn't see it sitting around anywhere. "Has she gone to the other side of town to that fancy, uppity Presbyterian Church now that she's married to Jack?"

Carol wondered if that preacher harangued on and on about burning in Hell. But she decided he would have to try a different method with the fancier crowd that went there. "Annalee would be out of place in that church." It pleased Carol to think that way about her ex-friend.

Carol knew her ex-friend had stepped out of familiar territory, married to that fancy-assed engineer. "Like going to the Twin Oaks Country Club to a fancy-dancy dinner-dance, like she bragged about right to my face." Carol felt herself getting angry again. Her heart raced, thinking of how she'd been treated by all of them.

Not seeing Jack's fancy Oldsmobile that Annalee drove about in these days at the Baptist Church, Carol decided to drive past the small boarding house, The Village Green Rooms, where that good-looking Harold Lines was staying. As she drove slowly past, she saw no sign of a fancy vehicle that had DC plates and said *Phaeton* on the side. "He's probably over to Annalee's, playing with Gerald's kids again."

Disgusted, Carol headed back to her house. Even today, nothing had gone right. The baby kicked so hard, she gasped for breath and clung to the wheel as she pulled into her drive. "Oh, God, will this child ever be born so I can get this load off me?"

She gasped the words as she dragged herself out of the car and headed into the house. Getting up the steps was becoming a problem for her these days. And she worried about the spot of blood left on the seat where she'd been sitting.

Chapter 21

It was Sunday morning and, somehow, after the long night of passion spent in her husband's arms, Annalee had not found the energy to attend church services. Her parents were due to come and see the children, and they would be along soon. Her mother would view her lazy Sunday morning in the worst possible light. Annalee expected words of censure and another lecture about her sin of omission on this Sabbath morning.

Last evening, after a wonderful night at the country club, and with the house so empty and the children gone, Annalee had spent a surprisingly wonderful night as a real wife to Jack. The long hours in his arms had almost completely erased the cruel memories of her first husband. Jack had proved to be a fine and able lover and, still in the throes of her heated memories of last night, she walked about in a mellow glow this morning.

She couldn't get herself to do much more than dream as she went about half-doing her work in the kitchen. Still in a state of disbelief, Annalee stood looking at Jack as he sat in the living room reading the Sunday paper.

She kept going over in her mind all that taken place last night. The dinner-dance at the Twin Oaks Country Club had been a wonderful experience. She'd met new people while wearing a daring and lovely new dress. But, best of all, she remembered swaying to that lovely music in her husband's arms, while he whispered lovely things in her ears. Never in her life had she experienced anything as fine as that.

She felt like a whole new person this morning while her new husband sat in the living room reading the Sunday paper the same as every other Sunday morning. He looked so quiet and calm, but she remembered so well the quiet, yet subtle power of him. His body had a devastating strength and the memories held her in a soft glow, still completely amazed at the gentle way he'd taken her. Over and over, she thought about how she'd trembled at his touch. How easily he'd driven her wild with need. Then the careful way he'd sent her over the edge into unbelievable heights of ecstasy as he'd taken care of that and everything else in an unbelievably lovely way.

She had never known or even guessed about those wild sensations and the way he'd made her feel. Married to Gerald, she had never experienced anything remotely like that. But remembering those friendly words of encouragement from a woman who'd enjoyed a long and happy marriage, Annalee decided that Mary must have known all about these things. If not, she could never have given Annalee the sort of advice she had.

Her advice had been little more than hints and mere suggestions about such things. Annalee wasn't sure it was possible to describe wild sensations like that to anyone and Mary, that shy, modest woman, had gone out on a limb with the little she had tried to say.

Annalee shivered inside remembering how it had come about after they'd gotten home. He'd calmed her fears, gentled her, and had finally changed her way of thinking about those lovely, intimate things that could happen between a man and a woman.

Feeling as she did right now, nothing in the world could bother Annalee today. If God had made man and woman to be together and created those marvelous feelings, who could argue with it? And that included her parents.

Annalee heard Amy's car pull into the drive. The children were home, and just in time. Her parents were coming, and Annalee expected them to arrive fairly soon. She had made some sandwiches and planned to have them stay for lunch.

Amy brought all three of Annalee's children inside. They were happy to be home and, after kissing her, they ran to Jack as a group. Her children had fully accepted him as their new father. He and Bucky were the men of the family now, and Annalee loved the growing male camaraderie she had seen between them. She had long believed that a boy needed a good man around to grow up properly, and so did a girl.

That ended his reading the paper. But soon, she heard him reading aloud. She looked in to see the three children close around him, Bucky sitting on the arm of the chair and both girls in Jack's lap, their heads against his chest. He held out the funnies as he read about Buck Rogers, Major Hoople, and Mandrake the Magician.

Annalee figured they had no real idea about those characters, but they did enjoy being held in his arms and being read to by a deep, soft, masculine voice. She imagined the girls felt it rumbling in his chest. How well she remembered hearing that comforting sound herself.

Annalee smiled at the sight and loved him all over again. What they might have understood, she had no idea, but they quietly listened to his reading.

She thrilled again at the sound of his soft, deep voice. Her children had never known that closeness with a father before, and she blessed Jack all over again for his kindness.

The doorbell rang just then and, not wanting to disturb Jack from his reading, she hurried to answer. It would be her parents, and she felt her pulse race because of it. Her mother had always managed to find fault with her, no matter how hard Annalee might try. Her father just went along with her mother, as though he had no opinions of his own and not a lot of backbone either.

Annalee opened the door to them. "Hi, Mom and Dad. Come in and have a seat." She waved toward the long couch across from Jack and the three kids sitting with him. "The children are home now."

Her parents came in and sat down. Jack lifted the girls off his lap, rose to shake her father's hand, and nodded to her mother. "Please, make yourselves at home," he offered.

The three children stood, quietly staring at the new people in the room.

"Bucky, why not shake hands with your grandfather?" Annalee said.

The boy gravely walked up and shook his grandfather's hand without seeming to notice his grandmother. "Hello, Grandfather."

He said it without any sign of joy in his eyes or voice. Sarah just stood there, staring at them. Annalee noticed she had her thumb in her mouth again.

"My, how they've grown since the death of their father," her mother said. She made no move to go to them or hold them in her arms. She merely sat in her seat and looked at them. "I can certainly see their father in their coloring." She kept referring to their dead father, a subject that added to Annalee's consternation.

She needed no reminders of Gerald and found her mother's continual references objectionable and almost painful. "I hope that's all you'll ever see of him in them," Annalee said quietly. She couldn't help saying those words. It was how she felt. She hoped and prayed continually never to see anything of Gerald in her two children. Then she asked her mother, hoping to change the subject, "How have you been? We were sorry to hear your car was broken down for our wedding." Her mother made no reply but seemed rather edgy and uncomfortable. To break the tension in the room, Annalee asked, "Would you like to see the rest of the house and their rooms upstairs?"

Her mother nodded. Annalee led her to the stairway and they went up. At the top, her mother turned to her. "We went to that little Baptist Church this morning. I noticed you weren't there. Why weren't you? These children should be in Sunday school every Sunday. Are you planning to raise a bunch of heathens, now that you're living so high and mighty?"

"I try to go each Sunday, but I just couldn't this

morning. The children weren't here either." Annalee led her mother to Bucky's room, hoping she would be pleased for the boy. "Look what Jack has done for my son, Mom. He is the best man I've ever known, and the best husband, too"

"Yes, I see how kind he is, all right," she huffed. "It looks to me like Buckley is being spoiled rotten and you're allowing it, Annalee," she ranted on further. "And I must say, I am very worried about the way you are living now. It doesn't seem right, somehow, you getting married so soon with your husband just dead and barely in his grave."

Annalee felt her fury rise. "Well, it was a choice I had to make, Mom. It was marry Jack or come and live with you. I chose the lesser of the two evils, if you will forgive me for saying that. Finding a decent man, who will take care of me and my children, has been the best break I've ever had in my entire life." She glared at her mother. "I don't know how it happened exactly, but I believe right now, I am the luckiest woman in the world, despite what you may have to say about it." She couldn't stop saying what had burned on her mind for so long. "I confess, I do not understand the why of it, but I'm very sorry you can't find it in your heart to be happy for me."

She watched her mother shrink before her eyes and felt pity for her, but Annalee was finally saying what she had held in for too long a time. "If you can't handle the truth of that, I feel very sorry for you. Forgive me for being an evil, wayward, no good daughter, but when I needed help from you, I got the cold shoulder. I got nothing from you. You had no pity or help for me when I was married to that monster, Gerald Lines, a man who beat me and cheated on me. Even his children were terrified of him. And now you have nothing good to say about my life when I'm married to the best man I've ever known."

"Well, if that's the way you feel after all we've done for you, I guess we'll be heading back to Arnott where we belong."

Annalee saw a tear gleaming in her mother's eye and felt terrible about it. She believed she'd had the right to say what she had. And along with that, she wracked her brain trying to figure out what all they *had* done for her. "I wonder. Do you remember that I had no wedding dress for my first marriage? You said it was too much to pay for silly nonsense like that," Annalee said, reminding her mother of another thing that had hurt her so much in the past. Her mother turned to head down the stairway, and Annalee asked, "Didn't you want to see Sarah's room?" There was no furniture in it yet, but she had to say it, anyway.

"I think I've seen enough for today, Annalee. May God forgive you for the terrible things you have said to your poor, old, mother." She kept on going down. When she got to the living room, she beckoned to her husband and, with her head held high, she and Annalee's father walked out the door.

Jack looked up from where he sat with the children, reading to them again. "That didn't go so well, did it?" He studied her with his deep gray eyes in that way he had. "I heard the two of you up there, darling. I guess you had a few things to get off your mind."

Annalee nodded. She wanted to cry her eyes out in shame, but she felt it had been warranted. Her parents had never been happy for her unless she was suffering the tortures of the damned, as in her first marriage. It hurt her to think of her folks that way, but what other way was there?

Then she looked at her children, all three of them happily sitting in their daddy's arms, enjoying his low soft voice and the feel of his strong arms around them. In spite of the sorrow over her parents, she felt more blessed and far happier than she had been in her entire life. And she owed it all to that handsome man sitting with the children.

He loves me! He'd said it over and over last night in her arms. She couldn't remember Gerald ever saying that to her. Right now, she wanted to take Jack in her arms and let him do whatever he wanted. She was filled with eagerness to explore further those fantastic sensations that Jack made her feel. But she would have to wait for the dark of night when the little ones were asleep. The way she felt toward Jack right now, it would be a long wait.

Annalee wouldn't have believed how it could be with her husband last night, in spite of what Mary had said, but she believed it now. Jack hadn't hurt her, but rather with patience and gentleness he'd slowly made that union between man and woman a blessed, wondrous thing. If these things were truly as God had intended, she wondered about her parents. By the sour outlook she'd seen in her mother, she believed they had missed out on one of the finest blessings life had to offer. Annalee had nothing but pity for them.

She found herself frequently looking at Jack, as he read the papers to himself, played with the children, or read to them. A time or two he caught her lingering gaze and returned a sly smile, filled with intent for later on, when the children were sleeping.

A sight like that had once chilled her through and through. But now, his look, so full of meaning, filled her with a sense of thrilling needs. He only had to lift an eyebrow to make her blush like a young girl.

Still in a state of disbelief, her heart was so full right now she wished she could share it with someone. With Jack, she could speak freely and already had. That was a new thing for her, too, knowing he remained her friend, no matter what.

Annalee's thoughts led to Mary. Annalee planned to see her in a day or two. She longed to thank her for her wise advice and understanding and to let her know Annalee had finally learned to no longer fear the marriage bed.

She went to Jack. "I think I really need to do some serious shopping for Sarah. She loves to sleep with Cecelia, but a girl needs her own space."

"Of course, you are right, my dear." He said the words in the way that sent her heart pounding in her chest. The children had gone up stairs, and he reached out to pull her across her lap. "My God in Heaven, An, if you aren't something." He kissed her near to death and had her in a burning heat within moments. "I don't think I'll ever get enough of you. I don't see how I ever could."

Annalee giggled. "I know my mother believes I am going straight to Hell for living in your lovely home. We had an argument about it, Jack"

"I heard something of it while you were up there. Will you be able to make it up with them later on?"

"I don't know. It seems my mother believes you

have to be tortured and half-starved to find your way to Heaven." She kissed him slowly. "I think I have found my way there already, Jack." She giggled a bit more. "You are one handsome devil, Mr. Harrison. I had no idea that something like this would ever happen to me." She laid her head on his chest. "I still can't believe it, Jack."

"Oh, my darling girl, there is so much more to come. Just you wait until the coast is clear." He punctuated his words with deep passionate kisses that went all the way to her toes. His mouth had the power to turn her mind and body into mush. "You will sleep in my room tonight, then?"

She felt her face burn as she nodded in agreement. "If I can wait that long."

She struggled to get off his lap but he wouldn't let her go.

෨෨෨

Derrick and Amy came for a short visit. They were headed for a long drive in the county with their children, a popular activity for a Sunday afternoon.

Seeing how it was with the newlyweds, they made their visit short.

The day wore on. Annalee made supper of fried potatoes, slices of ham, and a slaw. Inside, her nerves were on edge. How would he be tonight when the house was quiet and the little ones asleep? She'd waited all day for this hour with trembling fear, and eagerness combined. She had gained a lot of trust in her new husband because of how he had been last night and she would never have believed herself taking part so willingly. She imagined how her mother would view such goings on and blushed while standing at the kitchen sink, wiping dishes.

But how would he be tonight? Those memories of earlier days lingered in her mind. She shivered as she recalled the roughness, coldness, and almost hate, with which Gerald had taken her. She recalled feeling mauled and injured in heart and mind. The dirty bastard had laughed at her while he did those things. She had come to believe he had wanted her brought down low for some unknown reason of his own. She wondered. *How can I rid myself of these dreadful fearful thoughts? Will these memories of a man's way of inflicting pain and degradation on a woman he'd sworn to love ever go away?*

She went up to check on the babies, for no matter how masterful Bucky was, he was still a very little boy to her, just past his babyhood. They were asleep, tired out from a busy day of playing. She smiled as she remembered hearing Jack read the funnies to them aloud in his soft, low voice.

As she turned from looking in on Bucky, she met Jack face to face. She felt her heart race as she looked into his eyes. She saw nothing predatory there, only the warm glow of his desire.

"Jack," she gasped as he took her gently in his arms.

His seeking lips claimed hers for a long moment. "An, I have thought of this moment all day." He held her close against his chest. "I honestly was not in love with you when we married. I had the utmost respect for the woman I knew you to be. I believe you know that. But now things are so different I can scarcely grasp the meaning of it. I planned to honor our arrangement, I truly did."

He chuckled softly. "It was that kiss at the altar that set me off. Annalee, you have charmed and bewitched me until I am nearly out of my mind. I have to watch myself at work these days." He grasped her for another deep, lingering kiss. "I am hopelessly in love with you, woman."

She went willingly into his heated embrace and met him fully. "Jack, I never imagined I would ever be able to speak or feel like this about..." She still couldn't say the words. "I didn't know these marvelous sensations even existed."

She returned his kisses with all she had to give and felt him sweep her up into his arms. She knew where he was headed and no longer worried about what he would do to her there. She wanted everything he had to give her and let herself go, body and soul.

Chapter 22

Annalee awakened to the feel of the soft, aching sensations of a body well used in the acts of love. She leisurely stretched her arms in the air, feeling softened, and somehow, completely fulfilled as a woman. Jack had gone to work, and she was ready this morning to finally go out and find something for Sarah's room.

Happy now that she had the means to get those things she needed without worry, Annalee lay there for a moment, imagining the pleasure of decorating a little girl's frilly bedroom. She wanted wallpaper, bedding, pictures, and maybe a small lamp at the bedside, all in colors and patterns to delight a little girl. Those were things she'd never had, but that she wanted for Sarah. Sissy already had them.

Annalee piled the little ones on the back seat of Jack's nice Oldsmobile sedan and drove about the small village until she spotted a small, neat-looking furniture store, The Furniture Mart. She'd never had the occasion to visit a store of this kind before and had no idea if it contained what she was looking for.

They went in, and she told the man who met her inside what she was looking for. She saw him glance outside at the nice car she drove, and that gesture made her wonder about the man, especially when she saw him lick his lips. Seeing that, her eyes narrowed. She wasn't sure he was all that trustworthy.

He pointed to a small white set, the only one he had suitable for a little girl's room. The bed was a twin, which might be fine for one person, but not for two, should she need the space. And she would, if they had more visitors over time. Sadly, she thought of her parents and wondered if they would ever come again.

Annalee didn't see anything else to her liking and was ready to leave the store, when she saw Carol heading her way, her gait, slow and lumbering, with her pregnancy now well advanced.

"Well, my goodness, if it isn't An, out shopping again and spending Jack's hard earned money?"

Carol edged closer and Annalee saw her grossly swollen feet, facial features, and even her hands. The sight of Carol, bloated and disfigured, shocked Annalee and aroused a feeling of pity, though she tried not to show it.

"Well, Carol, I'm surprised to see you out and about." Annalee's voice was cool, even icy.

She couldn't help how she felt. She no longer trusted this woman's friendship. Not after Carol had done her best to hurt her by burning her house down and shoving that damning note in her face. However, Annalee hadn't been as hurt by that note as Carol had wanted and having her home burned had only had resulted in her being married to the best man she could possibly imagine. She had made very sure that Carol knew it.

"So how are you feeling these days?" Annalee had to ask, alarmed at the sight of this poor soul.

She no longer had warm, friendly feelings toward Carol, but wondered if the woman was doing all right. It didn't look to Annalee like things were going along normally with this pregnancy. Things didn't look good as far as Annalee was concerned. Could Carol be in some kind of danger?

"Oh, I have a few problems, I guess," Carol confessed. "That doctor is so bossy. He won't let me have any salt or anything fit to eat. He fusses about things so much I hate to go to him anymore." She sighed and shrugged. "But of course, I have to go."

Carol seemed rather edgy to Annalee, fidgeting with her purse handles and twisting about.

"Are you sure you're doing all right, Carol? You're so swollen and puffy. Isn't that a bad sign? I was told to be careful of that when I carried my two."

A poor friend Carol may have been, but Annalee managed to feel pity for her condition. Carol was a woman having a child and she was alone with no father to help her raise it. It made Annalee all the more grateful for her marriage to Jack.

"Actually, I'm sort of scared, An. I found a blood spot on my car seat the other day, as well as on my clothing. I haven't told the doc about that yet. I'll see him in a couple more days."

"When you see a sign like that, you are supposed to

see the doctor about it right away. That is not natural or normal. I'm quite sure about that. I think it could be a sign of danger."

"Oh, An, you have always been such a worrier, worse than anyone I know."

Carol tossed her head, but not as she usually did. Even that small gesture was slowed by the severe bloating of nearly her entire body. Annalee felt a sense of alarm. An expectant woman ought to know that pregnancy, at any time, was often a chancy thing.

Annalee had often read in the papers where both mother and baby were lost on the delivery table. She hoped this wasn't one of those times, but she was sure that something was wrong. With the passage of blood, things were definitely not as they should be.

"You'd best get yourself over to the clinic right now, Carol," Annalee cautioned. "What are you doing out running around town when your due date is obviously so close?

"I get sick of being cooped up. No one comes to visit me anymore." Carol looked down at her swollen feet. "I have written to my brother, Henry, asking him to come. Maybe if I tell him what's happening, he might come. I don't know, though. We never got along."

Annalee couldn't feel sorry for Carol on that score, but since her voice was so filled with defeat, it made Annalee wonder what had happened between them? Knowing Carol, it probably wasn't anything good. Thinking of that crumpled note Carol had shoved in her face, Annalee wondered if she still had that evil thing from Gerald hanging around. Why had she kept it at all? Did she see it as a trophy or something?

"An, I am so sorry for waving that note at you," Carol said in a low voice. "It wasn't a nice thing to do. I really am sorry."

Annalee noticed she didn't say she was sorry for sleeping with her husband—no, she didn't mention doing that little deed.

Carol shifted her stance. "I guess I'd better go. I really drove around town hoping to run into you. I miss you so much, An. I really miss our friendship, I do."

Annalee thought she saw a tear forming, but she wasn't sure. "Well, I'm out today trying to find that bedroom furniture for Sarah. She needs her own room." She sighed. "Not having any luck so far."

"Well, good luck with it." Before Carol turned to leave, she asked, "Has that brother-in-law of yours gone back to DC? I haven't seen him around town any more, either."

"Yes, he left yesterday I believe it was, right after the dinner and dance at the Twin Oaks Country Club."

Annalee couldn't help herself, she had to mention that lovely night out in good company, dancing in Jack's arms.

❦❦❦

Carol left the store, headed for her car, and piled her bulk into it with Annalee's warning words ringing in her ears. *Am I headed for trouble?* she wondered. But she hadn't seen any more blood since a week or so ago, when she'd found a smear on her car seat. Lately, she had found it difficult to keep track of things. Her mind had gotten fuzzy at times.

The doctor, Andrew Childs, had told her to call if she had any concerns, and he had named several of them, including headache, swelling, bleeding, and even confusion. But she didn't really like the man. She thought he was bossy and his hands were too rough when he had done the last pelvic exam, early in her pregnancy.

Carol decided she'd better go see the doctor. "But I'll go in tomorrow. I'm so tired hauling this bulk around, I can barely move around anymore, especially not today," she muttered.

She drove toward her home, ignoring the tremors in her hands, and groaning with her severely aching head.

ℰᔆℰᔆ

Annalee took up the paper after she'd had a chance to relax once she'd arrived home. She had fed the little ones some peanut butter and jelly sandwiches and made them each an orange drink from some powder the Watkins man had brought.

The outing had tired them, and she put them down for naps. She scanned the ads and found what might be the answer for Sarah's room. The ad claimed it had a full sized bed, a dresser, mirror, and nightstand suitable for a younger child. It was in a cream shade, which in Annalee's mind made it just right for a little girl. And the price was right. Annalee answered the ad and asked the woman to hold it until her children were awake. She would then drive over and have a look at it. That settled, she went up to Jack's room and pulled the sheets off the bed. She smiled. They definitely could use a good washing.

While in the room, she saw a picture of Jack with his first wife, Amelia, sitting on top of a large chest of drawers. His lost wife had been a pretty blonde girl, with short curly hair and deep set eyes. Annalee had heard they'd been blue, but in black and white or Sepia, the coloring didn't show in the picture. She felt no jealousy on seeing that picture and her heart went out to Jack. He had suffered a terrible loss in losing a beloved wife.

That she and Jack had come together was still a miracle in Annalee's eyes and nothing she had ever thought possible. That they had formed a loving, intimate relationship was totally unbelievable. How had she gotten so lucky?

That picture of two people so in love and working on a family together brought tears to her eyes. Life had some tough surprises in store for some. How well she knew that. Remembering how he was with her last night, and every night since the dinner dance, she wondered how he could whisper his love for her so ardently when he had loved Amelia so much.

She shrugged and wondered about Jack and men in general. Could they love two different women so much that way? Gerald could love more than one woman, but in his case Annalee couldn't imagine it was love. Not in any way. He hadn't enough love in his heart to give to any woman. She wanted to ask Jack about his wife. They were that comfortable together now and she knew she could. She wondered what he would say.

જ્જ

With her children in the car, Annalee drove to the

house with the young girl's bedroom set. She had considered it to be that before she'd ever seen it. Once inside, she met the lady, Helen Morgan. Annalee introduced her three children and told Mrs. Morgan the set she was looking for was for Sarah. Little Sarah's chest puffed out a bit at the attention when her name was mentioned.

A trim, sad-faced little lady nearing old age, Mrs. Morgan led them into a small bedroom and pointed to the set. Annalee was instantly delighted with what she saw. It was far nicer and better quality than the one she'd seen in the furniture store.

"Why are you selling it?" she asked the woman.

"My daughter once had this room. She grew up sleeping in this bed. Last year, she married a nice young man and—" The woman choked back a sob. "Of course, she moved away after that. I had thought to keep it for her little girl, but we have lost her since then, so we no longer need it."

"What do you mean, ma'am, by you 'lost her'?" Annalee asked.

The little girls were tumbling about on the bed, giggling. It was lovely, with painted floral designs on the front and back.

Bucky stood, quietly looking about, a frown on his face. He saw nothing in this girl's room to delight a young boy.

"My daughter has passed away now. It happened a few months ago," Mrs. Morgan replied.

"Oh, I'm so sorry to hear that." Annalee had to ask, "What happened to her, if you can tell me about it?"

"She was near the end of her first pregnancy. All was fine until near the last month. About then she got so puffy and swollen, even her hands and face. She started having some awful headaches, too. We didn't know a condition like that could be so dangerous. When I had my three, I never had so much swelling and such." The woman's face had grown nearly white as she told Annalee the story. "Her doctor had warned her to come in if it got too bad." Mrs. Morgan let out a sob then stifled it. Annalee wanted to stop her, but the lady put up her hands. "Sorry, please don't mind me. It hurts me to tell it all over again, but in some ways, it helps me, too," she went on. "By the time her husband called us, he had taken her to the local clinic. She had suddenly gone into terrible seizures at home. He got the neighbor man to help him get her to the clinic. They took her to surgery right then to take the baby, hoping that would stop her seizures. The ether they gave her did stop her shaking." Mrs. Morgan slumped into a chair. "Taking the baby didn't help her. They said it was too late for my Betty. They couldn't save her life, the doctor said. They saved my grandson, just barely. My daughter never woke up again that terrible night. Our son-in-law called us as soon as he could. When we saw her right after that, she didn't even look like herself. Her face, hands, and feet were so swollen and pale. Even her lips and nose were swollen all out of proportion." Mrs. Morgan blotted her tears with a handkerchief as they rolled down her cheeks. "I'm sorry to tell such a sad tale, but thank you for listening."

"Mrs. Morgan, thank you for telling me about this. I have a friend who might be in a similar situation. From what you have just told me, I am worried to death for her. Her condition sounds just like your daughter's." Annalee felt she needed to hurry to Carol's home immediately.

"Oh, my dear, if you can save someone else from what happened to my daughter, God bless you."

"We've been friends for years, but recently we have had a falling out. I saw her earlier today, however, and I know she is frightened, though she wouldn't say so. I wonder if she would listen to me or even admit she might be in trouble after I tell her about your daughter?"

"I think you should go to her and tell her to see her doctor sooner than planned, if she is able. Don't let a little misunderstanding hold you back. This is too important. I was told quite a few women die each year from this very thing.

Just then, they heard the wailing of a very young baby. "Oh my goodness, he's awake," Mrs. Morgan said. She smiled. "Take your time deciding about this furniture. I was saving it for a granddaughter, but as you can imagine, that's not going to happen."

The woman left them standing beside the very nice little bedroom set and hurried away.

Annalee worried about Carol, but feared she wouldn't listen to her advice if she went over to warn her. Carol was so stubborn.

Annalee checked out every drawer in the small ornate dresser and nightstand. There was a small white lamp that looked like something she would like for Sarah and decided to ask about it, also. The joints of the furniture seemed tightly glued and it had no nicks or scrapes she could see.

She decided she would love to have this set for Sarah.

Mrs. Morgan came back, cuddling a tiny baby next to her chest. "This is James Hamilton, my grandson." She held him out to Annalee. "He's about three months old now."

"He's just lovely, isn't he?" Annalee held him down for the girls to see.

Bucky crowded close to have a look, too. "He ain't very big, is he?" He had a skeptical look on his face, seeing someone this small.

"No, son, but he will grow bigger, just like you did," Mrs. Morgan assured him. "You were just about this size when you were a baby, too. Someday he'll be a big boy like you." She smiled at Annalee. "Life goes on, doesn't it?"

"Yes, it does," Annalee replied. "I believe this pretty set would do just fine for my little one." She beckoned Sarah to her. "Honey, how would you like to have this nice bed in your own room?"

"Yeth, if Sissy can sleep with me." She nodded, especially admiring the lamp.

Annalee turned to Mrs. Morgan as she stood holding her tiny grandson. "I would love to have this set if you can part with it."

Mrs. Morgan nodded. "I'd love you to have it. I hate to sell it, but I have this boy to raise now, with his daddy, of course. He is living here with me and his son at this time, but I imagine one day, he will re-marry and take this precious child away. But for now, I cherish every day I have with this little boy."

The deal made, Annalee ushered her little brood into the car and headed home. She had left a nice roast in the oven and it was time to make the rest of the dinner. She did her best, but her mind stayed on Carol, and the danger she was in.

When Jack came home, Annalee had dinner ready. He looked at her and asked, "What's going on? What's got you so tied in knots?" His face had gone a bit pale, and Annalee didn't want him to think it was anything about him, or one of the children.

"Jack, I found a nice bedroom set for Sarah today. It has been used, and for quite some time, too. But it's like new and very beautiful. It's better built than anything at the furniture store. It had been used by the lady's daughter."

Annalee kept on talking. She had to tell him about her fears for Carol. "But then this woman, Mrs. Morgan, told me what had happened to her daughter and how she'd lost her. It struck home with me because I had just seen Carol. Her bloated, swollen condition was scary enough, but more so after Mrs. Morgan told me about the way she lost her daughter. It sounded so much like the situation Carol is in. I'm afraid for her. If it's the same condition this woman's daughter had, it might be fatal for both her and the baby." She flung out her hands. "I know we've had things happen between us, Jack, but I'm speaking of her life and that of her child, too. She could die from something like this."

"Will she listen to you?" Jack asked. "Does she have family anywhere that you know of?"

"I don't know, Jack. She's never mentioned any family, but just today she did happen to say she had written to a brother. She is so stubborn and devious, maybe she is on the outs with him—and no doubt for good reason. I already told her she should go in to the clinic because she looks that bad, even now. She is swollen everywhere, even her lips and hands. According to Mrs. Morgan, that is how her daughter was in the last month of expecting. She died because of it, Jack. Her baby boy lived, but she didn't."

"Why not call Carol and see if she is doing anything about it?"

"I think I'll call Amy in the morning. We'll both go see her. Maybe she will listen to the two of us.

Chapter 23

The next morning Annalee called Amy and told her what she knew about Carol, adding what Mrs. Morgan had told her. "I'm so worried for her. Do you think if we went over together, she might listen to us?"

"We can only try. I'll be right over and I'll bring Marie. I wouldn't want the kids to see Carol that way."

"Yes, I agree. It would be too much of a shock."

Annalee hung up and got the kids dressed. It was late summer, by now, but Amy's children weren't in school as yet.

Amy came and they drove away, leaving their children in Marie's capable hands. On the way over, Annalee had a terrible feeling about what they would find. They parked in the drive and hurried to knock on Carol's door. They waited, knocked again, but heard nothing. Annalee knocked harder. Hearing no answer or stirring within, she pushed on the door. It opened so they hurried inside.

The house was messy—dust on the furniture and papers lying about. This was not Carol's usual style at all. Annalee grasped Amy's arm. "I'm worried, Amy. Her car is sitting out there so she must be here, but where is she?"

They heard a moaning, gargling sound emanating from the bedroom and rushed into the room to find Carol lying sprawled across the bed. She didn't see them or acknowledge them. She eyes were closed and she seemed to have stiffened with her back slightly arched. Her hands were clenched tight. Her eyes opened right then and rolled back.

Annalee touched Carol's cheek and nudged her shoulder. "Carol, can you hear me?" Shaking her shoulder but receiving no kind of answer, Annalee cried out to Amy, "Get some help. Call Jack and Derrick! We have to get her to the clinic and we can't do it by ourselves."

Carol blew out a few moist breaths, her lips flapping loosely. Her eyes opened again, but she didn't seem to see anything at all and they stayed rolled back. Annalee was terrified. She had never before seen anyone in the dreadful state in which they'd found Carol. Annalee truly believed Carol had the same fatal condition as Mrs. Morgan's daughter, or very close to it. Her friend, or not, this young woman faced a damning situation.

Amy returned. "They're coming, An. How is she? Any changes?"

"No, nothing and I'm scared to death for her, Amy. Look at her! Oh, dear God, this is the worst thing I've ever seen. If we hadn't come over here when we did, I believe this would have been a terrible tragedy. I hope they get here really quick. I don't think there is any time to waste."

"I'll go wave them in." Amy hurried away to open the door.

Annalee watched Carol start to shake and arch her back farther. Carol muttered a few words through thickened lips that made no sense. Her speech was garbled.

"Look at that," Annalee cried. "Oh my God, I think she's going to go into seizures," she said in her increasing fear, remembering Mrs. Morgan's words. "Is this the same type of thing that happened to the woman's daughter?"

It sounded so much like what Mrs. Morgan had described that Annalee trembled at the sickening reality of what was happening before her. She had never seen anything like this in her life and didn't know what to do.

Carol's tongue hung out the side of her mouth, and Annalee saw flecks of foam when she blew out her breath. "Oh please God, where are they?" she cried out in fear for the bloated creature on the bed.

Annalee heard a car door slam and then, quickly, the rush of male footsteps as Jack and Derrick appeared with Amy. They rushed into the bedroom and took one look at Carol.

"My God, this is bad," Jack exclaimed. He issued orders. "Amy, call the clinic and tell them who we are bringing in, and that she may be having seizures."

He and Derrick wrapped Carol snuggly in a blanket, partly to control her shaking, but for modesty as well. Annalee heard one of them utter a grunt or two as they hefted the bulky form between them and headed out the door to the car. It was Derrick's Buick, because Jack drove the Model A these days. Surprised, Annalee hadn't known they each had their own car.

They carefully loaded Carol into the back seat. Jack knelt on the floorboards to hold onto her and urged more speed as Derrick drove. "My God, man, are we going to make it?"

Amy called the clinic and gave them what information she could. She then turned to Annalee. "Does she have any family or someone we can call?"

"I don't know for sure, but she did mention a brother, Henry. I can't remember Carol's maiden name. It would be his, too. Let's see if we can find something."

They went to Carol's desk, pulled out drawers, and rustled through papers. They found an address book and took a look.

"Here's something," Annalee said. "It says, 'Alberta Hensley.' Do you know who that could be?"

"Does she have a phone number?"

"I don't see one." Annalee found a letter. It was a funeral notice. "Well, it won't do much good to call that Alberta person. Here is her funeral notice. Must have been someone she knew, an aunt, maybe."

They were very worried about Carol and left off hunting for an address or phone number to call.

"Let's go see how things are going," Amy suggested.

They loaded into Amy's car, and headed to the clinic. They entered to find Jack and Derrick sitting in the waiting room.

"What's going on, fellows?" Amy asked.

Annalee looked at Jack. He sat there quietly, his face pale.

"They took her in right away and called for some specialist from Rapids," Derrick said. "She is sedated enough to stop her seizures. They were just at the beginning, they said, if that means anything. They also wanted to know if she has family and where they are."

"We looked through her desk, Derrick," Annalee said. "But we didn't find any relatives just yet. As far as I know, she never talked about anyone except a brother somewhere. And even at that, it sounded like they were estranged. So far, we didn't see any name we recognized in her address book." She sat down beside Jack, shaking and trembling. He put a consoling arm around her. "If she is going into surgery, Jack, I'd like to wait to see how she does before we leave."

Just then, Dr. Andrew Childs came out. "Mrs. Woods is in rather serious trouble," he informed them. "We believe she has a condition, frequently common to first pregnancies, called pre-eclampsia. Her seizures were only beginning, so there's hope for a good outcome. The baby's heart rate is high, but steady so far, but it is experiencing stress right now as well. We are awaiting the arrival of a specialist from Wisconsin Rapids," he continued. "He should be here shortly and will perform a cesarean section on her to relieve her of the fetus. That is what must be done in a case like this. She is quiet at the moment, but her condition is grave. I must warn you of that. I understand she is a widow. Has she no family at all?"

Annalee leaned toward Jack and into his warmth. His big body gave her the comfort she needed right now. "We are trying to find someone. She has a brother named, Henry, somewhere. We'll keep looking."

Within a few more moments, a car screeched to a halt out in front. A tall, thin man in his forties came rushing inside and went to the front desk. "We've been waiting for you. Follow me," the receptionist said hurriedly.

She led him through the double doors, where he disappeared. They sat waiting for an hour or more, until the tall thin man came out and addressed them. "I am Dr. Charles Lincoln. I did the best I could, but I'm sorry to tell you, Mrs. Woods has expired. I'm very sorry, but these cases are fraught with danger for a woman in that situation, and in her case, we were just too late."

"What about her baby?" Annalee asked.

"He seems to be doing well enough. He is small, a week or two early, but so far, I think we got him out in time. But I must say, that was very close, too."

The doctor began to reach behind his body and untie the strings of his surgical gown as he walked away, back through the double doors.

"So what now for that poor little child?" Annalee asked. She felt dizzy with all that had happened. It was all so tragic and so sudden. "What will happen to him if he has no one?"

"If no one claims him, I imagine he will become a ward of the state. They usually do in these cases. It's so sad."

Annalee's thoughts went spinning inside her head. *That child is a half-brother to my children. What can I do? How could I prove it if anyone asked?*

She turned to Jack. "Do you think Harold Lines would want to adopt this child if no one comes forth to claim him?" she asked. "He is an uncle, too. Carol told me that in no uncertain terms."

"I don't know, but I have his card," Jack told her. "I'll give him a call."

Annalee nodded her head. "I think that's a great idea. He'd be a good father. I wonder what his wife will say."

She then remembered. "Carol has a brother, too. We'd need to see how he feels about this before any steps are taken. He is also the uncle of this child." *The legal uncle*, she thought to herself and wondered what the trouble between Carol and her brother had been.

A nurse came out. "I am so sorry about your friend." She hesitated a moment, then asked, "I wonder, would you folks like to see this baby?"

They all stood up at once.

"Yes, ma'am, we would," Jack said.

She led them back through the double doors to a small, white, room. In a bassinet, lay a tiny red-faced baby, his wrinkly face screwed up, squalling for something to fill his belly, or perhaps for some time in a pair of comforting arms.

The nurse had a small bottle of milk with a nipple on it ready for him.

"This will be his first feeding. So far, he's only had water and I think he's upset about it." She picked him up, sat in a rocker, cuddled the tiny body in her arms, and put the nipple in his mouth. The baby latched on and began to suck vigorously. "He's a strong one for all he's been through." She laughed softly. "Look how he's eating. He's already got a man-sized appetite." She looked at Annalee. "You look so familiar. Aren't you the lady who got cut crawling through her window that morning your home burned?"

"My goodness," Annalee replied. "Yes, that's me. You certainly have a good memory." She gestured at her companions. "We are here because this baby belonged to a friend of mine. We are trying to contact his uncle."

What she didn't say was, *His mama burned my*

house down and this poor child is my dead husband's baby, however, she thought it.

The nurse hugged the tiny body closer as he fed him from the bottle. "It's a sad thing to lose your mother at such an early age. I hope and pray for the best for this little boy."

Poor baby. He would never know the comfort of nursing at his mother's breast and would never know his mother or his father. He made his little pulling baby noises, indicating he liked his belly full. Annalee noticed how black his hair was. *He's his daddy's image all over again.* She idly wondered what kind of man he would become. *Will this child become a very handsome, smooth, well-dressed, educated man, or a handsome man with a cruel streak all the way through him?*

They left the clinic and the men went back to work. The day was mostly over, and Annalee needed to get home and make dinner. But before they left the clinic, she said to Amy, "We should go back to Carol's house and see if we can't find that brother she mentioned. If she has a bible around, he might be named in that."

She remembered seeing that crumpled note lying on the bedroom floor as well and decided to pick it up. It might be important, later.

"Do you remember what Carol's family name was in high school?" Amy asked. "Wasn't it Sturgis or something close to that?"

"Now that you mention it, I believe it was. Now that we know what to look for, we might have better luck. We won't be in such a hurry and might do a better job of it. Let's go back there, then. We need to find him and notify him."

Annalee couldn't stop wondering if Carol had more relatives than the brother she'd mentioned a time or two. She rode with Amy and, in short order, they pulled up to Carol's house.

Reentering, Annalee had the sick feeling of tragedy. She kept seeing Carol sprawled across the bed in those last dreadful moments of her life. It had ended so badly. Amy followed Annalee. They went straight inside and found the address book where they'd dropped it before they'd hurried to the clinic.

"See anyone named Sturgis in there?" Amy asked. "She said she had written to him, so he must be in there."

"Here it is. Henry Sturgis and he's got a phone number, too, thank God. We'd better call him. He has to be notified as to what happened."

Annalee picked up the phone and heard the operator's voice. "Number please?"

"I'd like long distance, please," she replied.

"Just a moment, I'll connect you," the operator said. Annalee waited until she finally heard another voice say, "This is long distance. What number please?"

"It is Amherst 3045 in Madison, Wisconsin," Annalee said.

"Just a moment, please, I'll connect it for you."

Finally, after many rings, Annalee heard a male voice say, "Yeah? Who is it?"

"Sir, this is a friend of your sister, Carol Woods."

"I ain't got no time to waste on that filthy, meddling bitch!"

"Sir, I'm calling to tell you, she has had some serious trouble."

"I can believe that. It's about time. Sounds like some

of her nasty tricks finally caught up with her."

"Sir, what I'm trying to tell you is that, Carol has passed away."

"She *what?*" Annalee heard a scuffle, a choking sound, and finally, "Say that again." And in another minute, "Now tell me what happened, and who you are."

"I am a long-time friend of Carol's. She was having a baby, sir, and she developed some very severe complications at the end. They did emergency surgery, but they couldn't save her. I'm so sorry to bear such dreadful news, but you seem to be the only family member we could find."

"She was having a baby. I never knew a single thing about that. She never spoke to us after—did it live?" His voice had a slight slurring sound to it, and Annalee wondered what had caused that. Was the man a drinker?

"Yes, sir, she had a baby boy. He is small, but seems to be healthy enough. He's eating very well."

"I guess we'd better come up there and see to things."

"Will you be here soon?"

"Take several hours, depending on how the car runs. It ain't much and a lot of that was Carol's doing, too."

Annalee had no reply to his last comment, though it sounded like it could have had something to do with another of Carol's machinations. Annalee wondered what had happened to cause that relationship to sour as deeply as it appeared to have. Nothing good, she guessed. "She is still at the clinic, sir. I guess that will do until you come. Would you like to have my phone number, so you can call me when you get in?" she added. "Her house is open, too, if you need a place to stay."

He did want Annalee's phone number and sounded a bit too excited about the house being available. Annalee told him her number before she hung up then said to Amy, "I wonder if he is the only heir. And what he will do about the baby?" She knew one thing, though. She needed to hold onto that damning note. It would definitely prove half of the baby's parentage, should that be needed. Annalee picked it up from the floor where she'd thrown it a lifetime ago, heaved a sigh, and turned to Amy. "Well, that's taken care of. I get the feeling he is a lot like his sister." She didn't elaborate further on that statement. It was just an instantaneous sick feeling she'd gotten from the telephone conversation.

Amy gave her a quizzical look. "What do you mean about the brother?"

"It's just a feeling I got from speaking with him— makes you wonder how they were raised. He sounded excited about the house, though. It was passed to Carol by her parents. That's what she told me." Then she added, "He had nothing but nasty things to say about her before I told him she was dead."

Amy shrugged as she drove. "Well, it was as much as we could do right now, wasn't it?"

They drove to the clinic in silence and Annalee went back over everything in her mind, trying to get an idea of the kind of man the brother might be. That damning note was safely in her pocket, now.

At the clinic, Annalee told them the brother was on his way. As they headed for her home, she was deep in thought. *The brother will be coming to Delano as soon as he can. Someone has to decide what to do about Carol's body. Who else could make those decisions? After all, he is family.* Annalee sighed, feeling somehow sort of responsible, but she couldn't figure out why. She would go home and make dinner. Maybe Jack would have something to say that would make sense.

Chapter 24

Annalee and Amy walked into the house via the kitchen door and were met by the tantalizing odor of cooking food. Surprised, Annalee saw the kitchen table set and Jack standing by the stove. He sent her a smile that said, "I'm so damned glad to see you."

Amy looked at Annalee and nodded. "You have one great guy here, my dear, and he can cook, too." She grinned at Jack, went to the stairs, and called up to Marie. "I'd better get myself home, and fix dinner myself," she said, coming back into the kitchen. She had tears in her eyes as she left with Marie.

Annalee felt like crying herself, thinking of that poor motherless baby in the nurse's arms. She had no tears for Carol. That had never even entered her mind. "Oh, Jack, what a terrible day this has been." She went to him, put her arms around him, and placed her head against his firm, broad chest. He smelled so good to her that she wished the children were in their beds, asleep.

He crushed her in his arms and put his head down to hers. "I know it has. You've been so brave, my darling girl." He kissed her soundly and laughed softly. "I've made a few things for dinner. I didn't think you should have to make dinner after the day you've had."

"Where are the kids?" She looked around and wondered aloud. "Is that Bucky playing hide and seek again?"

"They were here a moment ago. They came down with Marie." Then he winked at her and exclaimed a bit louder, "I wonder where those kids could be. I'm really worried they could be lost. I thought I saw a kidnapper lurking around here, looking for somebody's small children."

Annalee heard the giggles coming from the living room and she and Jack went in to search.

"Where could they be? I'm afraid our children are gone forever, Jack."

She heard a muffled shriek coming from behind the couch and leaned over the back to take a look. The children came tumbling out, giggling and laughing. Even Sarah joined in. That told Annalee her littlest one had become secure enough with Jack that she could be a normal happy little girl in his home without worry or caution.

Annalee looked at him with tears in her eyes. "You have done this, Jack. Look how happy they are." She scolded the naughty little ones and sent them giggling to the table then she went to him and hugged his big body close. "They are happy, safe, and secure. All of them."

"It's all because of you, An. Maybe some from me, but it's more the mother you are that has created the warmth and comfort of this home. This house was a dark and lonely place before you came into it," he said, and sent her a look that nearly curled her toes. "I'll show you just how much I appreciate you later, my wife."

His words held so much meaning for later in the night that Annalee could barely make it to the table. She sat in her seat, already numb with desire, while that big, handsome man of hers served macaroni and cheese, along with hot dogs for their dinner.

"Oh boy, this is the bestest supper I ever had!" Bucky exclaimed, his glowing eyes set on his step-daddy, Jack.

The rest of the little ones were every bit as happy as Bucky with the sumptuous feast.

Annalee gave Jack an indulgent smile as she cut the hotdogs for Sarah and Sissy. "Thanks, Jack. You've made a great meal for us."

As she ate and let her blood cool a bit, Annalee wondered what Carol's brother would be like. What would he do about the baby? She secretly hoped there was a chance he wouldn't want the child. He just might if he was much like Carol and thought someone else might want the child. But she would have to wait on that to know just how devious the brother might prove to be.

Jack kept looking at her. "What's going on in that head of yours, love?"

He had taken to calling her names of endearment, some of which belonged in the bedroom. Fortunately, his heated words went sailing right over the heads of the little ones. But the blush those words sent across her cheeks made Jack's eyes shine a whole lot brighter, thinking of the promise awaiting them both at day's end.

Annalee shivered in her seat at the supper table,

knowing how Jack could be in the quiet of the bedroom. The gentle, yet strong way he had with her, soothing her then heating her blood into a lovely torment of need. She now had desires she'd never known existed. And the powerful way he had at taking care of those—oh, Lordy, she wondered if she could wait. She now had that on top of his everyday goodness and care. It was no wonder she loved that man.

She'd had no idea what a good marriage could be like, but by the way he was with her, she had rapidly learned to trust him and to let herself go. Her memories of Gerald had been almost erased from her mind, until she had laid her eyes on his newborn son, lying all alone in the clinic. The sight of that poor infant had brought home to her how lucky she was to be free of an ugly relationship.

What would Carol's brother turn out to be? She pitied the newborn child if this Henry turned out to be as uncaring and devious as his sister. Would he even want the child? Did he have heart and generosity to want to raise his nephew to manhood?

❧❧

In the morning, Amy appeared with Marie and her children in tow. "Let's go see how things are with Carol's child."

She came inside to wait while Annalee grabbed her purse. With Marie watching the little ones, Amy and Annalee drove in Amy's car to the Delano Clinic.

Annalee was tense with worry over the outcome of this little trip. Her fingers gripped the edge of her purse.

"What do you think that brother, Henry, will be like?"

"I'm wondering that myself," Amy replied. She clutched the steering wheel as she turned into the clinic parking lot. "I'm worried he will be enough like Carol that the baby's future will be in jeopardy."

"I don't see another car here," Annalee said. "I wonder if the brother Henry came to Delano at all."

They went in and at the front desk. "We'd like to see the baby and find out if his uncle has come to see him."

"I remember you ladies. You brought the poor mother in yesterday. So sorry how it turned out." The receptionist shook her head and rose from her seat. "Right this way." She led them back through the double doors and pointed to the little white room. "He's right in here and, so far, we haven't seen the uncle. Oh, the nurse is feeding him again. He's been a hungry little guy." She smiled. "Nurse Ann Riley has him just now."

They walked in and stood quietly as the nurse fed the baby.

"How is he this morning?" Annalee asked. "They said out front that no one from Carol's family has come by so far."

"I'm Nurse Riley, and no, I haven't heard anything, or seen a soul so far." She had a bewildered look on her face. "Wasn't an uncle on his way?"

"Yes, we called him last night and he said they were coming. They weren't sure when they'd get here because of their car. It sounded like they had some problems." *Was it car trouble that made them so late?* Annalee wondered.

They heard a car pull up and voices in the front lobby.

Annalee stepped out of the room to see if the double doors would open to admit some of Carol's family. "Maybe that's them now."

She saw a man and woman come through the doors. The receptionist led them to the small, white room. "He's right in here, Mr. and Mrs. Sturgis."

Annalee and Amy stood back as a short, stubby-looking man about thirty or so came shuffling in, accompanied by a frumpy, poorly dressed, overweight woman, following in his wake.

The nurse nodded toward Annalee and Amy. "These ladies brought Carol here yesterday afternoon in a very severe state of illness. We did the best we could for her, but unfortunately, we only managed to save the child."

The man cast an appraising eye on Amy and Annalee. "So I guess you ladies were friends of Carol's?"

"Yes," Annalee said. "And we very were worried about her because of her swollen feet and hands. I had seen her a day or two before and she didn't look quite right. We told her she ought to see her doctor right away." She looked at him, frowning. "Yesterday morning we went by to see if she was doing all right and found her unconscious. It looked to us like she was starting to shake all over and stiffen up, so we thought she might be going into seizures. We called our husbands to help bring her in to the clinic." She held out her hands. "Sorry they couldn't save her."

"Let's have a look at the baby, then." He moved to the edge of the white crib and peered down at the tiny infant. The nurse had completed the feeding and laid the sleeping child down. "My God, Teresa, look at all that black hair," Henry said. "How can that be? Carol had blonde hair and Donald was a redhead. Something's fishy here." He looked at the nurse. "You sure she had this kid?"

The nurse narrowed her eyes at the man's suspicions. Her firmly set lips let him know how she felt about his questions. "Of course, she was the mother. I was right here during the surgery and afterward, also."

"Well, there's something wrong about this whole thing, I can see that." He crossed his arms and looked down at the sleeping infant again. "We're going to have to do some thinking about this, that's for sure." Henry and his wife turned to leave the room, and the nurse followed him out.

Annalee stood quietly wondering, her eyes wide as she looked at Amy. Speechless at the coldness in the man's demeanor, regarding his sister's remains and her surviving child, Annalee wondered if her brother cared at all about Carol or her child. Annalee felt sick all over listening to the ongoing conversation.

"Would you like to speak with the doctor about this, sir?" the nurse asked. "And what about your sister?" she also demanded. "What would you like us to do with her remains?"

"Oh, yeah, I guess something's got to done about that." He turned to his wife. "Teresa, we have to do some deciding. I am her only relative what with Donald gone, too. I suppose that also means what she has left is ours, then, wouldn't it be?" he added.

Annalee heard the sound of greed seeping into his voice and felt a creeping nausea. He was Carol's brother all right, grasping, greedy, and self-absorbed. Annalee felt nothing but sorrow, thinking these two would be rear-ing Carol's unfortunate child. And that thought had her wondering at their own upbringing during their younger years. What had happened to them as children to have created two such conniving, selfish human beings?

Not a trace of sorrow over the loss of a sister, only what he would get out of it. And it would be a sizable amount, if it meant that lovely home of Carol's, the nice furnishings, her car, and anything that might remain in her bank account as well.

Annalee turned to Amy. "What do you think about this business?"

Tears formed in Amy's eyes. "My heart goes out to that poor baby lying in that crib, I know that much."

Annalee nodded. "I almost hope and pray they refuse to take this baby," she said. "I know someone who would love to have this child. I'm absolutely sure of it. He's related, too."

"What on earth are you referring to, An?"

"I'm speaking of Gerald's twin brother. He said they have been unable to have children, and this child is his nephew. I have the note that pretty much proves it." Seeing the surprise on Amy's face, Annalee added another bit to the conversation. "Amy, she had me over for lunch the other day and waved that note right in my face, bragging about it, in case you wondered why we weren't speaking. Well, until this emergency happened. On top of all that, my neighbor saw her car near my home the night it burned. She nearly killed me and my children along with it.

"My God, An! I never knew about that. How can you possibly be sure it's the truth?"

"About the home burning, I only have my neighbor's

suspicions about that, but I believe Carol did it." Annalee shrugged. "She shoved that note at me, right into my face. She wanted me to read it, to show me she was a better woman than me. And I read it. Gerald was making a date to be with her again. It sounded like they'd been getting together like that for a long time. Donald found that same note and read it. He was so furious he kicked her out of the house during that terrible storm. That's why she came to my house for a few nights. It was the night of that terrible storm. You remember—he was killed that night by a flying tree limb that blew down on him.

"When Jack came back for his daughter, after two or three days, and found out who Carol was, he told her about finding Donald's body after a tree branch hit him. Carol turned white as a sheet because she knew he'd felt guilty about kicking her out of the house right into a storm. He'd run out there to bring her back inside. If that child is Gerald's own flesh and blood, Amy, of course his twin brother would want to adopt him to bring up if he could."

"I wonder if Carol's brother would go for that." Amy frowned. "I'm sure he would if he got something out of it."

"Jack has called Harold in DC. He is on the way here to Delano with his wife. I guess we'll find out in a short while, won't we?" Annalee told her. "Those brothers are so completely different. They are exact opposites. Harold told me they were mirror twins. Ever hear of that?"

"No, I never have, but about that note business and her setting your home on fire. Why haven't you ever told me about this, before, An?"

"Neither of these subjects is easy to bring up, is it?"

"Well, no, I suppose not. Derrick and I knew you were not happily married. You never said a word, but it wasn't hard to figure that much out."

"I couldn't talk about how it was, but he was brutal to me," Annalee said. "I was so ashamed and believed it was my fault for a long time. When I finally realized it wasn't, I was stuck in that marriage with no way out." She held back a sob. "I finally went to my parents, but they were no help at all. And now, if you can believe it, they came to see me since I'm married to Jack. My mother saw me in that dress I wore to the country club dance and called me a harlot." She gave a half smile and shrugged.

"Well things are sure different now, aren't they?" Amy said.

"In every way possible, Amy, I am so happy with Jack I can't believe it, or how lucky I am." Annalee grew serious. "How can he love me when he was so much in love with his first wife? I planned to ask him, but haven't done it yet."

"He did really love her, An, but I've never seen anyone that lonely after he lost her. His child was, too. I don't know about how a man can be in love more than once, but as you have seen, they can. I guess a woman could, too. Poor Carol. I guess she was never really happy with any man, including your faithless husband," Amy offered, shaking her head at the unanswerable questions they both had raised.

ೲೲೲ

A day later, Annalee answered her door. She welcomed Harold and met his tall, slender, dark-haired, and very fine-looking wife, Caroline, or Carrie as he called her.

After the first few comments and get re-acquainted tidbits of conversation, Harold got to the question that lay most heavily on his mind. "Tell us about this child you've had Jack inform us about."

He waited for an answer with an eagerness that aroused a sense of pity in Annalee. It was so easy for some people to have children, yet so tragically difficult for others. The child hunger she saw in them both nearly broke her heart.

"I know this child is Gerald's," she said. "I have a note to prove it. Carol herself told me her husband was not capable of fathering a child, and until she and Gerald got together, there was no child between Carol and Donald. What I don't know is whether or not Carol's brother will want to keep the baby?"

"Tell me about this brother, Annalee. If at all possible, this baby could be the answer to our prayers for a child. And he'd be of my blood, if not Carrie's."

She could almost feel his desperation about this child building in his mind. "I already have the idea Henry is very much like his sister," she said. "He was excited to be the sole heir to all she had. That includes the home, car, all the furnishings, and what money she had in the bank."

"I have an idea that might help him decide," Harold said with a gleam in his eye as he turned to his wife. "How would you feel about having this child? Of course, we have had this discussion more than once, but this baby boy is my nephew. He already *is* family."

"Of course, it would be fine. I think I could be a

good mother, and I have always wanted a child to raise and love. Especially if you're sure he's your nephew. How much better it is if the child is a close relative."

"I will show you the note." Annalee dug into her purse. "You need to be sure, and if it convinced *me*, it might do the same for you." She handed them the wrinkled yellow note. "Here you are. Maybe you will recognize the handwriting. I know I did."

Annalee watched them scanning the paper and heard Caroline cry out. "My God, Harold, it looks like you wrote this yourself!" She was shaking like a leaf. "He wrote nearly the same way as you do, dear."

Harold handed the note back to Annalee. "It is proof enough for me, except for the slight backward slant. You poor girl. Gerald must have been a sorrier bastard than I had previously thought and, as you already know, my thoughts were not that charitable before." Then he added, "Funny thing. I saw Carol in Mary Ellen's café where I had breakfast most every morning. She was a terrible flirt, even in the family way. I had the idea right then that she and Gerald were rather well acquainted, so to speak."

"Yes, they were all of that," Annalee quipped.

"I wonder if we could arrange to see the child." Harold's anxiety was so obvious, his hands trembled.

"I imagine you could. He may still be at the clinic. It didn't seem like Henry was all that eager to take him."

They herded all the kids and themselves into Harold's huge, luxurious auto. Annalee sank into the plushy leather cushions. She wanted to ask what kind of car it was and, moreover, wondered what kind of position he held that he could afford such a vehicle. But instead, she directed him to the clinic.

They entered the clinic, and, immediately, Annalee caught the odor of antiseptic, cleaning agents, and the usual hospital smells. She spoke to the receptionist. "We are inquiring about Carol Wood's infant."

"Yes, I remember. You are one of the friends who helped her that awful day. He's still here, but the people from St. Michael's Orphanage in La Cross have been notified. We were at a loss to know what to do with him, as the uncle has never bothered to come back in to see him." She looked puzzled. "It's as though they don't want to bother caring for him, at least not so far. He hasn't been back to check on him and, usually, we only keep a newborn in cases like this no more than seven to ten days."

"Oh what a shame," Annalee exclaimed. "I think we'll go speak to him about this. Please, when are the orphanage people coming?"

"Not for another few days. We had no other choice as he has to have someone to care for him."

"May we see him, please?" Harold asked. His hands trembled and his lips were tight. He was the picture of eagerness, wanting to see this child of his twin brother.

Chapter 25

W ho are these folks, then?" the receptionist asked, nodding to Harold and his wife.

She needed to know who was seeing the patient. It was the right thing to do, and they all knew it.

Annalee explained their presence. "They are the baby's relatives, also, and would like to see him."

"I don't understand. I thought the uncle was all he had."

"It's a bit complicated," Annalee replied. "But we have the needed proof if there would ever be any question."

"All right, you can follow me, but the little ones must remain here. We must be careful, you understand. With all the childhood diseases the younger child is likely to get, we can't be too careful."

"You children cannot go back there," Annalee told Bucky. "Will you keep watch over the girls here for a little while?"

"Yep, I can do that, but why can't we see that baby?"

"Because they said you can't. So you can't. That's all there is to it, dear. Don't worry. I will be right out as soon as I can."

The receptionist was the same one from the other day. She knew Annalee and nodded. "I'll keep an eye on them for you."

Annalee left the children sitting alone as the receptionist led them through the double doors. She introduced them to Nurse Riley, the current nurse on duty. At present, she had the care of the baby as well as any other patient they might have. "He's doing just fine," Nurse Riley said. "He has a good appetite. Is there any news on whether or not the uncle is taking him?" she asked, as she led them to the baby's crib.

"We aren't sure of anything just now, ma'am," Annalee said as she looked into the crib, along with Harold and his wife.

"My God, Caroline," Harold said, his voice hushed. "He's just beautiful, isn't he?"

His face had a glow of excitement over it as he gazed at the tiny mite. The child lying there was all that remained on this earth of his twin brother. Annalee saw how he reached out as if to take the child in his arms as well as into his life.

Caroline gasped. "He sure is. Honey, it's amazing. He looks just like you. Oh my God, Harold, he could be your son, he looks so like you."

Annalee saw that her face had instantly taken on a motherly glow as she looked down at this tiny infant and kept repeating how much he looked like her husband. Inside herself, Annalee prayed they'd be able to adopt this little boy and take him to their home in Washington DC.

"Any chance we could hold him—just for a moment?" Harold asked the nurse.

His request was so filled with longing she couldn't help but say yes. "Just be careful to support his head. He's only four days old, and that's very young, you know." She reached down, scooped up the baby, and placed him in Caroline's arms.

"Oh my goodness, how heavy you are already," Caroline cooed as she looked into that tiny face. "Oh Harold, do you think…"

Annalee saw tears in her eyes.

"I'll turn heaven and earth upside down to make it happen, darling. Here, let me hold him, too."

Caroline transferred him carefully to Harold's waiting arms. Annalee smiled at seeing him hunch his shoulders over in fear of dropping the infant like so many inexperienced new fathers seemed to do.

"Be careful with him dear, he's very tiny," Caroline said.

At that moment, the infant opened his black eyes and looked right into their faces. "He's so beautiful, Carrie dear," Harold breathed softly. "I can't believe what a miracle he is," he gasped, and added, like a silly fool, "Look, honey, he knows me already."

Annalee looked at the nurse. They both understood the instant love this couple had toward this baby boy. Annalee prayed again that they would be the ones who would take him home to rear as their own son.

After many moments of gushing over the infant, the nurse suggested they should leave.

"Why don't we go see Henry about this?" Annalee

suggested. Once outside, she warned them, "When he sees this fancy car, he is going to want plenty of incentive to let that baby go. He obviously doesn't want his nephew to keep and rear, but he is a greedy soul. So be prepared."

"I have an idea how to handle this," Harold said.

They herded all the children back into the car and Annalee directed them to Carol's house. They drove slowly through the streets of the small berg to reach Carol's home and parked in the driveway behind her dust-coated, green Ford sedan.

It already had suffered from neglect as the coating of dust and grime plainly showed. Annalee wondered how it could have gotten that dirty looking in only a few days, until she remembered they hadn't had rain for several days.

Annalee didn't really want to subject the children to anything inside that house, but her own curiosity kept her, with the children, moving toward the front door, along with Harold and his wife.

Harold knocked on the door. For a while, they heard nothing. Then the door opened a slight crack. "What'd ya want here?"

It was Henry's voice, and Annalee believed he'd been drinking by the slurring sounds he made. Thoughts of that poor child in this home with Henry and his wife made her shudder.

"We'd like to speak with Mrs. Carol Woods' brother, if we might," Harold said, his tone sounding as officious as he could make it.

They heard the sounds of shuffling inside, as well as the clinking of bottles.

Then the door opened wider and the short, slightly tubby Henry bade them, "Come on in, then, and let me know your business."

Immediately, Annalee caught the scent of days' old booze and the fresh, sour tang of beer as well.

Harold introduced himself and his wife then gestured at Annalee. "I believe you have already met this lady, but perhaps not her children."

Annalee nodded her head. The children clutched at her skirts. "How are you doing, Henry? We were wondering if there will be a service for Carol and when. She was a friend of ours, as you know."

"Well, we ain't decided yet about that. She's over to the funeral home now. Guess we ought to get moving on that." He looked the worse for having spent the night in a drunken haze. Annalee was very familiar with how that was, having seen plenty of it from Gerald.

Harold opened the topic of interest. "We were wondering about the child. What are your plans regarding his welfare and up-bringing?"

"Just what business is it of yours, if I may ask?"

Henry's eyes narrowed and Annalee saw his wife take a look out of the front window. Her eyebrows rose when she spotted the fancy car.

"My wife and I would like to adopt the child," Harold said. "We could give him the best of everything and are prepared to do just that."

"What possible right have you got to horn in on what happens to be our kinfolks? That kid is ours if Carol was my sister. We can take real good care of that kid ourselves," Henry replied, his chest out and his face taking on a heated, ruddy shade.

Harold's voice was smooth as silk. "You realize, of course, all that was his mother's now belongs to this newborn child, by right of succession. I am in the law and have a comprehensive knowledge of how these things work."

Henry's face went white at Harold's words. "A little baby ain't able to attend to things. How can he inherit everything?" he asked then gasped out angry words, exposing the hurt and anger he held toward his dead sister. "After all the dirt she did to me, I got the right to her stuff now. Ain't no damned slick lookin' lawyer goin' to cheat me out of it, neither."

Annalee had wondered at the strained relationship between Carol and her brother. By his outburst, Annalee decided it must have been a doozy of a dirty trick—one of Carol's best.

"She went and done me out of this house, too, when Mum died," Henry said, continuing on with his tirade. "Our mother had told me it was mine before she went. Dad was already gone by then." He paced the floor, his fists tightly clenched. "But that sneakin' bitch, Carol, went and tore up the will. And then she and her husband Donald camped out here until I had to give up and leave. Damn her soul to hell for the dirty bitch she was." His face, reddened with anger, nearly glowed as he raved on and on.

Annalee stamped her foot and admonished him, "Mind your talk, mister. We have little ones here and that foul language of yours is not fit for their ears."

Henry had the decency to flush a bit. "Sorry there, kids. I sorta got carried away."

Annalee saw Bucky smother a giggle into his hands

at the bad words he'd heard, while the girls clung to her skirt in fear at Henry's angry outburst.

Harold spoke up. "I can see you are not quite decided about the child, and you have a lot of other things to handle as well. We will return tomorrow, and with the authorities should they be required."

He took his wife by the hand and, with Annalee, they shepherded the children out the door. Henry and Teresa followed them outside.

Annalee saw him gasp at the sight of Harold's long, low-slung fancy car with the word, *Phaeton*, written in scroll across the side in what appeared to be silver.

"Henry just got a good look at this car, Harold," she said, her voice low. "He will be after some real money tomorrow. You can mark my words on that."

"He won't be a problem, dear, not at all. And this car is actually made by Ford, but I don't think they make a lot of them." He uttered a soft chuckle along with a quiet, intense look across his dark features—so like his twin, Gerald.

Annalee always felt a slight shock when she looked at him though she had learned Harold was an entirely different man. She wondered at his confidence. "How can you be so sure?"

"There is nothing so easy to work with as good old fashioned greed, my dear. Even though this baby is his sister's, he obviously cares nothing at all for that little baby boy we have just seen and held in our arms."

"It's so sad. It breaks my heart," Annalee said and Caroline nodded in agreement.

"That's because you have a heart, Annalee. Not everyone does."

Harold opened the car door and they entered the plushy interior to return to Annalee and Jack's home. She asked them to stay with them and assigned her old room to them. It was a bit feminine, with the pink, rosy wallpaper and matching bedspread, but it had a double bed, room for two.

❧❧

Jack and Harold sat together, hashing over the day's events.

"I think you have a good case for adopting that baby," Jack commented, "But let's call the best attorney in town. He's a friend of mine and he's damned good."

Harold nodded. "I agree, Jack. That boy is the spitting image of my brother, Gerald, and I can't bear the thought of him growing up in that utterly miserable household we saw today." He visibly shook as he went on. "My God, man, that brother of Carol's, Henry, is a drunk! We saw it with our own eyes."

"Blood ties are strong, Harold, and you only have that note to prove your claim. You need a damned good lawyer and Homer Sells is your man." Jack leaned forward in his chair, almost as an emphasis. "I've seen Homer win almost impossible cases. And it looks to me like you really have a good shot with that damning note and a good lawyer, plus the fact that this Henry most likely doesn't want the child, anyway. That note and his greedy nature are two very positive factors in your favor."

"Thanks, Jack. I'll give him a call and may I use you as a reference?"

"Of course. Better yet, I'll go along with you, if you like."

Annalee and Caroline were busy in the kitchen, preparing dinner. The children sat at the small table eating a hastily prepared supper of macaroni and cheese, made especially for them. Sarah continued to peek into the living room at Harold as she ate.

Harold had continued trying to attract little Sarah, but she always went to Jack and the poor man flung up his hands in frustration. With Bucky, he had little problem.

The boy no longer held any fear of him, finally realizing this man was not like his father. Bucky saw no raging temper or heard angry words from this man and understood there was nothing to fear. And upon seeing approval from Jack, Bucky had shyly gone to his uncle. But he remained quiet, with his boisterous side held in check, even when he took Uncle Harold up to see his room.

Annalee smiled, knowing that Jack had already become the anchor in this family, not only for her, but for her children as well.

Caroline grinned. "Harold is trying so hard to make up to those two. He's a failure with Sarah. He's doing better with Jack's little Sissy, poor man."

"He'll be a wonderful father when you take that baby home," Annalee replied. She really believed they would.

Caroline had tears in her eyes. "God help us, I know it. We have never managed to conceive and right now he is beyond happy that we might have a chance to be parents. Annalee, he can barely stand it."

"Let's hope this local attorney will be enough help to make it happen."

సౌసౌ

Jack and Harold entered the offices of Homer Sells. They were escorted into his office, duly lined with thick tomes filled with legal matters and pictures of important men on the walls, including the current president of the United States, Herbert Clark Hoover.

Jack introduced Harold to his good friend, Homer, and they sat down to discuss the case. Jack had the letter written to Carol Woods from Gerald Lines and, after all the discussion was through, that note proved to be the pivoting factor in Harold's case. It proved, as near as was possible, that he was the uncle on the father's side.

"I'd like to give Donald's doctor a call," Homer said. "The only other deciding factor, aside from this note, is proof of his sterility. Do you know who Donald Woods saw here in town?"

Jack had no idea and Harold lived in DC. "No sir, we don't." Jack added, "I don't believe Annalee would know that either."

"Never mind," Homer said. "I'll call around. I know about all the docs here in town. I can find that out easily enough." He went on a bit more. "You say the adoption people have been called in this baby's case?"

"That's what we heard at the clinic," Harold said, a sick pallor spreading over his face. "My God, they can't take him, just like that, can they?"

"We'll make sure that doesn't happen. Let me get to work on this. I will draw up adoption papers and have them ready for Henry Sturgis to sign if we can convince him that way. We might be able to wrap this up in short order."

Jack saw the glow of hope spreading across Harold's face. They left the legal offices, and Jack said, "Let's catch some lunch. How about it?"

"Yes, let's," Harold said. "But I'm so damned nervous I doubt if I can eat a thing."

Jack saw the sweat breaking out across the man's forehead. "Hey, man, quit your worrying. It'll be all right. You'll be holding that little mite in your arms before you know it. Think of the stuff your wife will have to go shopping for when you take that child home to DC."

"Oh, God help me, I hope you're right about that. I don't think I could stand it if I had to see that baby in the hands of that drunk and his slatternly wife. It would absolutely kill me, Jack."

"It will have to go before a judge before it's all done. Homer can expedite all that of course, especially after Henry signs the adoption papers. If he does, I don't think there is much left to do before a judge except make it legal."

Harold held back the fearful thought, *What if he won't?*

"Well, there will be a christening and a hell of a big celebration to take place after it's all done," Jack said.

Both men laughed, hopefully, at the thought of it.

Chapter 26

Jack took the day off. He wanted to go with Homer, Harold, Caroline, and Annalee to see what could be done. Amy elected to take the children for a while to free up Annalee for the day as the men and Caroline wanted her along.

Harold paced about. "Let's drop by the clinic and check on the baby first thing," he said, his voice filled with anticipation.

"Sure, we can do that."

They headed out in Harold's car, and Homer followed in his own. When they walked into the clinic and asked to see the child, the receptionist's face turned white and her eyes widened.

"He's gone. His Uncle Henry came for him early this morning." She fluttered about in her indecision. "Let me get the nurse for you," she said and turned to head toward the back, hurriedly pushing through the double doors.

Harold and Caroline stood there nearly speechless.

"That devil of a brother is planning to make me pay an exorbitant price for that little guy," Harold said. "I know he is."

Homer smiled and patted Harold's arm. "Don't worry your head about this for a moment, Mr. Lines," he said, making his voice soft as feathers. "I know how to handle guys like him."

Jack waited to see how things went, but his dander was up. He'd seen the shock and fear on Annalee's face when they discovered the child had been taken by a known drunk and his slovenly wife. Maybe they had a family right to him, but as far as the man and his wife were concerned, they were in no way fit to be his parents.

The nurse came out. Her face had gone pale as well. She told them how it happened. "The brother of Mrs. Woods came early this morning for the infant. I tried to tell him that we usually don't release a newborn for nearly ten days. That is, of course, for the baby's sake. We want to be sure he is thriving properly and his umbilicus is healing as it should. This is only his fifth day of life, after all. But that man threatened us with kidnapping and demanded we turn over the child. We had to let him go. After all, he is the legal uncle and Mrs. Woods only surviving family member."

"We understand, ma'am," Harold said. "You did what you could. We'll go call on the uncle and check on the baby while we're there."

He put his arm around his wife and turned for the door. His features were pale, and his shoulders slumped in defeat, and disgust, at this unexpected turn of events.

Henry was definitely hoping to exact a big price for the child, and Harold was ready for a fight. He had the sick feeling that Henry had his heels dug in and was ready and waiting, planning to see what he might gain from this situation.

They returned to the car, and Harold drove in silence. Obviously, no one felt like talking after what they'd learned at the clinic. Annalee, merely the observer in this heartbreaking fiasco today, offered no comment. But she too felt the tightness of apprehension about the outcome.

They pulled up in front of Carol's home and, as a group they headed for the front door. Harold went first and knocked solidly on the door. With clenched hands and tightened lips, he waited.

Henry opened the door. "Well, my goodness, look who's come to call," he said, his tone nearly mocking. "Hello there, come on in." His voice was chipper and full of power as he stood back to allow them entry. "Welcome, come on in to our new home but then, it should'a been mine, all along." A snarl crept over his face as he said it.

He had assumed control of Carol's home, without any reading of a will or going through probate. Annalee wondered what the lawyer would have to say in that regard, if it was mentioned at all. So far, he had made no comment either way. She hoped he was as good as Jack thought he was.

She looked about, hoping to catch sight of the little newborn, but didn't see Henry's wife or the child. Annalee assumed Teresa must be back in one of the bedrooms with the baby.

Harold stood straight and tall in front of the chubby, runty brother. "We came to see about the child of your sister."

"You mean of course, my nephew," Henry said. "We brought him home this morning. Wanted to get him before she called the orphanage people or whatever. Never know about sneaky folks like that, once they'd get their hands on 'im." His nose was as high in the air as he could manage, and his chest swelled with his importance.

"That child is also my nephew, and we can prove it," Harold said.

"You're a damned liar, you are!" Henry's face flushed red with his angry outburst. "What proof have you got? Just some dirty gossip, most like, or somethin' like that."

Annalee saw no bottles of beer or empties lying about. They had cleaned up their act. She had to wonder whether Henry actually did want the baby. She found that hard to believe.

Homer spoke up. "I am Mr. Lines' attorney. I understand you live in Madison. Is that right?"

"I don't see what the hell b—business it is of yours, m—mister," Henry stammered. "Why do you want to know that?"

"Just checking my facts, Mr. Sturgis. I want everything to be straight and above board about your taking custody of the child in question."

"What the hell are you talking about, child in question and taking custody?" Henry's face grew beet red as his fists clenched. "Now you just listen here, mister smart-ass lawyer, my affairs are none of your damned business, and if you keep on, I'm going to have to kick you and your bunch of nosy friends ta hell outta here."

"I put in a call to the local sheriff in Madison, regarding you and some of your activities around that town.

I must say he had a lovely tale to tell me. Are you sure you want to kick my ass out the door?"

Henry's face turned white as a sheet. "What do you mean? What lovely tale are you talking about?"

Just then, Annalee heard the cry of a baby coming from Carol's bedroom. She and Caroline ran that way and entered the room. The baby lay on the bed in a wet, filthy diaper, crying. He was red in the face and angry, by the little fists waving in the air. The dressing covering his unhealed umbilicus site had gone awry. It was soiled with urine and feces, and the site looked far too red. That ugly wound frightened Annalee.

She feared that umbilicus would become infected with all the filth around it.

Teresa looked at both ladies in alarm. "He was asleep, but now he's awake, hollering his little head off, and won't shut up. I'm trying my best, but no matter what I try, I can't get him to shut up and go back to sleep."

"Let me try," Annalee said. "If he just woke up, he's most likely hungry." She looked about for a clean diaper. "He needs some alcohol and a clean dressing for his cord site. Where are his diapers and his bottle?"

"We already used up everything that came with him from that clinic place. I've tried to get Henry to go get some more, but he said he doesn't know what to look for. And if I go, he's afraid to left alone with this kid." She held up the bottle, empty except for about an ounce of curdled milk. "This is all we got left."

Annalee shuddered at the sight of that foul bottle. "Do you have any milk at all in the house?" she asked then added, "And can you find some clean dishtowels? They are usually nice and soft after so many washings."

She watched Teresa rush out of the room, just as Harold came in. He looked at his crying nephew and nearly broke into tears himself.

"My God. Don't these people know anything about babies?"

Annalee looked at him and shrugged. "Doesn't look like it."

She removed the squirming baby's soiled diaper and took him to the bathroom. She saw no clean cloths suitable, so she held his little bottom over the sink and ran warm water over his reddened genitals. He stopped his crying and looked up at Annalee. He looked so much like Buckley when he was a newborn, she cried out, "Harold, he looks just like my boy, Bucky, did as a newborn!"

"Of course he does. They're half-brothers, aren't they?" He smiled down at her as she patted the baby's bottom with toilet paper. "You have a gentle way with babies, don't you?"

"I've had a lot of practice." She soothed the baby's hair and stroked his downy cheek as Teresa returned with a pile of worn dish towels.

"Here you are, but this was all I could find. We're out of milk, I'm afraid."

"These will work." Annalee took a towel and tore it into a strip for the umbilicus site. She found a bottle of alcohol in the bathroom and cleaned the wound with it. Then she wrapped the worn but clean towel around his belly.

She looked at Teresa. "Where are his pins? Are there any pins?" For now, she tucked the loose end into the rest of the dressing and deftly folded a worn, soft towel into a make-shift diaper. She lifted the baby's legs to place it beneath him. "He needs powder, and lotion, along with the proper milk formula. Where have you put his pins— ones he came with?" Teresa glanced about but came up without any pins. "I'll do the best I can," Annalee said to the flustered woman. "Could you boil some water then? He has to have something in his stomach until we can get some milk for him."

Angered at the numerous requests, Teresa cried, "Oh God, where in blue blazes did I put those damned pins?" She shrugged. "Let me look around. Maybe I can boil some water for him." As she wandered off, Annalee and Harold heard her murmur, "Oh, God, that damned kid is driving me nuts. What I wouldn't give for a damned good slug of whiskey! I need a drink so damned bad I'm about to go crazy."

Annalee looked up at Harold, shaking her head. "You've got to get this child out of here."

"I'll go see how things are going out there."

He left the bedroom after another look down at the baby. The longing and fear in his eyes made Annalee wince. The baby was hungry and no soothing words would settle him, not anymore. She washed her hands and stuck her little finger in his hungry mouth. He latched on, but she knew from experience, he wouldn't be quiet for long.

The lawyer had Henry sitting across from him at the dining room table. What they were saying, Harold couldn't hear, but Henry looked pale and sick. Things weren't going his way and his face was white with fear. Harold moved closer. He had to know what was being said. It meant more to him and his wife than anyone in the room.

"Now, what you have right here, is a nice home, a good car, and all the furnishings. Why jeopardize all that for a child you really don't want?"

Homer's voice was soothing, confidential, and strong. Harold realized that Homer was working to close a deal that meant the world to him and his wife, Caroline. He sat there, desperately awaiting the outcome.

The voices droned on, until finally, Henry snarled— at least Harold thought he did by the way his lip turned up—picked up a pen, and signed a paper. Homer stuck out his hand, and they shook.

Then he heard the lawyer say, "You are a wise man, Henry. You have done a fine thing today. It will have to be legalized by the courts, of course, but I'll get that taken care of in a few days."

They rose from their seats and Homer patted Henry on the back. "You won't be hearing from me anymore, not at all." He turned toward Harold and said under his breath, "Let's get that baby and get him somewhere where he'll be safe." He smiled and nodded. "It's all settled with Henry Sturgis. You'll be able to adopt this child. Henry has signed away any rights he might have had to the child. Now we must go before the local judge and make the boy legally yours."

Harold had tears in his eyes as he shook the man's hand and turned to Henry. "Thank you more that you'll ever know."

This time, Harold was he sure heard Henry snarl. "Your lawyer is a Goddamned shyster if I ever met one. He outta be locked up!" he added, then he went into the kitchen and slammed the door.

Harold returned to the bedroom, where Annalee still

waited for the safety pins and milk. "It's over. He'll be ours. Come on, Carrie, my darling new momma, let's get him to Annalee's house." He laughed quietly, a crowing sound in his voice, relaying his elation. "To hell with the damned pins. I'll get him that and everything else a baby could ever need."

"He needs food more than those darned pins anyway," Annalee said. She still had her finger in the baby's mouth.

Then he said to Annalee, a sheepish expression across his face, "Will you help us? We haven't a clue what a baby needs."

She let out her breath, laughing in relief. "You bet I will. This is a happy day for all of us!"

Annalee picked up the baby, cuddled him closely in his blanket from the clinic, along with his stinking bottle. She carried him out to Harold's plushy car. They left Carol's house for good as off in a corner of the kitchen, she saw Teresa hoisting a bottle to her lips. Annalee heaved a sigh as she cuddled the tiny boy in her arms and murmured, "You'll get use to riding in style soon enough, little man."

In the car, Harold said to Jack, "What on earth did that lawyer say to Henry to get him to sign those papers like that? I figured we were in for a long fight, and with that poor baby crying his heart out while we dickered with that sleazy uncle."

"I have no idea," Jack said. "But I hear Homer never loses a case."

"We could use a man like that in Washington. He'd put that bunch of losers we have in there now out to pasture."

Jack laughed. "Maybe he'll run one day. I'd sure vote for him."

When they reached the house, the baby was crying in hunger again. Annalee hastily scrubbed the pathetic bottle and filled it with cow's milk, hoping that was what he'd been getting. She fed him, he fell asleep, and then she called the nurse at the clinic.

She told Jack, Harold, and Caroline, what she learned. "They said to give him for starters, two ounces of canned condensed milk, but not the sweetened kind. Put a small dollop of the dark Karo syrup in the bottle and fill it with boiled water. The syrup is to keep him open if you know what I mean." She shrugged. "Luckily, we have some things on hand, but we'll need to go shopping for a few others." She looked at Caroline with a smile and raised eyebrows.

"What are you going to call him?" Jack asked Harold and Caroline.

"We haven't quite decided, but I'd like one of his names to be, Jackson, if that's all right with you, Jack."

Caroline spoke up. "Why not call him Derrick Jackson Lines, or how about Jackson Derrick Lines? I love both names and can't decide. Let's ask his half-brother."

Annalee called up stairs to the children and, in a tumbling mass, they came down, giggling, with hair mussed.

"Yep, Momma, we're all right here."

Sarah and Sissy held onto each other's hands and waited for Bucky to tell them what to do. Harold looked at them with shinning eyes, but Sarah still eyed him with suspicion.

"Which name do you like the best, my young man?"

Harold asked Bucky. "We want to name this little baby boy. He is going to be ours from now on and he needs a name. We like both names, Derrick and Jackson. We wondered what you thought. Which name should be first?"

Bucky stood still, his mind busy with his thoughts. Then his eyes lit up. "I think he should be Jackson and then Derrick. We have a new daddy, and his name is Jack. I think that's a real good name for any baby boy." He squinted and his forehead curled a bit as he struggled with the question. "Is that baby gonna grow enough to have a big man's name? He's awful small now, ain't he?" He looked at Jack for conformation.

"You were that little once, yourself, Bucky," Harold assured him. "But look how big you are already. You will be a big man named Buckley someday, and this baby will be a big man named Jackson Derrick Lines one day, too."

"I hope so. He's awful small now. Can't even talk or nuthin'," Bucky said doubtfully. He turned away and looked at the girls. "Come on, we got that fort to build."

With that, they raced for the stairs.

"That boy is the best thing that ever hit this house," Jack said, chuckling. "My Sissy hasn't cried once since he came to live here. I have the idea she thinks he hung the moon."

"He's the picture of his dad, but of me, too. What a handsome lad," he said as he uttered a joyous laugh.

Annalee saw Harold as a man who now felt completely blessed and Caroline along with him.

The baby had fallen into a good sleep, still wearing his clothes from the clinic and the worn, dishtowel diapers. "Will you fellows keep an eye on Mr. Jackson Der-

rick Lines, while we go find enough things for his imme-
diate needs and his trip home to DC?" Annalee asked.

The men stayed home to keep an eye on all the little
ones, and Annalee took Caroline shopping.

They took her car and headed for the nearest thing to
a shopping mart. Claiborne's Emporium seemed like the
best place to start.

"You need a proper crib of course, but wouldn't a
good sized basket do to make the trip home?"

"What a great idea, An. Why don't you just walk
around and pick out whatever you think he needs right
now? This is all so new to me."

"Well, I've had two and have come to believe that
when you have a baby, the instructions, in so many ways,
seem to come right along with them. It doesn't take long
before you get into their routine and know what they need
and when they need it. You might like to have a pediatri-
cian check him over, mainly so you have a doctor who
knows the child if he does become ill. And believe me,
they often do."

"Annalee, this is all so new to me," Caroline repeated. "Do you think I can do this?"

"Of course, you can. I suppose it's different, when
you didn't carry him, but you can be his mother. You
have the heart for it, and that's what counts."

Annalee spotted a large oval wicker basket. "Look at
this, Caroline. He'll fit in there just fine. Babies like to
feel surrounded, sort of like before they are born. It will
fit nicely in the back of your car, too."

She walked on until they came to baby clothes. "He
needs a few things from this counter." She laughed a bit.
"Just enough to get him home. You must have friends

who have babies. They will be a lot of help for you as well."

"I doubt anyone will ever be more helpful than you have been, An." Caroline picked up baby shirts, a couple of thick packs of diapers, several bottles, nipples, lotion, and powder. Then she picked up one thick blanket and held up a thinner one. "These will be nice for inside, won't they?"

"Nice going, Caroline, good choices. We mustn't forget to get some dark Karo and more canned condensed milk. How many days does it take to get back to Washington?"

"At least two days, with a stop-over for the night. We will need to heat his bottle, too." Caroline smiled at Annalee. "It's pretty complicated, taking care of a baby, isn't it?"

"Yes it is. And you've already seen the pathetic condition in which we found the poor child. Henry's wife had no knowledge of infant care at all. Furthermore, she hated the job of doing it. It made me nauseated and so angry at the way she let him get messy, hungry, and crying his eyes out. Her big worry was when she could get the next drink." Annalee was still upset at what they'd seen. "I'm so thankful you folks have him, now."

They finished shopping for what they needed and returned to the house with all the supplies.

Jack saw the oval basket. "What a great idea, ladies. That's perfect."

Harold's eyes popped out at all the needed supplies.

"This is just the beginning, dear," Caroline said. "Are you sure that judge will make this child ours?"

"You mean, little Jackson Derrick Lines, my dear?"

"I already love this baby boy, who looks just like you, but I won't stop worrying until I know for sure I can be a good mother."

Harold went to her and took her in his arms. "Soon, dear, soon."

To Annalee, Harold so closely resembled that cruel man she had come to fear and despise, she felt a stab of anxiety until she got it under control. It still happened when she looked at him. But she knew better. It would take time for her to erase those memories, and Jack was right beside her to help with that.

The women ignored the men and the sleeping baby, as they got busy and fixed the basket with soft bedding and padded sides. Annalee found some old sheets to make bed linens for him. They laid the sleeping infant in his new bed and stood over him looking at his cherubic little face as his lips made little sucking motions.

Annalee saw the look on her husband's face and wondered how long it would be until she had one of their own to look down at as he or she lay asleep in a crib.

Chapter 27

Homer called Harold the next morning to let him know the court case was on for the following day at two o'clock in the afternoon. "Don't worry your head about it," he said. "I have found the doctor who took care of Donald Woods and have his affidavit regarding the sterility of his patient. That, along with Annalee's little wrinkled note, we can prove your kinship to the child. And then we have the signed document from the brother Henry. You and Jack can bear witness about the drinking and the condition we found that poor child in when we went to that house—if we need to use that but I doubt we'll ever have a problem. None at all."

While they awaited the court hearing, Sarah's furniture was delivered. The women had a wonderful time setting up the little girl's own bedroom with the frilly lamp, pictures on the wall, and even wall paper that Sarah had chosen from the wallpaper book.

When it was all done, Sarah rolled around on her bed

with Sissy right beside her. Bucky stood looking at them with a frown on his face. "Girls sure are funny, ain't they, Dad?" he asked Jack.

అలల

It went as well as Homer had predicted. Harold and Caroline were given full parental rights to one Jackson Derrick Lines.

The clinic gave them the required information and paperwork to apply for his birth certificate, and they were ready to head for their home in Washington DC. The night before they left, Harold finally enticed Sarah to sit on his lap. She had gone a bit pale, but Sissy and Bucky had sat on his lap before her, and she decided to allow it.

She was stiff and trembling, which made Harold wonder just what evil acts that little girl had seen. He cursed his dead brother beneath his breath as he cuddled her.

"Annalee, these are lovely children, and if you two won't mind us popping in on occasion, we'd like to visit fairly often. I feel like we've become friends, and now somewhat related as well. I am happy to see you settled with a very fine husband, as well."

"Thanks, Harold. You folks will always be welcome, and we would get to see little Jackson grow up that way in the bargain."

Jack was relaxed, holding a glass of wine. He handed one to Harold. "Here you go, Daddy."

Both men laughed as they raised their glasses in a toast to the joy of a good home, a solid mate, and fine prospects for the future.

℘℘℘

That night, in bed, Annalee turned to him. "Darling Jack, I never knew my life could ever be this full, this wonderful, but it is. You have made it that way for me." She sighed and pressed closer. "I never dreamed our marriage would turn out this way. I did not see this kind of union as I grew up. I guess I was so used to sorrow, pain, and disappointment, I couldn't imagine anything like what we have."

"Darling An, are you speaking of our lovely marriage of convenience?" He chuckled softly. "I loved my first wife and missed her so terribly I thought I would die of it. But that day I came to your door with my unhappy little girl, you made everything different for her, and in time, for me. At first, it was just enough to barely go on alone, and most of that was for my daughter. But then, like the naïve souls we were, we made that pact to live together, side by side, as strangers." He laughed in his joy and reached for her. "That silly pact was destroyed utterly by that first kiss at the altar." He held her closer yet, nearly crushing her. "Was that ridiculous pact destroyed by that kiss for you, too, my darling An?"

"Right then, I only knew we wouldn't hold out for long, Jack. I was so terribly afraid. But I must admit there was something about you that mesmerized me right from the start. Yet you were so big and so terribly handsome and had those marvelous deep gray eyes, that I was even more afraid of you. And then, there was the threat and fear of those unspeakable things a man does to a woman in the dark of night. All that held me back."

"Unspeakable things, eh? An, you came into my life

when I had this terrible need for my daughter. I sought you out and it was a business deal all the way, until that kiss." He grabbed her hard and kissed her deeply. "Unspeakable things?" Jack chuckled. "Girl, you have set a fire inside me that burns day and night. God help me, I'll never get enough of you. Yes, darling, I know you were wondering about my first marriage, wondering how I can be so in love with you. The truth is, we never had the intensity you and I have, not at all. She was a fine woman in every way, and I will always cherish her memory, An. But this thing between us is something completely unexpected. How can anyone ever explain it? I can't. But until we are old and gray, darling An, I don't believe these lovely feelings will ever go away."

He took her softly, gently, and thoroughly, as the night wore on.

Later, Annalee lay quietly satisfied and deeply happy, though she wondered, *Will that little baby be right handed or left handed*?

About the Author

Ramona Forrest is a retired RN. She keeps busy writing novels—and traveling whenever possible. Forrest has resided in the back country of Arizona, assisted in roundups, worked in Saudi Arabia, and has had the pleasure of traveling extensively. She now resides in Phoenix and spends much time in gardening, writing, entertaining friends, and family.